And even though she really, really should, she just couldn't regret it . . .

She walked into her room and sat down on the bed, and it seemed everything felt and looked different, as though the world was lit by fireworks.

She'd had her first kiss. No, not that, exactly; *had* implied a passive acceptance of the action, and once things had gotten started, she'd *taken* her first kiss.

From a duke, no less. If she thought of it, which she hadn't much, she would have assumed her first kiss might be from someone of her class, someone she'd met through the agency, or a neighbor. Not a gentleman who was only a step below the Queen, a man who had the power to change law, rule over counties, destroy a reputation by raising an eyebrow.

Imagine if he employed both of them, what type of destruction he could create.

Not to mention employing his virility, his commanding voice, his arresting good looks, and yes, his exceedingly nice backside.

By Megan Frampton

THE DUKE'S GUIDE TO CORRECT BEHAVIOR

The Duke's Guide to Correct Behavior

Megan Frampton

AVON
An Imprint of HarperCollins*Publishers*

This book is a work of fiction. The characters, incidents, and dialogue are drawn from the author's imagination and are not to be construed as real. Any resemblance to actual events or persons, living or dead, is entirely coincidental.

AVON BOOKS
An Imprint of HarperCollins*Publishers*
195 Broadway
New York, New York 10007

ISBN 978-0-06-235220-0
www.avonromance.com

First Avon Books mass market printing: December 2014

Printed in the U.S.A.

10 9 8 7 6 5 4 3 2 1

Acknowledgments

To Scott, who is the best husband and gin-wrangler a woman could have. Thanks for going for long walks and eating ramen with our son so I could write this book.

Thanks to Louise Fury, my amazing agent, who is everything I am not. We make a great team, lady.

Thanks to Myretta Robens, who might have read this book more than I did, and told me to keep writing every time I freaked out. Which was often.

And thanks to Lucia Macro, my editor, who totally gets my writing and has given me an incredible chance to share it with readers.

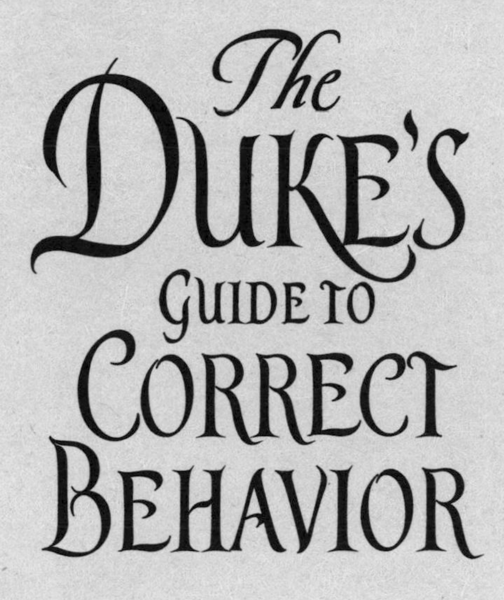
The
Duke's
Guide to
Correct
Behavior

Dukes, like generals, butlers, and other men in charge, should never be seen actually doing *anything. Dukes are here for the ordering of others, and while they should not abuse that privilege, they should exercise it enough to ensure full understanding of it from all nondukes.*

They can therefore do whatever they want by not doing anything.

—THE DUKE'S GUIDE TO CORRECT BEHAVIOR

Chapter 1

~~At the bottom of a brandy bottle~~
Two-thirds of the way through a brandy bottle
A duke's ballroom
London, 1840

Marcus felt his lip curl as he surveyed the signs of debauchery in his ballroom. Which was not, he knew full well, used for parties, balls, or social events of any kind.

Empty brandy bottles lingered to the sides of the chairs at random angles around the room; various articles of women's clothing were scattered around, including one cleverly placed corset on a statue of one of his very male ancestors; a few plates of half-eaten food were on the tables, one of the cats that refused to leave (or more correctly, that he didn't have the heart to make go) nibbling delicately on them while a second cat twined about his ankles.

"So you were saying how difficult it is to be a duke?" Smithfield's tone was as dry as—well, as his own throat felt.

He could fix that. He drained his glass, then attempted to scowl at Smithfield, one of his two new boon companions. The other, Collins, was currently fast asleep on one of the sofas, the results of imbibing a substantial amount of the brandy one of Collins's ships had brought in. Marcus himself had fallen asleep earlier, so he wasn't entirely exhausted. Not entirely, at least.

"It sounds ridiculous," he said, then felt himself smile as Smithfield looked at him pointedly. "It *is* ridiculous. I am a duke, I have no financial issues, I am unmarried, in prime health, and can do nearly whatever I want."

"But?" Smithfield said as Marcus paused.

"But all that is required of a duke is that we wed properly and start fathering little dukes-to-be, and that particular scenario is enough to make me want to wrap that corset," he said, gesturing to the statue, "around my throat and strangle myself. Bad enough I have to live a life I had never planned on; to do it at the side of a woman I would, in the best case, amicably dislike, and in the worst case utterly loathe, is not to be considered."

"That is terrible," Smithfield replied, still in that dry tone. "To have to marry and swan about being a duke when you could—well, what did you do six months ago, before you inherited? Or better yet, what would you rather be doing?"

Disappearing. Leaving. Being free of all responsibilities and cares. Never having to answer to anyone. "I used to walk a lot, just . . . walk. That made me almost happy." Marcus knew, in the back of his mind, that he wouldn't be talking this frankly if it weren't for the quantities of Collins's brandy he'd drunk. But Smithfield was asking, and maybe if Marcus were lucky, neither one of them would recall just how he'd bared his soul so pathetically. Again, thanks to Collins's brandy.

"Is that what you did before inheriting? Walk?" Smithfield's tone was now . . . less dry. As though he understood that what Marcus was saying was nearly important. Even if it still felt as though it wasn't really what Marcus wished to say.

But that would require that he knew what he wished to say, Marcus thought, which would require him to know what would make him happy. He could say, with certainty, that it was neither drinking, gambling, nor fornicating. Even before he'd come into the dukedom so unexpectedly, he had searched for satisfaction through drinking, gambling, and fornicating. He'd traveled to other countries, where he'd drunk, gambled, and fornicated. He'd returned to London where he'd at least had the comforts of his own home while he drank, gambled, and fornicated.

Except for the quality of the brandy, and the soft, luxurious fur of the inherited cats he seemed to have grown fond of, he'd been disappointed.

"Walking, yes," he replied, then glanced over to Smithfield. Who had fallen asleep. Marcus shook his head, drained his glass, and reached out to scratch the black and white cat on the chin. The cat was far more interested in the food on the table, however, which left Marcus to his own devices. As usual. *As he preferred,* he assured himself.

"I used to walk all the time, just on my own, with no one looking for me, no one worried about me, no one caring for me," he said, speaking to the uninterested cat. The dukedom had included the cats, whom the previous duke had acquired. Sometimes he thought they were the best part of inheriting the title. He poured another measure of Collins's brandy in his glass, but didn't drink. "Until my father told me to stop 'wandering about like a vagabond,' that it wasn't suitable, even for me."

He took a sip. "And then my father died, and my brother died, and suddenly I was next in line to inherit when the duke died. A man I'd barely met. And here I am, living in his house, with his title, with his cats, spending his money." His throat tightened. "I don't even feel as though I belong here, even though there is nowhere else I belong better."

The cat, wisely, did not respond.

He felt a surge of anger—at what, he wasn't entirely certain, just as he didn't know what he wanted.

But meanwhile he knew what he did not want, and that was for the two sleeping men in his ballroom to be there any longer. The cats could stay.

"Get up," he said sharply, walking over to poke Collins in the chest. The man frowned, brushed Marcus's finger away and emitted a loud snore. Marcus poked him again, this time in his soft belly, and he bolted upright, slamming his feet onto the floor, which echoed in the cavernous space of the ballroom.

"I'm up!" he said, brushing his fingers through his hair. "What's happening? Did Smithfield die?"

"No, not that I'm aware of." Marcus spared a glance toward Smithfield. Still breathing. He returned his gaze to Collins. "But you both need to leave."

The good part about being a duke, he'd discovered, was that he didn't need to explain why anything had to happen. He could just say it. "You need to leave." Or, "I want strawberries," in the middle of winter. Or, "Swap out all the furniture from one side of the house to the other." He hadn't said either of the last two, not yet at least, but it was a possibility if it seemed that it might, at last, bring him happiness.

He was reserving that last order for when he was well and truly desperate.

"D'ya have someone visiting?" Collins asked, apparently not understanding that being a duke means never having to explain himself.

Marcus didn't bother to answer, he just went to Smithfield's sofa and poked him. Unlike Collins, Smithfield's belly was flat and hard, but it had the same effect; he sat up and blinked, his disheveled hair sticking up in a few gravity defying directions.

"Out."

Smithfield nodded and swung his long legs over the sofa to the floor. He stared at the floor for a few seconds, then stood up, wobbling but at least not falling over.

He strode to Collins's sofa then and held his arm out. Collins took it and stood also, both men now at least upright.

Smithfield regarded Marcus with a cool, steady

gaze. "I hope you find what you're looking for, Your Grace." He didn't wait for any kind of response.

Good thing, too, because Marcus didn't have one, knowing that if he did, he'd damned well be off doing that. Instead, Smithfield just took Collins's arm and led him toward the door.

They all halted, however, at the sound of a firm knock.

Now what?

"Enter," Marcus said, turning his back to the door as he spoke. Cats couldn't knock, and that was about the only creature he would tolerate seeing.

And when did he become such a grouchy creature himself? If forced to, he could probably pinpoint the exact moment—he'd been about eight years old, and he'd overheard his father talking about him, saying he wished he was more like his brother Joseph. Less like himself.

One would think that wouldn't sting as much twenty years later, with everyone but himself gone from this world. One would be wrong.

Marcus heard the door open and his butler clear his throat. That was something, at least; Thompson did not clear his throat for any but the most interesting of reasons. He turned his head and felt his mouth drop open.

This was definitely an interesting reason.

A girl. A little girl with dark hair, a grimy gown, and the hugest eyes he'd ever seen on a human stared back at him.

"This," Thompson stated, "is Rose Dosett."

"Get out," Marcus said before Thompson could continue, but winced as the butler placed his hand on the girl's arm as though to escort her away. To God knew where. "Not her, them," he clarified, gesturing to the two standing men without taking his eyes off the girl.

Who had not, as it happened, taken her eyes off him, either.

The men walked swiftly to the door, only knocking over one bottle as they went. Marcus heard the soft drip of the brandy's dregs drop onto the floor as he and the girl continued their mutual observation.

Thompson cleared his throat, then spoke. "Your daughter, Your Grace."

The girl's face was relatively clean, at least in comparison to her gown. What he could see of her shape was thin, but not emaciated. And her face—her eyes were unblinking, solemn, huge.

He felt a pang of something, he had no idea what it was, flicker through him, like a half-remembered emotion that was pleasantly poignant. Like a dream where it was very urgent he do something, and yet he couldn't remember what it was. But he wasn't required to do anything. He could do whatever he wanted, now that he was him. Or more specifically, his title.

He hadn't done anything, and he already felt lacking. But that had been true since he was young, so why was he reminded of it now?

He shook off that feeling of urgency, as best he

could, and realized that just as he was staring at her, she was staring at him, as though she suspected just what he might have been up to. And didn't trust him not to do it again, in her presence.

Although that could be his own guilt talking. The cats looked at him that way, on occasion. But— "Dosett, you said?" he asked. Still without removing his gaze from the girl.

"Dosett, Your Grace," Thompson confirmed. "Her mother . . . well, her mother . . ." He trailed off as though aware that the girl was right there. Unspeaking. Unmoving. Unnerving.

Fiona Dosett. Marcus had nearly forgotten. She'd conceived when they'd been together, and he'd settled an annual sum on her and her offspring. He hadn't even known what gender his issue had been. Hadn't wanted to know, in fact.

Suddenly, regarding the small, still girl in front of him, that struck him as terribly wrong.

"Shall I place her in the blue bedroom?" Thompson asked, as though she were an unwanted package that just needed putting somewhere. The truth of which made Marcus wince, inside.

The girl—Rose—squeezed her eyes shut as Thompson spoke, making Marcus's chest tighten. That look she had on her face. He knew that look. The look of loss. He'd seen it in the mirror when he was younger, albeit his face was a lot less filthy. That look that said "I don't need love or caring because no one is here to love or care for me."

Although that could be just what he thought he saw.

"No, not in the blue bedroom," Marcus replied,

trying to soften his voice. Something he'd had little to no experience with. "Miss Rose and I shall take tea in the second salon." And he held his hand out to her until she reached forward and placed her small fingers into his.

Feeling, as she did so, that he had been given something that could prove extraordinary. If he could figure out what it was and what to do with it.

The Quality Employment Agency wishes to announce it has opened its office at 135 Plum Lane, and welcomes all clients into its establishment.

The Agency will match reputable servants of any type with employers who have immediate need for assistance. We specialize in ladies' maids, butlers, housekeepers, and governesses. The Quality Employment Agency is owned and managed by a group of well-bred ladies who understand what the Quality desires.

Quality is our company name, and our commitment to the public.

Chapter 2

The bell on the door jangled, letting Lily know that someone had entered the anteroom outside of the small office where she'd been working on the ledgers. She stood, feeling her back complain about her having sat for the past few hours. Each of the three proprietors of the Quality Employment Agency took turns at organizing the invoices, and this was her week.

The agency had done well since its inception just a few months ago, providing work (and the occasional falsified reference) for women with unfortunate pasts. They'd placed no fewer than six young women, all of whose reputations had been sullied for one reason or another. Lily and her partners were well-aware of what an unfortunate past could do to a person's livelihood, since each of them had unfortunate pasts themselves.

She walked out of the office to see a young man, garbed in a footman's clothing, holding a piece of paper and a snooty expression.

"Got this for whoever sends out ladies for governessing."

She unfolded the paper, feeling her eyes widen as she read its contents.

Need governess immediately. Send applicants to Duke of Rutherford, Mayfair.

She took a moment to read it, then read it again, just to be sure. And felt her mouth drop open in shock. A duke! An actual *duke* was turning to the agency for help. So far the agency's most prestigious client had been the cousin of a baron. He might as well have been a rat catcher compared to a duke.

This was what they needed to make the fledgling agency into a respectable business.

If the duke was pleased with the work, the agency's reputation would be made, and she and her partners could find more work for all the unfortunate women who came to them. It was an opportunity the likes of which they could never have dreamed of.

But she couldn't get ahead of herself.

Lily was not normally a person who took risks—the exact opposite, in fact—but she knew that this was no time to be the precise woman she'd shaped herself into since shedding—forever, she hoped—her own unfortunate circumstances.

Risk-taking when it meant jeopardizing your and your family's livelihood, well, that was one thing. Something her father had already done, to her family's detriment. But she couldn't think about that now, or how her sister had suffered, and how her mother had just given up afterward.

Unlike her father—*because* of her father—she had to do what needed to be done, and she needed to do it now. The agency was fresh out of suitable unfortunate women who could governess, and she couldn't afford to let this chance slip away. She had to take a risk. With her own self.

"I'm to wait for a reply," the footman said in an aggrieved tone of voice.

Ah, apparently she was ruminating too much. That was something she would likely never be able to shed.

She spun back around, clutching the piece of paper to her chest, as though someone would step in and steal it from her. "You will not have to wait, I have the perfect applicant. She will arrive within half an hour."

No need to inform the snobbish footman it would be her.

She made sure the door was shut before she ran around the small office in circles, waving the duke's note and yelping.

Not her most dignified moment. Her precise self was horrified.

But who could blame her? If Annabelle and Caroline were here, they'd be joining her in the yelping. This was why they'd started the agency, after all (well, not for the chance to yelp, but for the chance to aid unfortunate women), but she hadn't expected this kind of chance would come so soon.

She grabbed a piece of paper and a pencil and

outlined a few details about where she was and who their new client was, addressed it to her partners, grabbed her cloak, locked the door, and headed to her new position.

After emitting one last little yelp, of course.

Lily's excitement about the opportunity dimmed somewhat as she mounted the stairs to the sizable front door. A duke's house—his mansion—was larger than any private residence she'd ever seen, much less been inside.

She was already intimidated, and she hadn't spoken to anyone yet.

After taking a deep breath, she banged the knocker. She heard it echo within and felt herself tremble at making such a noise at such an impressive door.

Yes. She had to admit it. She was impressed by a *door.*

The door in question swung open and an older gentleman, his head placed at the properly dismissive attitude, looked at her. Noting, likely within seconds, her very worn cloak, barely a whisper of protection against the raw temperature, and the not-so-skillfully darned gloves she had on.

"I am here—" she began, only to have him interrupt.

"I know, and you should have come around to the back entrance. But since you're here, please do come in."

Was every person the duke employed entirely too full of themselves? Or perhaps it was just the two servants she'd met thus far. Still, it was worth keeping in mind when she spoke to the man in question.

She followed the full-of-himself butler inside, trying not to stare at all the grandeur inside.

"Wait here, I'll let the duke know you have arrived." The butler walked into one of the rooms to the side of the foyer, leaving Lily alone to get more intimidated by the foyer.

Imagine how she would feel when she actually saw one of the rooms.

She counted no fewer than ten doors leading off the entryway. It was hard to fathom just what purpose each room had; perhaps the duke allotted separate rooms for each one of his digits? "Oh, no, Mr. Thumb, it's not your turn. We'll be in the ring finger's room today." Or did he spend one day a week in each room, with the balance of the three left for holidays, birthdays, and . . . Incredible, she couldn't even dream up what purpose so many rooms could serve. It must be very hard work to be a duke, given everything one had to do.

Pairing digits with rooms, or making sure nobody used Boxing Day's room on Michaelmas. Or vice versa. Things like that.

The butler reappeared, making so little noise Lily jumped when he spoke. "The duke will see you now," he said, managing to imbue his words with the proper amount of correctness plus a healthy dollop of disdain.

He walked ahead of her to one of the many doors and flung it open. "The lady is here, Your

Grace," he said, then gave her a sharp nod that indicated she should enter.

She did, and immediately decided this was the pink room, because nearly every item in the room was pink. And not the healthy pretty color of a late summer rose; no, this was the insipid pink of a wan begonia that had gotten too much sun and not enough water.

It was . . . well, it was tremendously pink, and exactly the opposite of how she presumed a duke would choose to live.

But all thoughts of interior design fled her head when she saw him. Just him; the child was not there.

But his presence was enough. He looked exactly the opposite of how she presumed a duke would look.

He stood next to a spindly escritoire, pink of course, and his whole self was so . . . tremendous, that it seemed he might just knock everything in the room over with his presence.

He was tall, and very, very, very handsome. Extremely male. No, entirely and absolutely virile. That was the word. Virile, with all the connotations that brought the pink to her own cheeks. At least she better matched the room.

Goodness. She'd seen pictures of gods and soldiers and kings and other leaders of men, but she'd never actually felt the impulse to follow one of them anywhere.

This one, though, she might consider following, even though that way led to things a young lady should not be thinking of. Especially a respectful governess who needed to make a good impression.

He had dark hair, straight, which brushed his collar in an unkempt way that nonetheless looked utterly dashing. His eyebrows were straight black slashes over his eyes, dark brown, which were intently gazing at her as though he could see to her soul.

And if he could, he knew what she was thinking about him, so that could be problematic.

The sharp planes of his chiseled face were further accentuated by the stubble on his cheeks, giving him an even more dangerous look. The Dangerous Duke sounded like a character from a gothic novel. And he looked like just the sort of man who would lure women to do Dangerous Things.

One of his slashing eyebrows had risen, and she realized she'd been staring at him. Didn't that happen to him frequently enough for it not to cause comment? Perhaps not in the sanctity of his own home. Or maybe there was a room made for staring, and she was not in it.

"The governess," he stated, as though it was in question. He did not sound as though he truly believed she was one. Which made two of them, despite her having had experience with children, namely her sister, which was why she didn't have experience with any children past five years old. The familiar pain reminded her just what circumstances had brought her here. *It's a worthwhile risk,* a whispered voice in her brain said. *Be strong.*

"Your references." He held his hand out as he spoke.

"References," she repeated, knowing the pink in her cheeks was increasing. Perhaps this was the Room for Blushing, but if it were, she was doing all the work. He looked absolutely confident, that one eyebrow still lifted as though it had noticed her blushes but he himself had not.

There was a silence as they continued to look at each other in what felt like a facial standoff.

His other eyebrow joined its mate. "I presume a reputable governess from a reputable agency—I saw the advertisement in the papers, and my butler knew of the agency's reputation—would come supplied with references?" He lifted his head and crossed his arms on his chest. "Are you saying my butler is misinformed? Are you saying I have made the wrong decision?" His tone was nearly incredulous.

She still did not speak. She knew what to say—she'd coached enough of the unfortunate women to be able to recite it in her sleep—but she just couldn't, not with him, and those eyebrows, and all that . . . *virility* just a few feet away.

She was very far from reputable at this moment, she had to admit.

His lips—the fullness of which she'd just been admiring—thinned. "I need a governess. Not for me, mind you," he added, those lips tilting up in a crooked smirk, as though this duke had a sense of humor, "but for my . . . my charge. A young lady of approximately four years." A frown. "Or more or less, I'm not precisely certain."

This was for the agency, she couldn't falter now. Or open and close her mouth like a hungry fish. Either action would not be useful.

"Yes, of course, Your Grace." She made a slight curtsey, just as she instructed the women to do. To reinforce the client's importance so he or she would be beguiled into forgetting all about needing . . . "References. I regret to say I hastened to assist you without pausing to collect them." She had been too busy yelping to remember anything she might actually require. "I will certainly rectify that at a later date. Please know, for now, that I am skilled in the charge of girls, and if I could just meet the young lady in question, I would be able to prove my mettle."

His eyebrows lowered as he seemed to consider her words. "Prove your mettle in some sort of governess competition?"

She replied before she thought. "It is not as though the teaching of girls is something one can be competitive about. Either they learn or they do not. I assure you, I am quite competent."

Oh, stupid, stupid Lily. Wasn't it an absolute rule that one did not talk back to a duke? Particularly when said duke had your future employment in his hands? Plus the future of the agency, the one she and her partners had worked so very hard to make a success?

She clamped her mouth shut before she could say anything else.

But he hadn't yet thrown her out, so . . . She held her breath, seeing how the corner of his mouth had lifted into what might nearly be a smile, how one eyebrow had arched up—honestly, his eyebrows were miraculously nimble—as though he were amused.

And exhaled as he nodded. "You will suit," he said.

Hearing that, she had much more admiration for the unfortunate women who came to the agency.

Without saying anything more, he leaned over the surface of the escritoire and lifted a tiny pink bell from the far corner. He glared at it—and really, who could blame him?—and shook it.

Not unexpectedly, it had a tiny, light tinkling sound, and Lily held her breath, wondering if anyone could possibly have heard it. Moments later, however, the butler opened the door.

"Escort Miss Rose here now." No please, no softening of his voice, but to Lily it was as though an angel had burst from the heavens and was promising her cream cakes and chocolate sauce.

Which reminded her, she hadn't eaten for a while. What would she do if her stomach growled? Was stomach-growling a cause for not hiring a person?

She hoped she wouldn't have to find out.

The duke did not ask her to sit, of course; she was a servant being interviewed for a position, not a guest visiting for tea. Once he'd sent the butler off to fetch Rose, he barely even glanced in her direction. Although she couldn't stop looking at him. It was really unfair that he was a duke, and lived in the Mansion with Many Rooms, and looked as he did.

Now, for example, he was examining some papers on the execrable escritoire, his long, elegant, yet still ridiculously virile fingers shuffling them while his other hand raked through his hair, making it both more disheveled and more dangerously attractive.

His nose—and really, when had she ever noticed the shape of a person's nose before?—was straight and sharp, and nearly too big, but was, again, dangerously attractive.

An attractive nose. She was engrossed by the study of his nose.

At least he didn't have a wart or anything. That would be no less engrossing, but definitely less handsome.

At last she heard the door swing open behind her, and she turned around to see a small, slight child wearing a shabby gown and clutching the remnants of some sort of pastry, crumbs of which were falling to the floor.

And her expression—she looked as anxious and terrified as Lily felt, and Lily immediately felt a bond to this little girl who probably couldn't even count as high as all the rooms in the duke's house. Perhaps that would be one of their first lessons. If she got the job.

"Miss Rose, this lady has come to discuss taking a position as your governess." His voice as he addressed the little girl was gentle, as though he knew just how intimidating he likely appeared to this tiny, pastry-eating waif. To females of all ages, she had to admit. Never mind that she wished she had a pastry herself. But that he knew enough to use a softer tone surprised her. She wasn't accustomed to gentlemen being anything but demanding. Especially at her last unfortunate position.

He could never know of that particular item on her list of prior positions. Not if she wished to keep her current one.

"Her name is," he continued, still in that soft tone, ". . . what is your name?" he muttered, sounding impatient.

Lily swallowed. "Lily Russell, Your Grace, but you can just call me Miss Lily."

"Miss Rose, this is Miss Lily." He chuckled, an entirely unexpected sound. "Perhaps I should be called the Duke of Gardening instead of Rutherford." The joke was even more unexpected than the chuckle, but Lily couldn't spare a moment to think about how Dangerous a witty duke might be.

"Hello, Miss Rose." Lily spoke softly, as he had, already aware she had to be gentle toward this obviously frightened girl. She could definitely sympathize—she was frightened as well, frightened she wouldn't suit, frightened she would end up like so many of the unfortunate women the agency hadn't helped.

Frightened she couldn't help this girl as she wished someone had helped her.

"It is a pleasure to meet you." She knelt down and extended her hand toward the girl. "I would like to stay here and teach you. Would you like that?"

Rose looked at Lily's hand, then nodded as she

took a few steps, reached out and held it. "Yes," she said in a whisper.

Lily heard the duke exhale behind her. "She's just barely arrived," he said, "and hasn't spoken a word yet." He was not at all the commanding duke who'd demanded her references, not now. Now he seemed almost . . . anxious. "Not even once, during our tea. I was worried that she was mute."

Interesting. So he'd just met his charge? Not that it was any of her business, of course, prim, methodical Lily reminded that other curious, yelping part of her. But still. Interesting.

She smiled at Rose, who returned the smile, albeit shakily. "I believe Miss Rose and I will have plenty to discuss." She turned her head to look at the duke. "May I assume I have the position, then?" she asked.

He glanced quickly at her, and the heat of his gaze seemed to penetrate to the fraud within, the woman who'd never really been a governess, just a young lady with a sister. Her stomach tightened in both hunger and anxiety.

"Yes," he said at last. He barked out an order, and both Rose and Lily jumped. "Thompson, take Miss Rose and Miss Lily to one of the guest bedrooms, it doesn't matter which one. That will be the schoolroom."

The girl's fingers were trembling, and Lily wished she could tell her that it was all right, that trembling in the presence of such a pink room and an arrogant duke was a perfectly normal reaction, only she didn't think it would be good for the child to know her new governess was a ninny who yelped and pondered noses and wan begonias and a vast number of rooms rather than concerning herself with proper conduct.

She would save all that for a lesson sometime in the future, when the topic was Foolish Things Your Governess Thinks of and Does when Panicking.

If a duke does happen to do something that might fall outside the bounds of what most people in Society would consider proper behavior, it is incumbent upon the duke to behave as though not doing that thing would be scandalous. People in Society will then assume the behavior is faultlessly correct.

—THE DUKE'S GUIDE TO CORRECT BEHAVIOR

Chapter 3

The door shut behind them, all of them, and he was alone, wondering just what in God's name had he just done—although he could answer that, couldn't he? He'd taken in his illegitimate daughter after her mother died, had established this was to be her home, for the time, at least, and even hired a governess for her.

Not really what he thought most men in his position were accustomed to doing. Especially if they had spent most of the night drinking with their now boon companions.

First of all, if there was a daughter, she was usually legitimate, and therefore came with a mother, who would handle the hiring of the governess.

Illegitimate offspring didn't require recognition, let alone a governess.

The governess. He was now even more glad he was unencumbered in the wife area. Something about her made him prickle nearly as much as he had when first seeing Rose.

Or perhaps he was just tired.

Twenty-four hours earlier, his primary concern

had been whether to anoint Collins or Smithfield his new best friend. He still hadn't decided, but he was leaning toward Smithfield, since Collins ate the last bit of roast beef and had the temerity to ask a question of a duke.

Smithfield had just snored.

But now he had a child in his possession. A child for whom he was responsible. When he wasn't altogether certain he was responsible.

But he wasn't going to let that deter him from doing what was right. For now. For once. He hadn't done anything about his new title except resent it, but if being a duke meant he could change this girl's life for the better? But he knew damned well he couldn't do it alone.

And so he had found her a governess. A governess who snapped back a retort, which no one had dared to since even before he'd become a duke. A governess who had turned into stone when he asked about her references, whose cheeks had flushed when he spoke to her. A governess who wore a gown that the nicest thing one could say about it was that it was made of fabric.

A governess who had intrigued him right away. Made him ignore the missing references, the flush, the worn gown; made him want, instead, to see what color her cheeks would turn if he kissed her, if he discovered what curves lurked underneath her clothing. What she would say if he could get her to speak her mind all the time.

It was clear she had the goal of presenting herself as plainly as possible, but like an archeologist searching for a lost treasure in a pile of dirt, he could discern the beauty underneath. And that intrigued him as well. Luxuriant hair, the color of the most delicious chocolate, was pulled back into a severe bun, but several strands had fallen out, giving her a seductively disheveled appearance. Her eyes were hazel, but changed color as her emotions changed. In the height of the pink-cheeked moment, for instance, her eyes had gotten darker, while when she saw her new charge, he would have sworn they turned almost golden.

And her figure—her waist was small and trim, and as for her breasts—

No, stop, he reprimanded himself. What was he doing, waxing rhapsodic about his newest employee? She was here to instruct his charge. His *daughter.*

He was setting on a course of respectability, at least until he figured out what to do with his daughter. She deserved that care, at least.

Not to mention, the newest employee's demeanor was hardly that of a seductress, regardless of her disheveled hair or lush figure. More like when his prim-mouthed aunts had tried to temper his wild habits.

Clearly, he thought as he recalled what he'd done the night before, they hadn't succeeded very well.

Perhaps now that he was going to try to be a responsible parent, if just for a little while—not to mention a responsible employer, one who did not notice that the governess's eyes were the green of moss, the kind a woodland fairy might rest on—he might want to actually do something about his residence. He hadn't really cared that much before. Just as long as there were adequate rooms for himself and whichever boon companions he'd found, that was sufficient. That it be warm and have seating seemed reasonable. But anything else? He hadn't bothered. He assumed there would be time enough for all of that when he was settled. If he settled.

Besides which, he kept hoping he could someday just return to roaming, not having to worry about what people thought about him or what responsibilities he had.

It was momentarily terrifying, then, that Rose's arrival meant he might have to lose those vagabond dreams forever.

And who would he be if he were just the duke?

At least his current excesses—those antithetical to a responsible parent—were limited to drinking and gambling and not nearly as much fornicating as before. He had occasional dalliances, but he'd found, in general, it was too much effort for too little reward to embark on affairs with society ladies. Two minutes and it was over, and then he'd have to make conversation. Not worth it.

The thought had crossed his mind that if it only lasted two minutes, perhaps he was doing it wrong, but he hadn't been intrigued enough by anyone to conduct any scientific experiments. Besides which, how embarrassing would it be if he was doing it wrong? When he got married—*if* he got married—it would be too late for his wife to complain. Plus he assumed she wouldn't know, either.

Although if he could practice, perhaps with someone he'd just met . . .

No. Absolutely not. Drinking and gambling suited him just fine.

With that thought in mind, he strode over to the cart where this room's brandy was kept. No glasses; he vaguely recalled coming in here the night before to retrieve more for him and his guests. He shrugged, and raised the bottle to his mouth.

At which point the door was flung open and his new rigidly proper governess walked in, her expression reserved.

She was not here to help him refine his amatory activities, then. Pity.

"Your Grace," she said, clasping her hands in front of her, and then her expression changed to one of exasperation. "I was just—oh, for heaven's sake, just drink!"

Because he had frozen in mid-swallow, the bottle still tilted up, but his mouth had closed over the opening so no more liquid could travel down his throat.

At her words, he opened his mouth and the welcome burn of the spirit—unlike the unwelcome burn of his new employee's tone of voice—traveled down his gullet to nestle comfortably in his stomach.

He thought too late that drinking brandy straight from the bottle was probably not the habit of a respectable gentleman and father. Given that he'd only had a few hours being either, however, he thought he was doing rather well. Bottle-drinking notwithstanding.

He placed the now empty bottle down and looked more closely at her.

The severe hairstyle, the frown, the worn, ill-colored gown. No wonder she looked so glum.

He wondered what it would take to make her laugh. Or smile, even. A child needed laughter, did she not? He would just have to command her to laugh.

Which would probably go as well as when his aunts attempted to sober him up. Not in the way he needed it lately.

"Miss . . ." Damn, he'd forgotten her name.

"Lily," she supplied. Lily, of course, his garden of girls. Although this one was most definitely a woman, he corrected himself.

"Lily," he repeated. "What do you want?" He didn't mean to slip into his most arrogant tone of voice; if he were honest, he would have to admit that it just produced the quickest, easiest results. He wanted something, he announced his wants in that tone of voice, and usually within minutes he received it. That was true even before receiving his title. And being a duke meant never having to soften your tone.

Until now, at least.

"I am here, Your Grace," she said tightly, "to speak with you about the child. About Rose." When she said the girl's name, her voice softened. It seemed, actually, that her whole expression softened. He'd have thought about that more, about how she seemed to glow from the inside, just with saying the girl's name, but then he got distracted by—by her.

She was absolutely stunning when she wasn't looking as though she had just sucked on a lemon. And her figure really was lovely—shapely, but not excessive. As though there were secrets to discover underneath that drab gown, hidden curves and soft skin and unknown territory to explore.

But he had no business exploring his child's governess.

"What about Rose? You need to tell me if there is a problem with the—with my daughter." As he spoke, he felt his chest tighten. *My daughter.* He'd only just met his child, had spent barely an hour with her, but he already knew how it felt not to be wanted, and no matter what, he didn't want that for her.

Miss Lily shook her head, her lips curling into a slight smile. "No, there is no problem with her, as you say. She is a lovely girl. I merely wished to discuss how you wished me to proceed." A pause, then a more hesitant tone. "You said she has just arrived?"

They were both still standing. If they were to engage in any kind of lengthy conversation, he'd be damned if he'd conduct it standing up. With a servant, no less.

Although from what he knew about them, governesses inhabited an odd purgatory-like existence within a household—not lowly enough to be comfortable among the other servants, but certainly not part of the family.

Ah. No wonder Thompson had been even more rigid than usual. He needed to ensure the new governess knew her place. Thompson was likely irked that his employer didn't seem to know—or even care about—his place. Both in terms of his physical living quarters and his position.

He really would have to get around to redecorating one of these days.

"Do sit down," he said, gesturing to one of the chairs. He grabbed one that had fallen sideways and righted it, then straddled it backward. He'd found that was the most comfortable way to sit, the chairs being as uncomfortable as they were ugly.

The governess had no such option regarding the way she sat, of course, and lowered herself into the chair he'd indicated, smoothing her skirts and clasping her hands in her lap. At last, when it seemed she was settled to her liking, she looked up at him.

The directness with which she regarded him felt like she knew things about him, knew things he didn't even know. It felt prickly, like wearing a rough shirt, or attending church when one had no right to be there.

He hadn't done either thing in years, but he still recalled how it felt.

There was a long silence, until at last he realized it was his place to speak. In purgatory or not, no servant would begin a conversation when not specifically invited to. That road would lead straight to hell. Or unemployment.

"Have you had a chance to review what might be needed for her?" He made his tone as confident as he could, even though he was entirely unaccustomed to not knowing the answers. Or even to asking questions. This event, this arrival of a child who was shorter than the top of the execrable escritoire, was going to irrevocably change him. For better or for worse remained to be seen.

"I assume, Your Grace, that since this is the first child you've had living here—it is, correct?" she asked, the slight promise of a frown flitting across her face, as though she worried he was in the habit of collecting stray children. "I assume that we will need everything. Will you need an itemized list?" She tilted her head and her eyes narrowed in thought. "There will be papers, and pens, and chalk, and—"

"Fine, fine," Marcus said, interrupting. "Whatever you deem necessary. I don't need to hear the details. Just have the bills sent here."

"You will wish to hear how she is progressing in her studies." It was not a question, and he felt suddenly defensive. Because, of course, he hadn't thought about tracking her progress at all; if he were honest, he'd have to admit he hadn't thought about what would happen at all, beyond wanting to keep her there for the moment. To keep her safe, until he decided what was to be done with her.

And with him.

But keeping the child safe wasn't the same as keeping her well, a voice reminded him. His parents had kept him safe, but not well.

The governess was still gazing steadily at his face, and he realized she was waiting for a reply. Not that she had asked a question.

"A weekly report will be adequate."

"I will report to you, and not to your wife?" That was a question, one thankfully he could answer.

"I am not married."

"Oh."

Was he imagining it, or did her expression relax a fraction? Did she think he would— No, of course not. Dukes did not marry governesses, and vice versa. Definitely not this governess and this duke.

Not that he wouldn't mind pretending they were married. For two minutes, at least.

But she was not looking at him in any kind of pretend married way at all, or even in the way he'd grown used to—as though he was a rare breed, or some sort of fascinating bizarre species. He understood those looks. There weren't very many dukes, after all, and many fewer of them weren't gray-haired and married and gouty.

She was just . . . *looking*. It was refreshing, but also disconcerting. He felt as though he should be explaining how a man such as he had been able to remain a bachelor. He wanted to tell her how it felt to see Rose arrive in his house, how he saw himself in her face. How he knew how it felt not to be wanted.

But she was his newest employee, not someone he needed to confide in, or impress, or do anything except pay and expect to do her job.

He took refuge in his most obnoxious tone of voice. "Since you neglected to bring references, Miss Lily, perhaps you could instead tell me of your last position."

Had her expression been relaxed before? Now it was all tightened up again, as though someone were winding her face up like a clock, to spring it into action.

He acknowledged that he could be oblivious to other people, but there was no mistaking the tension in her face. In her entire body, in fact; her hands were coiled around each other and her posture made it appear as though she were going to leap out of the chair.

But she didn't do anything, just took a deep breath and met his gaze. "I was employed by a vicar's family in Littlestone. The Turnstones." The expression in her eyes got distant, as though she were recalling something. "It is a small village, but the vicar's wife wished her daughters to be able to make their way comfortably in London. I believe they are distantly related to a baron, they had hopes of arriving in town for the Season." She nodded, as though for emphasis.

And now what did he do with that information? He'd never actually hired a servant before, he'd left that up to whomever had taken care of it before he inherited. But this couldn't be entrusted to anyone but him.

"Hm." That seemed like an appropriate reply.

"I can obtain my physical references on my afternoon off."

As though they both knew when that was. Was it something that was understood? How had he gone this long—even being as feckless as he was—without knowing when servants had their free afternoons?

"Yes, of course." He was feeling more and more out of his depth in dealing with this woman. Perhaps there was a good reason he'd left the hiring to other people.

"When would you prefer me to take my afternoon?" she asked after a moment.

Aha! So it was not understood! He felt much better. "Tuesday." He said it as though there was no other possible day that would be nearly as satisfactory. He hoped it wasn't part of the unknown servant covenant that one never had Tuesday afternoons off.

"Yes, thank you."

Apparently it was not. He wanted to show how proud he was of this moment, but if he admitted his ignorance, his whole triumph would be rendered meaningless.

"And, if you'll excuse me, Your Grace," she said, biting her lip, "what have you said about Miss Rose?"

"Said about her?" He didn't think he'd said much about her, except not to throw her out and to escort her to one of the upstairs rooms. Had he already done something wrong?

"About her being here. With you. So—so unexpectedly," she said, nodding with a significant look.

Ah. They were to have the illegitimate child conversation already. He hoped she wasn't on the verge of leaving when she hadn't even begun.

"She's my daughter."

Miss Lily rolled her eyes and exhaled. As his aunts used to do as well. "I understand that, Your Grace, but what will you *say* about her?"

"That she is my young daughter?" He wasn't trying to be difficult, but he didn't see where it was anyone's business.

"Perhaps, if I might suggest, you could tell people that she is the daughter of one of your cousins. One who died in India, or somewhere else far off. Then your—then Miss Rose would not have to suffer as a result."

"Ah." The thought of having to even consider something like that made him furious, made him want to yell at her, but it wasn't her fault that the world chose to be so narrow-minded. "I see."

"Good, then." Her eyebrows knitted together in thought. "Not that anyone should judge where it is not their concern, but people will talk." From the way her face tensed, he wondered what people had said about her.

"Thank you." At least she wasn't offering her notice, not immediately, at least. And it seemed as though she might sympathize with Rose's situation. "Well, then." He rubbed his hands together the way he'd seen his father do when he was little—signifying the end of a conversation, or a wrapping up of a moment, or something so he didn't have to come out and say "Get out." Not that his father, and later Joseph, had ever hesitated to tell him to get out. But they were varied in their rudeness, he had to give them that.

"If I have your permission to return to Miss Rose, Your Grace?" she asked, rising from her chair.

That was the way to say one wished to leave another's company. He'd have to remember that the next time he had an inclination to be polite.

Marcus inclined his head. Feeling as though he had somehow wrested control of the moment from her, as though it had been at issue.

She nodded as she made a slight curtsey, then took herself and her prim lemon face out of his sight.

He gazed at the ceiling—replete with adorably pink cherubs—and thought about what he'd learned: that Tuesdays were acceptable for servants' days off, that his new governess was definitely a lovely woman, and that he had decided on a new best friend.

Not to mention he had a child in his possession, a child for whom he was purportedly responsible.

When confronted with an acquaintance who might become a friend, a duke must always ask himself: Is this person someone who might jeopardize the duke's standing? (And the duke must always refer to himself in the third person.) If the answer is yes, the duke will then have to decide if the person in question is worth the risk. Most times the answer is no.

—The Duke's Guide to Correct Behavior

Chapter 4

The duke, Lily could tell as she ascended the nearly-as-impressive-as-the-foyer staircase, had no idea what he was doing. Perhaps he was living his life according to *The Duke's Guide to Correct Behavior,* but he was definitely not a parent. Not surprising, given that it appeared he had only become one a few hours earlier.

Since she had never been a governess before, it seemed they had a lot in common. Not necessarily *good* things, but things in common.

She would not be sharing that information with him anytime in the near future. Or distant future, for that matter.

Thank goodness her father's estate had come equipped with a vicar, and that she could draw on her own memories to recall her mythical employer's family. She wished she could have pointed it out to him as an indication of just how clever she was, but then that would be counterproductive.

It would probably be even worse than arriving without a reference.

She felt herself start to smile, then realized she

was still walking. Really? All that thinking and she hadn't gotten there yet?

Maybe the duke should have hired a navigator instead of a governess. Should she have packed a snack for the journey? She really had to eat something, she did tend to get a bit . . . snarly if she was hungry.

The Snarly Governess and the Dangerous Duke. She stifled a snort of laughter as she reached the room, opening the door to a scene that stifled any laughter altogether. Rose was sobbing on the carpet, looking as though her entire world had just fallen apart.

"Your Grace, one of the gentlemen from earlier today has returned. Should I tell him you are at home?" Thompson ended his sentence with a disdainful sniff.

Marcus heard that sniff often, and suspected his butler did not appreciate his master's less dukelike moments. Which were most of his moments, if he were honest. But since Thompson was his servant, he didn't care. Much.

He waved a hand in response. "Certainly, send him in." Which one would it be? he wondered.

Within moments his question was answered as Smithfield strode in, an amused look on his face. "Your butler was not pleased to see me, I believe. And here I thought we had a bond, I do believe I gave him a coin when he returned with more brandy." Smithfield had a dry edge to his voice, an acerbic wit that matched Marcus's own.

He'd made a good choice in new best friends, at least. Although— "I don't have time for brandy today. Besides, aren't you tired? I know I am, and I got a few hours of sleep in. I was going to go rest, but then the child arrived."

Smithfield ignored Marcus's obvious hint and sat on the chair the governess had so recently vacated. Only instead of settling himself neatly down, he sprawled out in it and leaned back, balancing on two of the spindly pink legs. Hm. *He should try that position sometime,* he thought. It might be more comfortable.

"She is still here?" Smithfield sounded surprised.

"Yes." He paused as he remembered what she said. "She has just arrived, she's my cousin's child, and now my cousin is dead." He and Smithfield both knew it was a lie, but he had to start practicing. "What else should I have done with her?"

Instead of replying, Smithfield just gave him a knowing look, a look that said everything in both of their minds—aristocrats didn't usually take in their bastard offspring, they were far more likely to fling them out on the streets with a denial of their paternity, and what was he doing being responsible anyway, it wasn't as though he'd ever shown an iota of responsibility in his life, except for being responsible to his own comfort and ease of living. That it happened to coincide with his staff's ease of living was merely coincidental.

Or perhaps, Marcus reflected, that was just going through his own mind.

"I didn't think you were planning on being

a—a *cousin* anytime soon," Smithfield remarked, "at least not according to what you said last night." The way he spoke made it clear he knew the truth. And that Society wouldn't think twice about him casting her off, given the reality of the situation.

Why didn't that make him feel better?

Marcus shrugged. "It seemed impolite to toss her out, what with her mother having died and all." He winced inwardly at how callous he sounded.

Funny, he couldn't even remember Fiona's face, though he'd had her in his keeping for two months, at least. He did recall her remarkable ability with her mouth. And she'd been most reasonable when they discussed the babe. She hadn't even argued with the sum his money manager proffered as reasonable for the child's upkeep.

He would not share any of his memories of her mother with Rose, however.

"What are you going to do with her?" Smithfield sounded only mildly curious, as though Rose were an extra chair to put away or an out-of-style waistcoat. Plus he was questioning a duke. Apparently the "not questioning dukes" precept was less widely known than Marcus presumed. He'd have to speak to whoever compiled the ducal precepts.

"I've hired a governess." A beautiful woman. Not to mention, a woman who seemed as though she wished to challenge him. But someone who was also clearly competent to be in charge of a small child, judging by how Rose had responded to her, and how the child's face had grown more at ease seeing her. Was hiring a governess the first unselfish thing he'd ever done, or did it just feel like that?

Plus he'd felt a tingle of something in her presence, an awareness of what it was like to be in conversation with someone who wasn't intimidated by him. Might not even like him that much, actually.

What would it take for her to like him?

More than two minutes, he'd guess.

So perhaps he wasn't entirely unselfish.

"So you plan on keeping her?" Smithfield sounded startled. Hearing it so definitively made Marcus chafe at the permanence, and he had to squelch the urge to deny keeping her at all.

But the look on her face. He couldn't do that to her just yet, not until she'd gotten a bit more settled. Then he could decide.

"Is there anything I can do to assist?" Smithfield now sounded genuinely concerned. He'd even lowered himself back down so he was seated on four respectable chair legs rather than a shocking two. "My sisters are both married, they live in town, and both have offspring, I believe. If you need any advice or anything, I can ask them."

Perhaps he had made a good choice in a new best friend.

Although it wouldn't do to get all confiding in the man, given how they'd only recently met. But still. It touched him.

"Thank you, I will bear that in mind. For now, I just want her to get accustomed to being here. Her mother has just passed, I understand, and everything she's known is gone." She was like him, only his parents hadn't actually been dead. They had just paid so little attention to him that he felt as though he didn't have parents.

"Of course." There was a moment of silence, and then Smithfield spoke again. "You didn't happen to see my snuffbox, did you? That is why I originally stopped by, not just to question you about your plans in regard to your newly arrived urchin."

"Of course. Come with me to the ballroom."

Marcus flung the door open so he and Smithfield could enter. Unfortunately for Smithfield's property, the room was still in the postparty deshabille they had left it in. The servants hadn't yet been in to clean, what with Rose's arrival and his subsequent need to interview the governess.

It was, once he really looked at it, almost appalling. There were brandy bottles, half-eaten plates, and other indications of their time together. He focused his eyes on the larger table, the one with cat prints studding its white tablecloth.

"I'm certain my staff will locate it once they've had a chance to straighten up. Meanwhile," he said, almost before thinking, "since you mentioned it, would you and your sisters and their husbands like to come for dinner one night this week? I would be glad to have a mother's opinion on my charge and her governess. It would obviously be a small party, given the circumstances."

"That would be nice, thank you." Smithfield's expression turned rueful. "I apologize in advance if my sisters are dumbstruck by your presence—

they've never been within spitting distance of a duke, much less dined with one."

He hoped it wouldn't come to spitting. "Wednesday, then? Eight o'clock? Hopefully we'll have located your snuffbox by then."

"Yes, thank you." Smithfield unfolded his rangy body from the chair and stood, holding his hand out to shake Marcus's hand. "I admire what you are doing with regard to the child. It isn't every man in your position who'd take on that responsibility." He sounded genuinely impressed.

"Mmph, yes," Marcus agreed, feeling uncomfortable. When was the last time he'd been praised for something other than his ability to hold his liquor or play a hand of cards?

Never sprung to mind.

Did he really wish to change that?

It is not possible for a duke not to know all that is required of a duke; he is, by definition, the epitome of his title. How he is, is what a duke should be. But if a duke should happen upon a situation in which he feels as though he does not know all, he must never let on that he is less than completely competent. By assuming the mantle of knowledge, he becomes the knowledge. He is the knowledge.

—THE DUKE'S GUIDE TO CORRECT BEHAVIOR

Chapter 5

"What has happened?" Lily hurried across the thick carpet to kneel and clasp Rose in her arms. The girl was stiff against her body, and Lily fought against holding her tighter—that might only scare her. She could feel the warm tears falling onto the shabby lace that trimmed her gown.

"He left," Rose wailed, finally unbending her body and clutching Lily in a death grip.

"Who?" Lily asked, gently trying to pry Rose's fingers loose. A nonbreathing governess would not be helpful toward ensuring the agency's future. To say nothing of her own, she thought.

"Mmphhmph Smthph," the girl replied, sobbing more furiously into Lily's shoulder.

Lily slowly drew away and looked at Rose, who stared back with an anguished look in her eyes. "Who, dear? I couldn't quite hear that. I want to help."

"Mr. Snuffles," Rose said, as though Lily knew who that was.

"Who is that?"

Rose's expression changed from anguish to

exasperation. "The kitty! He was here, and I was petting him, and then he left. Bad kitty. Make him come back."

A cat. Thank goodness it was only a cat. "What does Mr. Snuffles look like?"

"He looks like a cat." Rose's tone made it clear she believed her new governess was an idiot for not knowing what a cat looked like. And, to be fair, if Lily didn't actually know, she would be one.

Lily pulled her handkerchief out and dabbed Rose's face. "What color is his fur?"

"All black, with white spots." So therefore not all black, but Lily was not going to point that out to the sad child. There was enough time later for pedantry of a feline nature.

"Should we go ask the duke?"

Rose's face brightened. "Yes, it must be his cat. He has to be a nice man if he has a nice cat."

Now was also not the time to point out that judging people by their animal ownership was not an acceptable way of gauging personality.

"Shall we go together?"

At that, Rose withdrew, crossing her arms on her chest and shaking her head. "You go. I want to stay here in case Mr. Snuffles comes back."

Lily stood, feeling her knees complain about her position on the rug. "Are you certain? You will be all right staying here by yourself?"

There were so many more questions she wanted to ask—how had she arrived, did she know anything about her mother, where had she lived before, why was she just meeting her father—but Lily knew that focusing on the cat's appearance or nonappearance was a good distraction from Rose's new reality, and she didn't want to jeopardize that.

The girl's expression turned scornful. "Of course, I'm alone all the time."

That was something worth investigating later on; it would certainly explain the look she'd had on her face earlier, if Rose had been neglected in the past.

But meanwhile she had Mr. Snuffles to locate. And a duke who might know where the missing kitty was.

If she was intimidated by the amount of rooms he had, just imagine how foolish she would feel to inquire about a missing cat.

But if it would make this little girl happier, she would do it, even if it meant speaking to the Dangerous Duke.

She kept that thought in mind as she descended the still enormous, still marble, always intimidating staircase.

The duke was not his house. Although the thought that he was even more intimidating—not to mention impressive—than his living quarters did nothing to assuage her tension. That he was the most male, most handsome, and definitely the most dukely man she'd ever met did not help her, either.

At this rate she'd be a heap of sobbing nerves by the time she reached the bottom of the stairs. What happened to her precise, methodical self?

Oh, of course. She'd tossed it away in a moment of impulse. Of risk.

"Calm yourself, Lil," she whispered, using her mother's nickname for her. "He is just a man"—a handsome, wealthy, important man—"who might know where a cat has gotten to. That is all." He would also discharge her on the spot if he so much as suspected about her unfortunate past. She needed to remain precise, prim, and methodical.

She really wished there was a word that started with *p* that meant methodical. It would make things so much more . . . *methodical.*

She took a deep breath, then reentered the putrid pink room, where she found him, as she'd expected. Only he wasn't lounging about elegantly on a settee drinking brandy out of a snifter; nor was he nibbling on some young woman's neck as he seduced her with lovely words spoken in that deep, resonant voice; nor did he seem to be in possession of any kind of cat at all.

Instead, he appeared to be buttoning a pinafore on a doll, a doll with brown hair and little black shoes, a doll that—unless she was entirely mistaken about the duke—certainly did not belong to him.

He looked startled when she walked in, then his expression quickly switched to chagrin, and then anger.

"What are you doing, just walking in like that? I could have been—I could have been . . ."

He paused, and Lily supplied, unable to help herself, "Cavorting?"

He glared at her, and then at the doll, and then back at her. "Cavorting, Miss Lily, yes." His tone was dry.

"Do you plan on cavorting while a child is in residence, Your Grace?" she asked as mildly as possible. She had no idea what cavorting meant in his world, but she was guessing it was not good for a child to be exposed to. Perhaps he had rooms for cavorting, and she would have to warn Rose—and herself—away from them.

She did not want to see him cavort. Did she?

A quick assessment of her thoughts told her, unfortunately, that she did. And she would be an unfortunate woman if she cavorted with him.

No cavorting, Lily warned herself.

"My behavior is not up for discussion, Miss Lily," he said, putting the doll down—gently, Lily noted—on the execrable escritoire. "Did you often walk in unannounced with your past employers?"

"My past . . . ?" Oh, of course, the vicar with aspirations. "Your Grace, I do apologize. I will be certain to announce myself in future so as not to disturb you." She sounded nearly as priggish as his butler did. He definitely would not wish to cavort with anyone as stuffy as she. *Good work, Lil,* she cheered herself. "I am here because Miss Rose is—that is, was—crying, and she wished I would ask you where your cat might be."

"Which one?"

Ah, so the Dangerous Duke appeared to have a clowder of cats. How very . . . unexpected.

Maybe each of his cats had their own room? What if he had other bizarre habits? First cats, then jungle animals. Or what if he decided to try to become a cat himself, and only drink milk, sleep, and groom himself? The first two might not be so bad, but images of the latter were hardly peaceful.

"She said his name was Mr. Snuffles."

One eyebrow lifted. "None of the cats have names, as far as I know."

Wonderful. Not only did he have a multitude of cats, he hadn't even bothered to name them. It was a good thing his daughter already had a name, or he might just be calling her "Girl" for the rest of her life.

"This cat is all black with white spots."

"So not all black, then." His lips curled into a smirk, and Lily had to tamp down the desire to smile back at him. Smiling back might lead to—well, it could lead to cavorting and luring and all sorts of things a proper governess should not be thinking about, much less doing.

Right. Back to the cat. "Do you know where it might be, then?"

"No. But I can ask Thompson."

The thought of the stuffy butler having to search for a missing cat for the child who'd just arrived because the even more newly arrived governess demanded it— "No, I will just take a look for it," she said hastily.

She could not afford to make enemies on her first day here. Later on, when she was more established, *then* she could make enemies. She tried to smile, which was difficult since she was also trying to remain distant, as a governess would. She probably looked like she had a queasy stomach. Of course, she could always blame it on the Pink Room's execrableness. Or her hunger. When would she get a chance to eat, anyway? "The cat will probably wander back. It's likely being fussed over by Rose right now."

He pinched the bridge of his nose, as if in thought. "Miss Lily, may I confide in you?"

Oh, dear. Was he about to tell her of some horrific habit he had, or perhaps admit his long-held desire to live as the Duke of Snuffles, perhaps?

"Of course, Your Grace."

"I have never been in proximity to a child before."

That was not a surprise. "Oh?"

"And I will therefore ask that you help me to deal properly with her."

That he admitted to not knowing everything, when she presumed that dukes were in the habit of knowing everything, or at least being told that they did, made her heart soften.

And the expression in his dark eyes when he spoke of Rose, well, that made her soften, too.

"I will promise you employment for at least three months," he continued in a distant tone of voice, "or until Rose is sent . . . somewhere. Whichever is the longer of the two."

Ah. So he was asking her for help temporarily. Just long enough for her to become established, and then she would return to the agency with a duke's seal of approval. It would be ideal, both for her and the agency.

It would, she told herself again.

"Here." Marcus picked the doll up and thrust it at her. "Take this. To Rose," he clarified, as though she might possibly think it was a gift for her.

She took it from him, their fingers touching as

they made the exchange. The contact sent images spiraling through his brain—he wanted to slide his fingers along the back of her hand, up her sleeve to her collarbone. To run his fingers along the smooth skin of her neck the better to clasp her to him and take her mouth in a—

"That's very kind of you. How did you find a doll on such short notice?" she asked, her hazel eyes warming up to gold.

Thank goodness she could not read minds.

"I asked Thompson if there were any toys lying about." He shrugged, feeling suddenly abashed. "It was a small thing, and I thought it would make her happy."

Lily smiled, revealing a dimple in the corner of her cheek. And also, Marcus thought ruefully, revealing his sudden desire to lick at that dimple.

Where were all these urges coming from?

Well, he knew where they were coming from—he squelched the impulse to look down at himself—but the better question was *why*.

He'd have to wait to be alone to even consider how to answer that question.

"It will make her very happy, Your Grace," Lily replied. "Now, if you'll excuse me, I should go see about finding Mr. Snuffles."

Mister— Oh, the cat.

"Of course." He watched as she turned to make her way to the door. "Wait."

She turned back, holding the doll to her chest. "Yes, Your Grace?"

"I would like to join you in the search, if I may."

He couldn't help but notice the wry smile that

played about her lips. As though she wanted to laugh but wouldn't let herself.

"Yes, I know it is not usual for men in my position to go feline-hunting," he said, answering a question she hadn't asked, "but if it will make the girl happy . . ."

"Rose," she said, those lips pursing into lemony primness again.

"Yes, Rose," he said, saying it deliberately loudly. "If it will make Rose happy, I would like to help."

"It is your decision, of course." She said it in a way that cast doubt that he could locate his own nose, much less a cat that had wandered away, most likely to hunt mice in the farthest regions in the cellar.

And he could locate his nose. He was certain of it. But just to be sure, he reached up and touched it. Now she looked as though she were shocked.

By his ability to find his nose?

"Perhaps first we should check in on Rose and let her know what we are about?" He thought that seemed very sensible, and judging by how her lips returned to their natural fullness, it seemed she did as well.

"Yes, that is a very sound idea."

"So glad you approve," he replied drily.

"Approve is far too generous a word, Your Grace," she said in a voice that was trying to be lemony, but instead just reminded him of lemon custard. Delicious, thick, rich, and with a tang that encouraged more devouring.

She turned back around, and he followed,

doing his very best not to notice how her trim waist flared out into lush hips, or how the skirts of her gown swung to reveal her ankles, clad frustratingly in thick stockings. Or that he could just see the nape of her neck, that soft tender place where he wanted to place his mouth.

Excellent work not noticing. Of course, not noticing was going to take some forbearance and constraint, two things he'd never had to have before. He would have to learn. Perhaps he should hire his own governess.

Although that, he considered as he continued not noticing, would get him into worse trouble.

Lily walked ahead of him, up the intimidating staircase to the room where she'd left Rose. She was acutely aware of him behind her—his height, his handsome face, his ability to ruin her life with the snap of his fingers—and she wished the agency's first duke had been someone much less virile. Even for just a few months, it was all going to be so difficult to navigate, what with her feeling as though she wanted to blush, even without going into the Blushing Room, and being so conscious of his being a handsome, wealthy, powerful titled man. A man who always got what he wanted—she could tell that even before she met him—and one who, she knew, would not hesitate if there was something—or someone—he wanted.

She couldn't think about it now. Not when she had to concentrate on finding Mr. Snuffles.

She opened the door to the room gently, not

wanting to startle Rose with a sudden noise. The room was as she left it, with Rose sitting on the carpet, holding a cat. A cat that was all black with white spots.

So not, in fact, all black.

"Mr. Snuffles, I presume?" the duke's resonant voice said behind her.

Rose looked up, tears still on her cheeks, but with a bright smile. "He came back right after you left, I think you might have scared him." This, the girl addressed to Lily, who opened her mouth to protest. The cat had disappeared long before she arrived, but she stopped when she felt his hand on her sleeve. A conspiratorial touch that warned her not to argue.

The touch felt so intimate, as though they were sharing something, some communality. As though they were already talking without speaking, that they both had something at stake and were united in their goals to get it. That was a far more frightening moment than when she had been admiring his nose, that was for certain.

She took a breath—a deep, precise breath—and turned to meet his gaze. Noting, again, how intense his eyes were. Dark, dark brown, almost black, with strong, expressive eyebrows above. "Thank you, Your Grace. I believe we can manage on our own for the moment."

She swallowed as she realized she had dismissed him. And, by his expression, he was not accustomed to being dismissed.

If only it were as easy to dismiss him from her mind.

"If you'll excuse me, ladies." His tone was clipped and precise. "I have some business to take care of." He nodded and spun around to the door, every line of his body indicating he was irked. Perhaps even peeved.

"Duke?" Rose spoke in a quavering voice.

He turned back around, his lips curling into a warm smile.

Oh, goodness, Lily thought, do not look at me like that or I will melt into a puddle on the floor. Which will just get the carpets soggy.

"Yes, Rose?"

"Thank you for taking me after Mama died." Rose said it matter-of-factly, as though it were an everyday occurrence to be brought to the Mansion of Many Rooms. She returned to petting the cat.

Leaving the two adults in the room entirely at a loss for words themselves.

A duke takes his entertainment as he wishes, as long as the entertainment is not detrimental to his reputation, his wealth, or society in general. Entertainment, therefore, should be limited to reading books of an edifying nature, ~~cavorting~~speaking with ~~in~~appropriate companionship, and perhaps the care and ownership of a ~~ca~~respectable animal.

—The Duke's Guide to Correct Behavior

Chapter 6

He didn't say anything more, just gave Lily one last look from those dark eyes and left her alone, at last, with Rose.

And Mr. Snuffles.

Lily knelt down on the rug beside both of them, resisting the urge to smooth her hand over Rose's hair, like Rose was doing to the cat.

"Oh!" Lily held the doll the duke had given her. "The duke wanted you to have this."

Rose's eyes widened and she stopped petting Mr. Snuffles to take it, immediately cradling it in her arms as though it were a real creature.

Lily did give in to her impulse then and smoothed Rose's hair. "You'll have to give her a name," *because goodness knows your father won't.*

Rose screwed up her face in thought and then nodded. "Maggie," she pronounced.

"Excellent choice." Lily hesitated, but she needed Rose to know that she had an ally in the house. One without fur or buttons for eyes, but a friend, nonetheless.

"I know we have just met, but I want you to

know that I will take good care of you. As your father will, as well," she continued, making a promise that was not hers to make. But one she would enforce.

"Mm-hm."

It might not mean anything to the girl now, but it meant something to Lily.

"Rose," she said, thinking about her own past, and how she wished just one person had asked, *How are you feeling?* "I know you just got here this morning. Did you get to ride in a carriage? I have never been in this part of London before," except to walk through and envy its inhabitants, "and this house is so large. Will you help if I get lost walking around?"

Rose nodded solemnly. Lily was opening her mouth to follow up with something else, something to help the girl feel more comfortable (besides a cat and a doll), when Rose spoke.

"Mama died this morning, and her friend said as how my papa needed to take care of me, and she put me in a carriage with two horses, one brown, one black, and then we were here." She nuzzled her doll's hair. "I miss Mama, but the duke said he would take care of me."

Lily knew she was the one who couldn't speak now, her words choked in her throat. If only there had been someone who could have taken care of a younger Lily, she wouldn't have had to find work in the only place she could. But her mother had just . . . drifted off after her father died, eventually dying, and there was no one else. Lily didn't want to drift herself. She wanted a purpose and joy in her life.

Not to mention food in her belly. Rose was now engrossed in introducing Maggie to Mr. Snuffles, or vice versa, so perhaps she could sneak away for something to eat. "Will you be all right just for a few moments?" She was hoping she could locate the kitchen in no fewer than ten doors. If she was lucky. "And then I will return and we will discuss what we will be doing in the upcoming days."

"I won't be alone, Mr. Snuffles and Maggie are here." Rose said it as though it was perfectly obvious, they were right there, and they actually were, Mr. Snuffles now engaged in chewing on a strand of Maggie's hair. It seemed the introductions had gone well.

"Of course. I will return shortly."

As she opened the door, she spotted a maid dusting one of the many pictures in the enormous hallway and asked her to come sit with Rose, who accepted the maid—her name was Etta—with as much stoicism as she'd accepted being there at all.

Relieved at solving that problem, she headed off to see if she could quell her starving stomach.

She found the kitchen in fewer than ten doors, and was able to introduce herself to the cook and finagle a cup of tea and a scone.

The cook, whose name was Partridge, was thankfully not nearly as stuffy as either the butler or the footman who'd brought the note. Partridge confirmed the duke telling her that Rose had just arrived and was his daughter by "one of them fallen women." And then the cook pursed her mouth in disapproval, reminding Lily once again what would happen if anyone discovered her own past.

Not that she'd *worked* in a brothel, but if anyone heard "worked in a brothel" they would assume the worst. Because why would anyone look beyond that, to the woman herself? That all she had done was manage the accounts, as she did now for the agency, was beside the point.

She had to make her own fortune, since her father had been so unfortunate as to lose everything he owned. The risk-taking fool. He hadn't taught her anything about looking ahead to the future, or done anything beyond showing her just what kind of person she didn't want to marry, much less be. The kind who just wanted to go off and do whatever he wanted, with no thought for others.

She had to remember her goals, and just what was at stake. Not just for her, but for her partners and all the women they'd helped in the past few months, and whom they hoped to help in the future. People who perhaps had been left behind by others who could have taken care of them—and didn't.

People who didn't have a duke for a father, or her for a governess.

She was on her way back up to Rose when she remembered—she had brought nothing with her, and she would be sleeping there tonight. That was certainly a risk, wasn't it? "Where is the duke?" she asked a footman, who was carrying some dirty glasses and what appeared to be a lady's corset.

She would not ask about that.

The footman to whom she'd spoken gestured to one of the other doors. "In his study. But—"

Lily didn't wait for whatever he was about to say. She knocked twice on the door, just to give him a head start on not cavorting, then opened the door and stepped inside, closing the door behind her.

He was not cavorting. He was—he was sitting in a massive chair, his long legs stretched out in front of him, with a gigantic orange cat on his lap. Petting it.

A cup of tea was placed on the side table next to him, and if it had been any other person sitting there, Lily would have thought it a sweet domestic scene.

Especially since he was crooning in some secret cat language in a soft tone of voice, not at all the autocratic, arrogant duke who snapped orders.

Only it was still him, with his attractive nose, and his sharply planed face, and the way he'd shown both kindness and autocracy, sometimes within minutes of each other, and how he'd made her blush, even if he likely wasn't the least aware he'd made her blush. But there was definitely blushing.

"Your Grace." She swallowed, and could have sworn his eyes tracked the movement in her neck. Watching as she gathered the courage to ask him.

"I assume that Rose is all right," he said, "and that you are here to have a question answered that no one else in my household can possibly answer."

His tone wasn't entirely mocking, but Lily would have to put it at about seventy-five percent mockery. She didn't want to even think about the other twenty-five percent.

She felt her cheeks start to get warm. She wasn't even in the Blushing Room.

"Yes, you see, I feel it is my responsibility to remain here, now that Rose is in my care, and yet I have realized I left all of my belongings, and I would ask if I might go retrieve them."

He frowned. The cat, no doubt nameless, seemed to sense his displeasure, since it leapt off his lap in what looked like a burst of orange fireworks. "Now? But it is getting toward dark, and you cannot go alone."

"Perhaps you might send a footman with me?"

Please don't let it be the grouchy footman. Unless that was the only kind he had. And then the grouchy footman would see where she lived, in not the most respectable of neighborhoods, and would report back to all the staff, and she would be unfortunate in an entirely new and different way. Wonderful.

"Unless . . ." Dear Lord. She was really going to ask this.

He raised an eyebrow, waiting for her to speak.

"Unless you knew of something that I might wear this evening? To bed? And then I could go gather my things tomorrow, first thing, after breakfast."

"So not first thing at all," he said in a sly tone of voice.

She could not get distracted by the fact that this

was the second time in only a few hours that she and the duke had shared a joke. Even if thoughts of laughing together kindled something warm, low in her belly.

"That is, if one of your female staff would be able—"

"I do not have any female staff."

"But you do, a maid is watching Rose. If you would give me your permission to ask to borrow something—"

"No." His tone was every inch that of a duke, even though he was the first duke she had ever encountered. She just knew that it was not possible for anyone who didn't have his rank, his power, his fortune—not to mention his looks—to ever speak so firmly, so commandingly, so certain he would be obeyed. And then, just as she was about to ask him just what he thought she should do, he told her.

Just as someone in his position would do.

"I have plenty of nightshirts, you will take one of mine." He rose as he spoke, and the combined impact of his height and presence and the shocking thing he'd said made it feel as though all the breath had been knocked out of her.

Except it sounded as though she were breathing faster, so perhaps not. And now she was imagining him in his nightshirt—not that she knew what a man's nightshirt looked like, especially not a duke's nightshirt, perhaps it was edged in gold or was made out of butterfly wings—but she could more than imagine what he would look like with fewer clothes on, and that was dangerous enough.

"I cannot," Lily said, trying to sound calm and in control and mildly disapproving, even though she knew she sounded startled and breathy and perhaps too concerned with what dukes looked like in their night garb. "It is entirely improper."

"More improper than asking to borrow a maid's clothing? Do you think they don't all gossip, and they'll wonder at the propriety of not only a young girl coming to live here, but that her governess seemed to appear out of thin air with no possessions?" His eyebrow rose as he asked the question, and she felt a moment of embarrassment for being so shortsighted. Beyond the grouchy footman scenario, at least.

But his nightshirt! "I have possessions, I just don't have them here!"

He shrugged, as though he didn't care. And of course he didn't.

"You can borrow my nightshirt, or not. What you sleep in is your concern, but now that the girl—Rose," he said with a special emphasis, "is here, I will not have speculation regarding anything related to the house." He seemed to get lost in thought for a moment. "It is time for everyone to behave with propriety."

So. In order to ensure that his staff did not gossip about him, he was asking her to do the most improper thing she could imagine—well, no, scratch that, if pressed she could certainly imagine more improper things—and wear his clothing to bed. Against her skin.

And if she were a woman who had no interest in her position beyond having a position, she would be leaving her post immediately, because if this was what he said the first day she was on the job, what would he be saying—not to mention doing—on her fifteenth? Her forty-seventh?

But she was invested, far more than he could possibly know, so she would take it and suffer him and his autocracies.

That it came with the bonus of being able to enjoy his looks and his presence, well, that was just a . . . a *bonus.* Rather like finding that one unspoiled apple in a bushel. And no, she did not want to take a bite of him. Well. Not much of a bite, at least.

"Fine. I'll take your nightshirt. And then tomorrow I will retrieve my own things," she said in a voice as frigid as she could make it without being outright insolent.

He waved his hand. "Why bother? If the rest of your wardrobe is anything like this gown, we will outfit you in new things when we go shopping for Rose. She has the same quality of clothing you do, one would suspect that you habituated the same establishments. Dowdy and Daughters, or something like that."

"That would be most improper, Your Grace."

His lips lifted into a knowing smile. "More improper than wearing my clothing to bed, Miss Lily? Hardly. So we will go shopping tomorrow, and we will choose some clothing suitable for your position. If you are clothed unsuitably, that will cause talk. And I have just said I wished for propriety, and since I can afford to buy it—I will."

There was no arguing with him, was there?

Of course it wasn't as though she had that many items of clothing to begin with. She had gowns that she categorized as more or less serviceable.

"An excellent plan," she said through gritted teeth.

She should not be so irked that he would be buying her new clothing, especially given the state of her old clothing, but it felt uneasily as though he would be buying *her.* And since she was well aware of what happened to women who'd been bought, she had to keep her guard up.

Although a part of her—that foolish yelping part—was absolutely delighted she was about to have some new gowns.

And wear his nightshirt to bed.

If it is in a duke's power to ~~buy his governess clothing~~improve his surroundings, and can afford to do so, he should, despite what ~~his governess's~~others' opinions might be on the subject.

—The Duke's Guide to Correct Behavior

Chapter 7

Provoking his newest employee was already more fun than gambling. He always won at the tables, presenting no sort of challenge whatsoever. But she—she was a challenge, that was for certain. She'd picked up on his jokes, when so many people just stared blankly at him, as though a duke couldn't have a sense of humor. She had dared to impugn, or at least come close to implying, he couldn't find his nose when he so clearly could. She had gotten Rose to talk within minutes of meeting her, where he had only gotten nods and shakes of the head.

And now he wanted to laugh all over again at the thought of what she'd asked, and how he'd answered. Very provoking of him, he knew that.

She so clearly wanted to rail (not night rail!) against him for his commands, and yet she did not. She just stood in front of him, her spine totally straight, those full lips clamped together in a tight line.

He hadn't had a challenge in his life since—well,

since one of his school friends had demanded he balance a spoon on his nose for two minutes.

Over the years, he'd wished that his father or his brother would care enough to challenge him to do anything. Balancing a spoon, riding a horse, playing a game—anything. The only thing they had done was insist he stop wandering around on his own for hours, since it wasn't suitable for a gentleman.

Apparently it was suitable for him to be ignored, and belittled when he wasn't being ignored. So when the spoon challenge had been issued, he'd done it for three minutes, not just two.

If only he could do other things for that long. But he shouldn't be thinking about that—he probably could get into trouble for it. Except that seemed it was all he could think about.

She was more than a spoon on one's nose.

"Come, then." He strode to the door and flung it open, holding it for her to exit through. Her skirts brushed his legs, and he caught the scent of her—a warm, delicate scent, something that reminded him of the best summer day in London—no, not that, London smelled horrible in the summer, perhaps the country, then. But he shook that off, studiously practicing not noticing as she ascended the stairs.

She paused at the landing and lifted her face to his, that lemon-sucking expression at its most lemoniest. "Where are we going, Your Grace?"

"To my bedroom, of course," Marcus replied, a wicked thrill going through him at the words. *To his bedroom.*

Her lemony face changed into one of shock, but not, he was relieved, of horror.

"I cannot go with you into your bedroom, you know that."

"Clearly, since I've just said that's where we're going, I do not know that. This way," he said, not waiting for her to argue with him any longer. She could sleep naked, if she wanted—and oh, goodness, but wasn't that an image that would haunt him this evening—but she would go with him.

He set off down the hall, not waiting to see if she would follow. His room was at the very end of the corridor, past all the disapproving portraits of past Dukes of Rutherford who likely could not believe the current duke was such a rascal.

He hadn't asked to be duke, he wanted to shout at them. But now that he was, shouldn't he at least enjoy all the privileges of the position?

Marcus stepped into his bedroom, feeling her close behind him. He put his arm behind her to shut the door, then spun back around to face his wardrobe. "Now where are my nightshirts?" he said, tapping his finger against his mouth. He knew their approximate location, but his valet usually got them out. It was too early for Miller to be at his post, which was what he was counting on anyway—not just because it meant they would be alone, but also so none of the servants would have a chance to spread any shocking news about the duke and his new employee.

"Do not concern yourself if you can't locate one quickly," she said in a terse tone.

He turned and raised an eyebrow at her. "Are

you assuming I do not even know where my own things are, Miss Lily?" He yanked the drawer open and rifled through it, not caring—much—that Miller would have to carefully fold everything again. He pulled a nightshirt out and held it over his shoulder, not turning to face her.

There was a pause, then he felt her take hold of the other end of it and pull, at which point he did turn around, separating them by his nightshirt.

If only that were so in a different type of scenario.

"Thank you, Your Grace," she said, not meeting his gaze. "I will return it tomorrow." She tugged again, but he only let it slide more through his hands, not let go of it entirely.

"No need, I have many more. It wouldn't be right, would it, for me to wear it after you've had it next to your skin?"

Did he imagine it, or did she shiver at his words?

He did let go of it then, and she snatched it, tucking it up against her chest in a tight little ball. "Thank you. And if you'll excuse me, I wish to check on Rose."

With that she fled, leaving him on his own to think about the two females he'd just allowed into his life. He had the suspicion—no, he *knew* his life was never going to be the same.

Lily scurried down the hall, resisting—just barely—the temptation to bury her nose in the linen she held pressed against her. Her bedroom was just beyond Rose's, and after she went in, she put the nightshirt on the bed before returning to Rose's room.

Rose lay splayed out on the bed, the covers halfway down her body, the new doll—Maggie—clutched tightly in her arms, while Mr. Snuffles lay at the foot of the bed assiduously licking himself.

"She fell asleep after about fifteen minutes, poor little mite," Etta said. "She's a sweet thing."

"Thank you for staying with her," Lily replied. Etta nodded and slid out of the room, every inch a respectable, innocuous maid.

Lily perched on the side of the bed, marveling at its size and comfort. It was easily twice the size of the bed in her own home, and this bed was only half the size of the duke's. That she'd seen. When she was in his bedroom.

The impropriety of it made her stomach roil. Or perhaps that was Partridge's scone.

Rose lifted her head, her eyes still heavy with sleep.

"Did you have a nice nap, Miss Rose?" Lily replied.

Rose nodded. "Etta told me a story, and Mr. Snuffles purred me to sleep, and Maggie says she likes it here."

"That's nice. Do you wish to tidy up for dinner? I am not certain when it is, but you must be hungry."

Rose twisted her mouth up in thought. "Not very, I had tea when I first got here. With the duke. There were scones."

Of course. Tea with the Dangerous Duke.

"Tomorrow we're to go shopping for new clothing."

Rose made a face. "Don't like shopping. Can't I just stay here with Mr. Snuffles?"

And leave me to shop alone with him?

"Perhaps, Miss Rose," Lily said, flicking her nose. "We will see how you feel tomorrow. It's been—" How to say it without mentioning what must have happened to land Rose here, yet to make sure she knew it was all right to talk about it? "—a day," she finished lamely.

"Yes, it has," Rose said, sounding as though she thought it was an obvious point. Which it was.

"Yes. Well." And in other conversational gambits, perhaps she could teach Rose all about tautology, pointing out not only that the day was a day, but that the cat was a cat, and the doll was even, oh my goodness, a doll.

She allowed herself to smile at thinking the duke would likely enjoy the joke.

"Tea, Thompson."

"Tea, Your Grace?" Thompson sounded as surprised as his properly stodgy self could, which is to say as though the bakery had delivered twelve rolls instead of a baker's dozen. A horror, likely, to Thompson's way of seeing things.

Marcus glanced up from his paper. "Tea." If he was going to be a respectable father, which he damned well was, he would drink tea, not brandy.

Which was why he was sitting in the library, not in any of the more convivial rooms, reading a newspaper and awaiting tea. As opposed to, say, drinking bottles of brandy with his new boon companions.

Or cavorting with the governess, a voice whispered in his head.

Hadn't he just twelve hours ago been dissatisfied with the course of his life? Been wanting some sort of occupation that someone with his title and responsibilities could engage in without getting engaged?

It felt as though he hadn't really done anything with his life. No, he *knew* he hadn't really done anything with his life. And now he had the chance to do something good, for another person. Perhaps then he would be able to allow himself to do something he wanted, even if it wasn't necessarily right.

Could he look at himself in the glass if he hadn't, at least, tried to do the right thing for his daughter?

The door opened before he could answer that, thank goodness. Thompson himself bore the tray in, setting it down on the desk just adjacent to where Marcus was sitting.

"Shall I pour, Your Grace?"

"No, thank you. I can take care of it." Because while he was intent on behaving more like a proper duke, he had no wish to be fussed over, no matter if every other duke received that behavior.

"Very well." Thompson made as though to go, but Marcus held his hand out.

"Wait. The thing is, if anyone inquires, Miss Rose is my cousin's daughter. The cousin has just recently died. If anyone inquires," he repeated. Which they will.

Thompson nodded. "Of course, Your Grace. If you need anything further, just ring."

"Mmph," Marcus grunted. Thompson left, shutting the door softly behind him, leaving him alone with the tea, the paper, and likely a cat or two hiding somewhere.

Mr. Snuffles, she'd named the all-black one. With white spots. He hadn't missed Miss Lily's answering smirk when he pointed out that an all-black cat would not be all-black if it had white spots, and he wondered when he'd last shared a simple joke with someone.

Oh, yes. The night before, with Smithfield. His new best friend. Who was—goodness, what had he been thinking?—coming to dinner next week, his best friend's sisters and husbands in tow as well. He'd have to make sure he sent out proper, written invitations—something he'd never had to deal with before.

If that didn't make him want to run away— Oh, wait, it did. But he would endure it, for his new-found propriety's sake.

She couldn't put it off any longer. She'd washed her face, brushed her hair, and tidied the already tidy room.

It was already eleven o'clock. Her duties would begin as soon as Rose awoke, and she had to be prepared.

She had to get undressed and put the nightshirt on.

She'd laid it right in the middle of the predictably enormous bed, where it remained, not doing anything.

Except to her peace of mind.

Her previous experience with men was limited to dealing with the tradesmen who'd supplied the brothel, most of whom had been married; she'd always worked in one of the back rooms, far away from the clientele, so she'd never run into any of *them*, thank goodness.

"It's only a piece of clothing," she said to herself. "It is not as though putting it on will mean anything, and it would be even more improper to sleep with nothing on all together." Put that way, it—well, it was still altogether too shocking.

She reached behind herself to undo the buttons of her gown. Undoing buttons at the back was normally an awkward task, but being so aware of the impropriety of what she was about to do added another element of difficulty, and she was perspiring by the time she got the sleeves off and was stepping out of the wide skirts of her dress.

She spared another glance at the nightshirt—it hadn't moved—and began to undo her corset, then removed her shift, biting her lip as all the thoughts of the day rushed in.

Meeting Rose, the duke, the agency's potential for success, the *foyer*, for goodness' sake, the doors, the pink room, and now this nightshirt?

It was enough to overwhelm anyone, much less

a precise, prim, methodical person such as herself. Or as she tried to be.

She picked up the nightshirt and put it on. There. She'd done it. As easy as donning the persona of a governess.

Or a fortunate woman.

While it might seem unreasonable for a gentleman to be expected to be dressed suitably at all times, it is nonetheless incumbent upon a gentleman who is also a duke to be dressed impeccably. If he is somehow caught being less than impeccably dressed, he should behave as though it is comme il faut *(even though he should not be speaking in a foreign language, especially French).*

—The Duke's Guide to Correct Behavior

Chapter 8

"Don't wanna go." Rose lifted her face, with its peeved expression, to Lily.

"I do not want to go," she corrected her, then caught herself at Rose's satisfied look. "That is, I am not saying you can stay here, but the proper way to say what you just said is 'I do not want to go.' "

"I do not want to go," Rose repeated, raising her chin in an unmistakable look of defiance. Lily tried not to laugh at how much her charge resembled her father at that moment. "I want to stay here with Mr. Snuffles and Maggie. We're having a tea party. With scones!" she added, as though that should be enough to convince Lily of the wisdom of her plans.

It did sound like fun. Much less disturbing, at least, than heading out on a shopping expedition with the duke to purchase clothing for both the new females in his household. And with more scones.

Rose must have seen how she was on the verge of relenting, since she put her sweetest smile on as she blinked her enormous eyes. "Please?" she said in a pleading voice.

"We shall consult the duke."

"He'll say yes," Rose said confidently. And likely he would, since he'd already said he had no experience with young children, and the prospect of taking a reluctant child out for several hours was enough to make even experienced caregivers blanch.

"We will see," is all Lily replied.

When he was presented with the issue by Rose, the duke shrugged. "If you don't wish to go," he'd said, "you don't have to. But you will have to trust that Miss Lily and I will choose the best things for you."

Of course he said yes. Because of course then Lily would have to spend time with him, alone, as he bought her clothing.

Rose nodded, engrossed in attempting to feed a kipper to Maggie. It was not going well.

He looked over at Lily, and she saw a glimmer of amusement in his eyes. As though he knew full well just what the prospect of them being alone together was doing to her. "Well, then, shall we say we will depart in half an hour?"

She kept her face as expressionless as she could. "Of course, Your Grace. I'll just ask one of the maids to stay with Miss Rose, if that is acceptable."

He waved a hand as though he couldn't care less. "Certainly. Whatever is best."

What would be best, she wanted to reply, is if he would not continue to unsettle her so. But that might be better said to herself.

After ensuring that Rose was safely ensconced with Maggie, Mr. Snuffles, Etta, and the orange cat Lily had seen the previous evening with the duke—whom Rose had named Orange—Lily met the duke in the foyer, where one of the footmen was waiting with her cloak. It looked even shabbier in the context of the duke's mansion. No wonder he thought she shopped at Dowdy and Daughters.

"There you are. Come along." The duke's tone was abrupt, and he strode to the door ahead of her. Well. He certainly was not the Duke of Politeness, that was for certain.

She trailed after him, unable to keep pace with his long-legged stride. Hopefully he would wait a moment before telling his coachman to go, so she had time to get in.

She was practically running down the steps to the carriage when she saw an arm extended from its depths. His, of course. Even his *arm* had an unmistakable aura of autocracy. She took his hand and got into the coach, sitting opposite him, so she was riding with her back to the horses.

It was darker than outside, and her eyes took a moment to adjust, but her ears had no such delay. "Sit next to me," he said, his voice equal parts boredom and command.

"Why— Oh, fine," Lily said in a frigid tone of voice as she crossed over.

His only response was a chuckle.

"Our first stop is the dressmaker's."

"There will be more than one stop?" she replied, wincing as she heard how her voice squeaked.

"That is, of course we can go wherever you wish, but I hadn't expected to be out for so long."

"Your charge will be fine. I appreciate your conscientiousness, but it seems to me that Rose needs time to adjust to her new situation, and she seemed quite delighted at the prospect of being with the cats and the doll."

"Where are we to go, then?"

She felt him shrug. "You said you needed some supplies for Rose, and I thought we could take care of it now. Plus, since we'll be out for a bit, I thought we would get lunch."

"Lunch? Together? That is hardly—"

"Proper?" he interrupted, his voice full of an emotion she couldn't name. "Look here, I am willing to forego all sorts of things in the name of propriety, but I will not be told I cannot dine in public with my child's governess." There was a pause, and then he spoke again, this time much less passionately. "I apologize. You don't deserve my ire."

"It is not my place to pass judgment, Your Grace." She gazed out the window as though anything outside were more interesting than what was within. Which it absolutely was not.

"And now you're reminding me you are merely a servant." He exhaled. "Cannot we agree we have at least one thing in common, and that is wishing for Rose to receive the best possible care?"

"Of course, Your Grace," she said in a repressive tone.

"And for goodness' sake, don't call me 'Your Grace' each and every time you speak to me. It's aggravating."

"What should I call you, then?" she asked. "Mr. Snuffles is already taken, and I hardly think you wish to be called 'Orange.'"

He laughed in response, and she felt that low chuckle resonate through her body. That he was this . . . improper when it came to being a lord—a duke, no less—was dangerous. Truly a Dangerous Duke, in that he was not very dukely at all, unless one counted the power, the money, the position, the air of command, and the many rooms.

Not that she was counting.

"Just leave off the 'Your Grace' two sentences out of three," he said, laughter in his voice. "I know you are cognizant of who I am, and I hope I am not so stupid as to be unaware that you are speaking to me, so we can dispense with so much propriety."

Now that thought definitely kindled something low in her belly. Dispensing with propriety seemed like a very . . . dangerous thing to do.

"Yes, Your— That is, fine."

"Excellent. Glad to have that settled." A pause. "Although if you wish to address me as 'Orange,' that would be acceptable." Now he was definitely teasing her. The worst part? She felt like teasing him back.

But she couldn't, not without risking things that should not be risked, such as her heart, her position, and oh, yes, her future.

He didn't think he'd ever had so much fun, at least not such proper fun. She was, in fact, about as proper as he could wish for, which was why he took such glee in riling her.

He couldn't let it go any further, but this—this was delightful, an entirely unexpected benefit to his having an illegitimate child, a need to be proper, and for his child to have a governess.

The carriage rolled to a stop at the dressmaker's, and the governess in question practically flew out of the coach, the rigid set of her shoulders indicating her displeasure with him and the situation in general, he presumed.

He just wanted to laugh again.

His footman opened the door and they walked in, the proprietor's face changing within seconds to disapproving—having seen Miss Lily first—to fawning, when he followed.

"May I be of service, my lord?" The proprietor was a middle-aged, not unattractive woman. She was wearing attractive fashionable clothing, a far cry from what Miss Lily had on.

"We need clothing for this lady, here," he said, gesturing to Lily.

And when had he started thinking of her as Lily, anyway? Oh, somewhere between thinking about what Miss Lily had on and indicating who she was. So right now.

The woman's face froze and her mouth pursed. "I am not certain, my lord, that my establishment is appropriate for what you are seeking."

"I am the Duke of Rutherford's governess, and he requires me to be gowned appropriately." Lily's voice was low and polite, the complete opposite of how Marcus wished to address the shop owner.

The woman's face cleared. "Ah, of course, Your Grace," she said, her tone changing to one of obsequiousness. "I have the very items. One of my patrons had a change of heart regarding her clothing, so as it happens I have some ready-made that will need only a few adjustments to fit the lady here."

"She will have new," Marcus began with a growl, only to be interrupted by Lily. Again.

"That will suit admirably, how fortuitous that you have them."

The woman glanced between them, clearly caught as to what to do. Marcus crossed his arms over his chest. "As she said, go ahead and fetch the clothing."

"Yes, of course, Your Grace." She went to the back of the shop, casting a quick look of awe behind her.

He hated those looks of awe. Far better to be regarded with an emotion not inspired by his title. And he knew the difference; until recently he'd been regarded with a much more varied range of looks.

Like the one with which his governess was now looking at him. "Why aren't you pleased?" he asked her. "I allowed you to have your way."

She uttered the most ladylike snort he'd ever heard. Not that he'd heard that many, honestly—most ladies did not snort. Especially in the presence of dukes.

He liked it.

"My way would be for you not to purchase clothing for me at all. It is not proper," she began, then her eyes widened as she realized what she'd said.

"Not proper," he repeated, moving closer to where she stood. "Not proper can encompass many things, Miss Lily. Would you like me to list them all for you?" Now he was within a few feet of her, a few delicious feet of her, but she stood her ground, not edging backward as he'd expected.

He liked this, too.

"There is no need, Your Grace," she replied through clenched teeth.

He advanced on her, not quite sure what he was about to do, but the shop's proprietor bustled back in with several items of clothing looped over her arm.

"These are the things, Your Grace, and of course I have bonnets and gloves and shawls and all the other necessary accessories to dress a young lady properly."

"Properly, hm?" Marcus echoed, knowing he was making her squirm.

"Admit it," he said when they were finished at the dressmaker's, "it wasn't that terrible. And now you are properly outfitted as a governess."

Lily smoothed the folds of her new gown. Mrs. Wilson had been able to make the necessary alterations while she and the duke chose clothing for Rose, and then he'd insisted that she change immediately.

It was nicer than anything she had ever owned. Green, with simple embroidery on the front and a not too wide skirt or sleeves looked like balloons. She hated those.

Entirely respectable, Mrs. Wilson had assured them, with a nervous glance at the duke, and she had to admit that it looked lovely on her.

She felt lovely in it as well. No, more than that, she felt *beautiful*, which she hadn't ever really felt before. Certainly she knew she wasn't horrible to look at, but seeing herself in the glass at Mrs. Wilson's shop made her breath catch. The gown fit well, highlighting her bosom and her small waist, and the color made her eyes seem almost emerald.

"And now you are a proper companion to Rose," he continued, startling her out of her self-assessment. "I would not have it said the Duke of Rutherford does not have proper employees." His tone of voice indicated he was teasing, although his words made Lily's breath catch again, but this time not in a pleasant way.

She was not proper, not at all. She had worked at a brothel and she was the owner of a small, struggling business that aided other unfortunate women. Women whose lives would be irreparably damaged if she failed.

Perhaps she should be worried less about his propriety than her own. She would have to behave as properly as possible, so as not to give anybody reason to talk.

He held his arm out for her. "I am taking you to Verey's for lunch, it is a respectable—proper, even—restaurant."

"Thank you, Your Grace." She resisted the urge to stick her tongue out at him when he glowered.

That would just be rude. Even though she wanted to. "You said every third time, and I have been counting. I will not say it again for a while."

He did not respond to that, for which she was grateful. "We will purchase what you need for Rose's schooling after we eat. I, for one, am famished."

The restaurant was entirely respectable, and once the host realized just who was dining, they were served with the utmost in proper service.

Lily had only ever eaten at pubs before, since arriving in London. In the country, her father had prided himself on serving the best table in fifty miles, but that wasn't saying very much. In those days, she had been acutely aware of just how much each meal was costing them from their ever dwindling funds. Until there was nothing at all.

This was the first time, then, that she'd had good food that didn't make her feel guilty. The duke ordered for both of them, of course, not even deigning to ask her what she liked to eat. And she loved every bite, from the tender roast chicken to the new potatoes to the littlest peas she'd ever seen.

"This is delicious. Thank you." She took a sip of wine, another first time for her—she'd only ever had tea at lunch. It felt decadent, and absolutely right to be here with him as she did it.

"You are welcome. Thank you." He leaned back in his chair and gazed at her. "I am grateful to have your expertise in dealing with Rose." He cleared his throat and glanced somewhere over her head. "My own upbringing is not a useful guide for a young girl."

He sounded almost wistful. As though being the heir to a dukedom—provided he wasn't a duke already—was a hardship.

"What was your favorite thing to do when you were growing up?" she asked.

"Besides terrorizing the peasants?" He grinned as he spoke, and she couldn't help but grin back. "I grew up in the country, a mid-sized country estate," he continued.

Like me, Lily thought in surprise.

"When did you move to London?" She had only been here a few years, and she did miss the country. But there would have been no opportunity to earn her living, nor was anyone there for her anymore—her mother died a little over two years ago, her father earlier than that, leaving his family nothing. Her sister—well, it had been at least fifteen years since she died.

She would rather be a not starved orphan than a starved one, she'd decided in those weeks after her mother died.

"I moved here when I inherited the title," the duke said, and screwed his face up in thought. "It's been close to six months, I believe. But I haven't lived in the country for long before that—I was sent to school, and I spent vacations there. Then I traveled in Europe for a few years."

She was opening her mouth to ask why, if he had a family in the country, he'd spent his vacations at school, until she realized that was far too intimate a question. And he might respond with questions of his own, which would be too dangerous.

"I've never been to Europe." *Unlike the country.* "What did you do there?"

He chuckled. "The same thing I did when I was growing up. I walked. I like listening to the quiet, if that makes any sense." He spoke in a soft voice, as though for her ears only, as though for her only.

She nodded. "It does make sense. London is so loud sometimes, and I wish I could just escape and be where no one is talking."

His lips twisted into a wry smile. "If you were a duke, you could just command them to stop talking."

She acted before she realized it, poking him in the arm. "Hush, you know you're all bark and no bite." She paused, then amended her words. "Or mostly no bite. Speaking of terrorizing, you came close with the dressmaker." She glanced down at her gown. Yes. It was still nicer than anything she had ever owned. "Thank you for this, by the way."

He smiled smugly. "I wanted to make sure that nobody would be able to cast aspersion on you or Rose for anything but your own personalities."

"Because we are both so dreadful on our own?" she replied, a teasing tone in her voice.

He shook his head. "That came out entirely wrong. I mean, I want Rose to feel valued. To feel as though she is being taken care of, and that she is not an afterthought. Even though—"

A silence. Even though she *had* been an afterthought, if thought of at all, from what Lily could gauge of the girl's history.

"Never mind. I just wanted to do the right thing," he said, taking another sip from his glass.

"Perhaps you would want to take Rose on a long walk sometime? To hear the silence?"

He met her gaze, a nearly hesitant smile on his face. "You think she would like that?"

Lily nodded, her throat tightening at the thought of her own father never once wanting to take her out for a walk to "hear the silence."

"I do," she replied.

~~A duke must never exhibit an unseemly emotion~~.
I'll do what I want.

—The Duke's Guide to Correct Behavior

Chapter 9

"I want to do it." Rose picked up the pencil from the table, her expression one of intense concentration.

They were in the schoolroom, Lily having arranged the various supplies she'd gotten on the table. They were reviewing Rose's education thus far, which was not as meager as Lily had worried. She had been loved, even if she lived in reduced circumstances.

Lily was grateful for that—she knew what it was like to be unloved, or at least not loved enough. Her mother had loved her, but when it came time to make hard decisions and try, her mother chose to just give up, essentially dying of fatigue.

It had made Lily even more determined to work as hard as she could. "Start at the top of the letter, it makes it easier to form." Lily reached out to touch the paper. "An A connects at the top, then goes down like streamers from a maypole."

Rose's eyes lit up. "I know those! We went to the fair last year. Mama looked so pretty."

She must have been lovely, Lily thought as

she regarded Rose. The child, now that she was cleaned up and sleeping well, was adorable, her huge, dark eyes like her father's, while it seemed—thankfully—she'd inherited her mother's up-turned nose.

"What did you and your mama like to do best?"

Rose kept her face bent over the paper, the emerging letter A needing her attention. "She told me stories. Like you do. I like those stories."

"That's very good, Miss Rose," Lily said, looking at the finished A. "And what stories are your favorites?"

Rose looked up. "Fairy stories. With princes, and dragons. I like the dragons."

"I like princes and dragons, too." She tapped the paper. "Do you want to try the next letter in the alphabet? What would that be, I wonder?" she said, tilting her head in thought.

"B!" Rose shouted, earning a smile from Lily.

"Yes, B, that's it. Do you remember what that looks like?"

Rose looked as though she was going to say of course she did, then she shook her head, as though reluctant to admit she didn't know after all.

She had inherited some traits from her father.

Lily took a pencil and wrote the letter next to the completed letter A. "Like this, a straight line with two equal bumps on the side."

Rose took her own pencil and started writing just below Lily's letter, her tongue sticking out of her mouth as she concentrated.

"What words begin with the letter B?" Lily asked. "Does 'cat' begin with B?"

Rose's expression was scornful. "Of course not, 'cat' begins with—with . . ." she said, faltering.

"Does 'bat' begin with B?"

"Yes, it does. And 'boat,' and 'best,' and 'biscuit.' "

"Very good!" Lily said. "And your B looks lovely."

Rose smiled at the praise.

They both turned as they heard footsteps—decisive, long-legged footsteps—in the hallway.

"Duke!" Rose exclaimed as he entered the room. "We're working on letters, do you know Miss Lily thought 'cat' began with a B?"

The duke's eyes glanced at Lily. "Perhaps you should be the one teaching her, then." His tone was humorous, and Lily saw the glint of laughter in his eyes.

"She writes letters better than I do," Rose admitted. "So maybe not."

"Ah, I see," the duke said, looking at the paper. "I was coming to see if you would like to spend a few hours with me, Miss Rose? Miss Lily has her afternoon off, and I have no other plans."

The way he spoke, as though he were genuinely asking, not ordering, made Lily's heart nearly hurt. And that was before she saw the expression on Rose's face, which was the most joyous thing she might have ever beheld.

"Yes, can we have something to eat first?"

"Of course." The duke held his hand out to Rose, who tucked her smaller hand in his. "If you will excuse us, Miss Lily, my lady and I have an engagement for the afternoon."

"Certainly, Your Grace," Lily replied, trying not to beam too much as she looked at the two of them.

"Lily, it's wonderful to see you!" Annabelle bustled over as soon as Lily walked into the office, her blue eyes sparkling, as they usually did, with some sort of general joy. "We got your note, and Caroline and I have been dying for you to come tell us everything. So what is your employer like? What is the charge like? A girl or a boy? And what—"

"If you'll let me speak, I'll tell you everything," Lily said, laughing. They made their way to the back office and Lily gestured for Annabelle to sit. She took the other chair, the one that the unfortunate women usually sat in when being interviewed by the agency.

She hoped it was not a portent.

She spent the next few minutes with only a few interruptions ("*how* many rooms?") telling Annabelle everything she wanted to know, only hesitating when it came to describing the duke.

Because words that weren't "impossibly handsome," "impossible," and "fascinatingly irritating" would have been inappropriate. And she didn't want to reveal to Annabelle—or herself, for that matter—just how true all of those words were.

Eventually, Annabelle's questions stopped and, at Lily's request, she enthusiastically began writing up a false reference from the Vicar of

Littlestone. Tapping her pen against her mouth, Annabelle asked, "Is it excessive to say you are entirely capable of handling children of all ages, from birth to eighteen years old?"

"Are you expecting the duke to present more children for me to care for?" Lily asked in a dry tone of voice.

"Excessive," Annabelle agreed, crossing out a few words on the paper. "Now I'll have to copy it over." She drew another slip of paper from their shared desk but paused before starting to write again. "Oh! You didn't say anything about your employer."

Drat that inquisitive Annabelle.

"No, I didn't."

Annabelle got to work copying the reference. "Is he nice? Have you spoken to him, or were you hired by his wife?"

"He's not married."

"No?" Annabelle replied, laying the pen down, an arch look on her face.

Lily glared at her. "As though there would be a chance for me to marry him. In case you have not noticed, he is a duke. And I . . . am not."

Annabelle fluttered her hands. "Well of course not, dear, if you were a duke you couldn't very well marry one." She snorted. "The idea of you being a duke."

Too late, Lily recalled her friend was far too literal.

"Even though I am not a duke," and could she believe she was having this conversation, "I will not be marrying one myself."

Hopefully that would settle it.

"Is he handsome?"

That had not settled it.

"I suppose so," just as she supposed the sky was blue, unless you were in London during the winter, and just as she supposed that if she had to keep answering such questions she just might burst out with what she was truly thinking. Things like: Why did he have to be a duke and look like that? Wasn't it enough that he had a tremendous title? Why couldn't he have been short and plump, perhaps with a wart or two? It would make her work much easier.

"You're not telling me anything," Annabelle said with a sulky look.

Precisely.

Thankfully, Annabelle was as mercurial as she was literal—you just had to wait until she cycled to another topic.

"Is that gown new?" she asked as she began to recopy the reference. Annabelle was the most fashionable of them—her own downfall had begun in a hat shop—and she somehow contrived to look nice despite having very limited resources.

"Yes, the duke—" Lily hesitated, knowing that Annabelle would jump on this tidbit of information. "The duke purchased it for me, since I will be taking Miss Rose out, and he didn't want my lack of a wardrobe to cause any comment. Because she is not—well, because she is illegitimate. He's saying she's the daughter of his cousin, to keep her from gossip, but she's actually his."

Annabelle narrowed her eyes and pointed the

pen at Lily. "You need to be careful, if he is the type of man to . . . to . . ."

"Cavort?" Lily supplied.

Annabelle nodded her head vehemently. "Cavort, yes. It is one thing to know you are not a duke, but you are a young, attractive woman, and you cannot allow yourself to get in any kind of trouble." They both knew firsthand what kind of trouble could befall a young woman with no resources. Thankfully, they had missed the worst possible trouble, but it only served to reinforce that Lily must succeed in her work, to secure the agency's future.

The trouble she could foresee would be in allowing herself to even speculate about why the duke sounded as though his childhood wasn't a happy one, or how they had a shared sense of humor, or what she felt when he spoke about his daughter.

Her concerns hadn't entirely subsided by the time she returned to the duke's house—her home, for the time being, at least—but she'd thought about what had to be done while she walked, holding her new, not-even-close-to-threadbare cloak around her in protection against the wind.

She needed to wrap herself up as tightly as she had the cloak, she thought, to protect her against any kind of danger of the dukely kind.

While knocking on the front door, she told herself she'd barely even noticed its magnificence. She rolled her eyes at her own foolishness, then schooled her features—prim, precise, methodical, so no one would suspect her of being less than a proper governess.

Thompson opened the door, his eyebrow raised in a pale imitation of his master's, then it almost seemed as if he might smile, and he gestured for her to enter.

"Your cloak, miss?" he said, waving a footman over to take it. "And how was your afternoon?"

Excellent. I got false references, told my flighty friend I am not a duke, and spent far too much time trying not to think about a certain gentleman.

"Excellent," were the only words that had run through her head that she actually spoke aloud, however. "Where is Miss Rose?"

"She is with the duke in the kitchens." He sniffed. "I believe Miss Rose expressed that she was hungry."

"I shall just run down, then."

"Miss Lily," Rose said, walking with the duke into the hallway. "You're back! We had pudding, I ate so much my stomach is huge." She clasped her hands on her belly and smiled.

Lily was glad to see the duke's belly had not suddenly bellowed out in a similar way.

"Did you have a nice afternoon?" he asked.

"Thank you, I did, Your Grace." She glanced at Rose, then spoke again to the duke. "I was wondering, do you have a conservatory? I was thinking that Rose and I would begin a study of flowers, and it would be very useful if we had actual specimens to see. Of course we could always go to a garden, but I was thinking—"

"Well, Thompson? Do we?"

The duke cut her off before she could meander any longer, thank goodness.

Thompson straightened his spine. "We do, Your Grace, but if you recall when first you took possession of the house—"

Now the duke interrupted Thompson. Perhaps it was his chosen activity this afternoon? Interrupting people?

"I do not recall, or I would not be asking. Do we have a conservatory?"

Thompson's lips thinned. "We do, Your Grace, but it has not been maintained in the proper way. At the time, you stated that the study of flowers was a useless endeavor, and that the space could be better used for other purposes. I believe you mentioned putting all the cats in there, if they were so determined to stay?"

Rose turned accusing eyes on the duke, who crossed his arms over his chest and returned her stare. "I didn't do that, though, did I?"

She seemed to consider, then nodded. "Mr. Snuffles likes it here."

He bowed. "I am glad we have that settled."

"About the conservatory," Lily began, feeling as though the conversation had run entirely away from her, "could you tell me where it is, and Rose and I will go investigate?"

Thompson began to speak, but the duke—of course—cut him off. "Just point me where it is, I will take our young ladies there," he said.

"Certainly, Your Grace." Thompson seemed to hesitate. "Although it is not in a state I would wish it to be seen."

"Haven't you learned by now that kind of thing doesn't matter to me?" the duke said impatiently. "Where is it?"

Thompson bent in a stiff bow. "Down through that door, then left, then right again."

"Thank you, Thompson," Lily muttered as the duke grabbed Rose's hand again and took off to where Thompson had pointed, without any indication that he had heard him.

Lily followed, hoping she had not just earned the irrevocable ire of the butler.

"This must be it," the duke said, grabbing the doorknob of the third room they'd passed through. He flung it open and stepped aside so Rose and Lily could see in.

In to where many, many plants were in their death throes. If not actually dead.

Lily paused at the threshold, suddenly feeling sympathy for Thompson. The room had large windows, but the glass was dusty, if not grimy. Random gardening tools lay scattered as though tossed, while varying sized pots of earth were placed on long tables.

"Well. No wonder Thompson didn't wish us to see this." The duke gazed around the room, his judging eyebrow lifted in disapproval. "It's not his fault, though, since I told him I didn't want to hear anything about it, and he told me until we got a new housekeeper he didn't have enough staff to clean it properly."

"There's one growing here," Rose said, poking a still living variety of rose. It wasn't in the best of health, but at least it wasn't yet deceased.

"That one is a rose, like you, Miss Rose," the duke said, giving her an exaggerated bow.

Rose's eyes widened, and she regarded the meager flower as though it were a bouquet of a thousand flowers. "It's so pretty." She reached her hand out and touched one of the blooms. "Soft," she added, her expression as open and happy as Lily had yet seen it.

Lily nearly jumped when the duke spoke in her ear. He must have learned stealthy walking from the cats. "The conservatory may be a disaster, but Rose doesn't seem to mind."

"No."

They watched the girl slide her finger down the stem, then yelp when a thorn pricked her. She turned even huger eyes to them. "Ouch," she said in a tone of righteous indignation.

"It is good to learn early on that very pretty things are not harmless," the duke said, pulling a handkerchief from his pocket. What did that mean? she wondered. He took Rose's hand gently in his and pressed the white linen against where the thorn must have pricked her. "Is that better?" he asked in a low voice.

"Mm-hm," Rose replied, nodding. Then her face brightened and she pointed to a far corner of the room. "Oh, over there, can I go see?"

Lily looked at where she was pointing and saw a hoop leaning against the wall. "Of course." Rose darted over and began trying to roll the hoop in the aisles between the tables, without much success.

Meanwhile, Lily walked up and down the

aisles herself, noting the few plants and flowers that were still alive. It was obvious someone had enthusiastically gardened here, just as it was obvious that no one had for a long while.

"We found a rose for Rose, are there any lilies for you, Miss Lily?" The duke stood on the other side of the table from her, hands on his hips as he surveyed his domain. Rather like a lion looking for something he could devour, she thought, if the lion were dressed in a suit and the prey was vegetative in nature.

"I loathe lilies," Lily admitted. Her sister had loved them, though, which meant there had been lilies at the funeral. "Their scent, their look, everything about them. Mostly their scent, though." She shivered at the memory. "Too sweet and too overpowering. And of course when people give me gifts, they think it makes perfect sense to give me a lily." She finished her sentence in a tone of mock outrage. Because if she didn't make a joke of it, she just might break down and cry.

The duke looked at her with an amused gleam in his eye. "How very unfortunate. Do you think you dislike the poor flower because of your name, or was that just happenstance? What if you had been named Scone, or Lemon Custard? That would have been truly awful."

Lily burst out laughing, then quickly covered her mouth with her hand, but still giggling into her palm. His eyes crinkled up in the corners, sharing the joke, and she felt the warmth between them—the dangerous warmth—unfurl inside her.

"Or Pudding?" she said when she could finally

speak, then cursed herself as she had another fit of giggling.

The duke flung his head back in laughter, reminding Lily she was doing a terrible job of keeping that cloak wrapped around her emotions.

A duke must always remember that everyone, save for the Royal Family, is lesser than he, and likely to be inhibited in his presence. It is up to the duke to ensure anyone in his company is at least comfortable, if not relaxed.

It is not advised to take inappropriate actions toward this goal, however.

—The Duke's Guide to Correct Behavior

Chapter 10

"You asked for me, Your Grace?" Lily paused at the threshold of the door, her heart beating faster than it ought to be. Given that she was just responding to her employer's request that she see him after Rose had been put to bed. That's all it was. Not that she wanted to actually see him.

"If I asked for you, do you think I want you hovering at the doorway? Come in." He didn't even raise his head to look at her, just uttered his command in that deep voice.

"Of course, Your Grace."

He did lift his head at that, both eyebrows raised.

Uh-oh. She had incurred the wrath of both eyebrows.

She entered the room, closing the door softly behind her. He didn't say anything, just watched as she came in.

It was unnerving, being the object of his scrutiny.

Well, unnerving and rather flattering, if she were being honest.

"Sit down."

Was this the Peremptory Command Room? Oh, wait, that was all of them. At least if he were in them.

She had been at his house for only three days, but it seemed more like three weeks. And of course every time she was in his presence she was acutely aware of him. The connection only went one way, thank goodness, because it seemed he didn't spare her a thought after ensuring that she was properly garbed for her position.

The rest of her gowns had arrived the day after they'd been to the shop, and she was wearing the nicest one she'd gotten—it was blue silk, and made a satisfactory rustling sound as she walked.

Cotton did not rustle nearly as nicely. Did not rustle at all, actually.

But she didn't have time for vanity. Not now, when it was time to do her duty and report to him, as they'd arranged. She glanced around the room, noting just how starkly different it was from the Pink Room. For one thing, it did not have a speck of pink in it.

It was an intensely masculine room, to match its current occupant, with large leather chairs and carts holding glasses and intriguing looking bottles of liquid.

But she couldn't pay much attention to her surroundings when he was there. He sat in the largest of the chairs, of course, his long legs sprawled in front of him, the habitual stubble on his cheeks even darker than usual. He'd removed his cravat, and Lily felt herself start to flush at the sight of his strong throat and the intimation of the beginning of his chest.

Oh, goodness.

She sat down quickly in the chair nearest to her, sinking down into where someone—someone much larger than she—had worn a groove into the seat.

"What can I help you with, Your Grace? Oh," she said, straightening in her chair even more, "I have my references upstairs, if you would like to see them."

Annabelle had done an excellent job.

"Never mind that now. We agreed you would report on how Rose is doing." He extended a hand in a summoning gesture. "So report."

She drew a deep breath. "Rose is a lovely child, she already knows most of her letters and she can count to ten correctly nearly all of the time."

Silence.

"That is it? I knew that already, from what Rose herself said. Nothing else to report?"

Lily felt herself getting flustered. "What else is there to say?" Was there something he knew about that governesses normally said about their charges? No, he couldn't, he was as new to this as she was.

He shrugged. "What did you normally say to the vicar?"

"The vicar?" Oh, of course, the family she'd supposedly been with before. The one who'd given her the solid reference written in Annabelle's hand. "The vicar! Of course. Well, I would report to the vicar's wife, and we would discuss how the children's studies were going, and what the plans were for the week ahead. The girls were older than Rose so there were more activities they were engaged in."

"Wives do all that, hm." He spoke in a musing voice. So she was not prepared for his next question. "Do you think *I* need a wife?"

"Pardon?"

"A wife," he repeated in an impatient tone. "Would it be to Rose's benefit if I were to find a mother for her?"

"That would be the only reason you would want to wed?" She paused. "And why are you asking my opinion anyway? I am your employee, not your marriage advisor."

He grinned, even as she was appalled at herself for her outspokenness. "But I have the feeling you have an opinion, Miss Lily." He rose and began to pace, his long-legged stride making short work of the walk from one side of the room to the other.

"You see, I have never felt an urge to wed. I don't know about your romantic entanglements"—at that he caught her eye and smirked, as though he knew she had no romantic entanglements—"but to me, marrying for love is so shortsighted. Because people tire of one another, and they change, and it's so messy. If I were to marry a woman who was well-aware of my feelings, or lack of them, before we spoke the vows, that would be far more realistic than if I were to profess an emotion I didn't have, wouldn't it?"

At that, he paused and stood just in front of where she sat, and she had to look away, anywhere but at him, with his virility, and his good looks, and his very practical reasons for wanting a wife.

"Well? What do you think?" He had that commanding tone again, so now she had no choice but to look at him. All handsomely tall, vulnerable, witty duke of him. All of that, wasted, because he had as much as said all he wanted was a woman to mother his child. Not someone to share his jokes, or caress his cheek, or find out more about this prickly, arrogant, intriguing gentleman.

She already felt sorry for the as yet unknown woman.

"I think, Your Grace, that you have already made up your mind."

"Perhaps I have," he replied. "Only—" He tapped a finger on his arm as he thought. "—that I might need some assistance in this process." And then that dark gaze was entirely focused on her, so she felt there was nothing but him and her in the world.

"And," he continued, repressing the urge to smile, "you will be just the person to aid me."

His governess's hazel eyes darkened, in dismay or anger, he couldn't tell. He tried to tell himself he didn't care which emotion it was, but he was lying.

"I am hired, Your Grace," she said, emphasizing his title, "to be a governess to your charge. Not to help you find a wife."

Anger, then. "I would hope I can select my own wife," he said with a snort. Something he wasn't planning on right away anyway, but she didn't need to know that. "No, I need help with something else, something I can only practice with a lady." He knew she couldn't disregard orders from her employer. Plus he did need help, he wasn't so arrogant to assume he didn't. At least, not entirely arrogant.

"Practice what?" She was leaning forward now, her shoulders rigid, her mouth pursed, every aspect of her demonstrating her ire.

Was it wrong that it caused a very different type of reaction in him? That he was hoping for her to snap out one of those prickly retorts, one that revealed her wit, her intelligence, and her refusal to indulge his autocratic behavior? She was a challenge, for sure.

He'd done his proper best to ignore just how reactive he was to her. Unfortunately, he didn't seem to be proper at all. Not as when it came to her, certainly.

"I am out of practice conversing with a young lady," not to mention other things, "and dancing and eating standing up at a party without spilling all over myself. You will help me." He cleared his throat. "That is, you could help me. If you agree. Besides," he said, uncrossing his arms and spreading them wide in front of him, "what else is there for us to do of an evening? You can't report on Rose's progress every night."

"Don't you have responsibilities outside the home?"

He lifted his eyebrow. "Haven't you noticed I barely have any responsibilities *within* the home?"

She made a *hmph* sound, but he saw her mouth curl up as though she wanted to smile as well. "Yes, actually. I have."

"And I am trying to change that." As he spoke, he realized just how true it was. "I want to become the kind of father Rose deserves, but to do that I am going to need help. You are the only one I can ask, Miss Lily. You are here, you are free in the evenings, and you are a lady."

She opened her mouth as if to argue, then snapped it shut again. "If I must," she said.

He smiled as though he hadn't noticed her reluctant tone. "Excellent. And since my friend Mr. Smithfield and his sisters and husbands are coming to dinner tomorrow, we should begin this evening. Now."

"Now?" she squeaked, finally standing up. She was close enough to touch, and he crossed his arms over his chest again so he wouldn't give in to that impulse.

"Yes, now." As he spoke, he felt something course through him, almost like an electric current.

Or a bolt of lustful interest.

She mirrored his stance, crossing her arms over her chest. But that just brought her breasts into higher prominence, easier to see out of the corner of his eye so she wouldn't know he was looking.

He was very glad they had gone to the dressmaker's. The gown she wore now was so much more flattering. It revealed her figure, which he'd suspected was lovely, much better than the dowdy sack she'd had on when she first arrived.

And she had quite lovely breasts.

"You said your friend is bringing his sisters and their husbands to dinner?"

"Yes, and I wish you to dine with us as well. You will bring Rose down later on."

She didn't even bother to argue—good, she was getting to know him—but continued, "But if the sisters already have husbands, you are not thinking of them as potential spouses—are you?"

He touched her arm as if to reassure her, but really, he just wanted to touch her anywhere that wasn't entirely improper. Well, he wanted to touch her improperly, as well, if he were being honest with himself. "I am not a sheikh looking to fill out my harem, if that is what you are asking."

She shook her head. "That doesn't even make sense. It would only work if they were still unmarried and you wished to marry both of them."

He shrugged, trying not to grin at how she had shut him down so thoroughly. "No matter, I have no intentions whatsoever toward Mr. Smithfield's sisters. But I do intend to make polite conversation."

"You are in need of assistance there," she muttered.

He grinned at her and she smiled back. That returned smile was far more gratifying than spoon-balancing, that was for certain. He wished he could just fling his head back and laugh, in the most unseemly way possible, perhaps even clasp her arm as they laughed together. Even in just a few short days she had intrigued him, engaged him, in a way he didn't think he had ever felt before.

That nobody had had this effect on him would be profoundly depressing if he weren't experiencing it now. He just wanted to learn more about her, to find out what flowers she might like and what had brought her into governessing in the first place.

"So," he said, clasping her arm as he lowered her back into her chair, "what does constitute pleasant conversation?" He returned to his own seat and placed his hands on his knees.

Nothing we've spoken about tonight, Lily thought, in answer to the duke's question. He regarded her intently, and she envied whichever woman would be the object of his scrutiny as a potential wife. Not to mention envying the woman who would be able to see more of the chest that was just barely showing above his shirt collar.

The woman he'd court—but never love—through polite conversation. She could do this. "You are not to mention how much or how little a lady has had to eat or drink, Your Grace." She cleared her throat. "Nor are you to discuss anything that could possibly be misconstrued," such as saying he wished to do something he could only do with a lady, "nor controversial, nor argumentative."

"What can I talk about, then?" He sounded amused.

She smiled in return. "Not much, honestly. The weather. The day's activities, as long as you haven't been doing anything too shocking. The pleasantness of the company, the food, and the dancing. If there is dancing, of course."

"And how will a lady know when I am particularly interested in her?"

Ah. That. "Well," Lily said, feeling her traitorous skin start to heat, "that is all a matter of nuance."

"Nuance?" Oh, dear Lord. His voice. He had lowered it to a deep timbre, even deeper than usual, and she felt as though she could actually feel it vibrating through her body, causing her to shudder in response.

She drew a deep breath. "Ladies are generally more attuned to nuance than gentlemen. For example, a man might wish to announce he has a particular fondness for a certain woman, but of course that is not polite conversation. But he can indicate, through his actions, how he feels, and that is entirely polite."

He twisted his mouth in contemplation. "So if I were to indicate my interest in a woman, I might—" He leapt up and held his hand out to her. "This requires practice."

Her mouth went dry as she placed her fingers in his, allowing him to draw her to her feet.

They were face-to-face, as close to each other as they would be if they were dancing. A polite distance, and yet . . . and yet . . . She felt anything but polite or circumspect or any of those things a proper governess should.

She had the urge to run her fingers through his thick dark hair, to scrape her palm against his cheek, feel the rough stubble against her skin. She wanted to lean against him, to give in to an emotion other than responsibility and love.

Desire. That's what it was. She desired him, and she wanted, quite desperately, to know what it would feel like, all the impolite conversation and cavorting and everything she suspected lurked behind those dark, expressive eyes.

"Miss Lily?" His voice interrupted her musings, thank goodness. What would he say if he knew what she was thinking, the governess whom he'd asked to instruct him on polite discourse?

She felt her breathing quicken as she thought about what he might say. Or, more to the point, might do.

For that matter, what she might say. Or do.

There seemed potential for a lot of things. Not all of them making for a precise, prim, or methodical governess.

Merely an improper one.

Any gentleman, whether a duke or a well-educated commoner, should keep in mind that ladies are not the same as men. First of all, they do not have the same desires and wants a man does. Nor do they have the ability to defend themselves against any unwanted passions. They are the weaker sex, and it is therefore imperative that a gentleman maintain oversight over any lady's behavior to ensure it is correct.

Unless the lady herself makes a request, at which point the gentleman has no choice but to accede to her wishes.

—THE DUKE'S GUIDE TO CORRECT BEHAVIOR

Chapter 11

"Of course, Your Grace. I was"—thinking about all the improper things I wished we could do together—"woolgathering. Most young ladies will not allow their thoughts to wander so, not when in your presence."

His smile, the one that made it appear they were sharing a delicious secret, deepened. "You find my presence so notable, then?" As though he weren't already the recipient of praise, he had to go ask for it? Hmph.

"You are a duke," she said in a dismissive tone, "so it wouldn't matter if you had warts and were bald. Any young lady would be cowed in your presence."

"But you are not." He still held her hand. She should take it away, smooth her palms on her gown, but she left it there. Soaking in the warmth of him, the feel of his bare skin—of course he wasn't wearing gloves, and neither was she—able to see every sharp, delineated plane of his face, that commanding nose, those expressive eyebrows.

Hearing his deep voice rumble through her.

"I suppose I should be cowed, Your Grace, if I really thought about it. After all," she continued, finally finding the strength to take her hand away, "you have the ability to let me go if I prove unsatisfactory." *Or knew I was thinking entirely improper thoughts.* "You have so much power over those who are deemed lesser than you, and with the exception of the Queen and her family, everyone is lesser."

He scowled then. "I would never abuse my position like that. You have my word."

She felt herself soften. "I know," she said in a quiet tone. And she did.

A silence as they stood there, still together, not touching.

"I believe you were to demonstrate how I could tell if a lady was actually interested in me? Beyond the happy accident of my title?" His voice was light, as though he had felt whatever it was, too, and wished to distance himself from it.

It was good that one of them, at least, was sensible. Although she never would have thought it would be him, the Dangerous Duke behaving more like the Demure Duke.

That would make her the Improper Governess, and she could not behave that way, not if she wanted to avoid scandal.

"Let us pretend we are conversing, Your Grace," she began.

"There is no need to pretend. We are conversing."

She rolled her eyes. "Yes, we are, but let us pretend we are at a function in the evening, and we are possibly intrigued by one another."

She couldn't help but notice his eyebrow had risen, as though he were about to confirm that they were intrigued by one another. She hurried to finish before he could possibly say anything that would make her blush again. "And I am a young, suitable lady," that he could not argue with, she most definitely was not suitable, "and you and I have found some mutual interests. What do you like, anyway?"

He shrugged. "I have not thought much about it, honestly. I suppose I would say I like brandy, and cards, and," a pause as he thought, "well, let us leave it at brandy and cards."

"A young lady is not likely to have much opinion about brandy and cards."

"Which is why I have never considered marriage before," he replied, walking to one of the carts in the room. "Or really worry about making polite conversation with a young lady. Until now . . ." He paused, and glanced back at her with a sly smile on his face. ". . . it hasn't seemed worth the trouble." He drew the stopper out of a bottle and poured a generous amount into a glass. Then smiled that secret smile again and poured a less generous amount into a second glass. He picked both up and handed the less full glass to her.

"This is not proper in the least, Your Grace," Lily said, the fumes of the brandy tickling her nose.

He chuckled, and she could have sworn he winked at her. "Upon reflection, I believe my best course of action is to take care of all the improprieties while practicing with you so there is nothing left but proper behavior when I meet a woman I might possibly consider marrying."

He held his glass up to hers. "May we never be out of spirits," he said, drinking after he spoke.

She took a sip, coughing as the fiery liquid burned down her throat. Trying not to think about what he'd just said. As the brandy warmed her body, she nodded. "That is quite good, once you get past the initial impact."

"So true about many things," he said in a soft murmur, one that did nothing to cool her heated skin.

She felt her cheeks begin to color, and set her glass down, bobbing a quick curtsey. "I should go check on Rose, Your Grace," she said, not daring to look at him again. Not daring to see what look might be in his eyes, the temptation of that bared throat, his tousled hair, his stubbled cheeks.

She fled from the room, fully aware of him watching her retreating figure. Knowing that no matter who he was—Dangerous or Demure—he was definitely a peril to her peace of mind.

"Pie for breakfast," Rose said, actually lifting her nose in disdain as Lily placed a piece of toast on her plate.

"No, Miss Rose, you cannot have pie for breakfast." At least she was standing firm in this matter;

ducal improprieties had nothing on the very possibility of a sweet in the morning.

"Then nothing," Rose said, crossing her arms on her chest.

Lily heard the footman—the one standing to the side of the room—stifle a laugh. He was not nearly as haughty as the other one, thank goodness. She shrugged in response, having learned at least one thing since entering the duke's household. "Pie is not what young ladies eat for breakfast. Isn't that right, John?" she said, turning to him.

The footman looked surprised to be addressed. Probably the duke behaved as though he were the only person in the room. "Not generally, miss," he said. "And young ladies need energy for—for whatever it is they do," he continued, clearly not up on what young ladies' days consisted of.

"Precisely," Lily said. "Do you want butter or jam?"

Rose still looked sulky as she answered. "Both."

That, she could accommodate.

She and Rose were finishing their breakfast when the duke entered the room, holding a letter. Lily's attention was immediately focused on him, that prickling awareness curling up her spine and low into her belly. He was very properly dressed today, and she had a moment of sadness that she couldn't see his throat and the beginning of his chest.

He walked over to Rose and kissed her on the cheek before sitting at the table. John filled his cup with coffee, and he took a deep drink before speaking. "I've had a letter from my friend Smithfield. He and his sisters are joining us for dinner tonight. Miss Lily will bring you down, too, afterward," he said, addressing Rose.

She beamed, and took the final bite of toast.

"One of the sisters' husbands is otherwise engaged, however, so if we don't mind, Smithfield is bringing a young lady who has been staying with his sister as well. We don't mind, do we?"

Rose shook her head as Lily felt that prickling awareness change into a feeling of dread. A young lady coincidentally available to dine with a duke. How fortuitous. That meant she definitely had to curb whatever . . . feelings he'd stirred up in her. He needed a suitable young woman to wed, and that woman was most definitely not her.

"Miss Lily?" the duke prompted.

"It is not our place to mind, Your Grace," Lily said in a demure—ha!—tone.

He frowned and shot her a glance, but didn't comment on her subservient reply. "I will write to Smithfield, then."

Lily didn't reply, didn't look at him again, but she felt his gaze on her, those dark eyes assessing what she might be thinking or feeling. Had he spent a sleepless night as well, pondering what kind of young lady he would court? Reviewing what qualities he required in a woman he'd ask to share his name, his privilege, his child—but not his heart?

Or had he thought about how close they'd been, what her hand had felt like in his, how they'd spoken—conversed—both properly and improperly. Was he looking forward to more practice, with her, or was he so jaded he didn't think about it at all?

And how did people manage to get anything done at all, with all this thinking and pondering and such?

When a duke—a proper duke, that is—entertains, he must ensure that all of his staff are on their most correct behavior. There is no fun to be had whatsoever, neither upstairs in the dining room nor downstairs amongst the servants, since fun could be viewed as improper. The food will be the ultimate in fashionable cuisine, which means that it will be laden with intricate sauces and difficult to eat without having it spill onto your clothing. Further, the conversation will be limited to the weather, the parties to be attended, and the duke's own consequence.

—The Duke's Guide to Correct Behavior

Chapter 12

"Thank you for the invitation, Your Grace."

Smithfield strode ahead of Thompson, who was holding the door to the drawing room for him and the rest of the party. Marcus didn't think he'd ever seen his butler come this close to an approving expression. Thompson nearly smiled when he told him that respectable people were to dine and directed him to make the preparations for guests.

His butler had directed what was to be served at dinner, as well, since Marcus hadn't bothered to hire a new housekeeper since the last one had decamped to a place, she said, "Where she'd be more appreciated."

Marcus didn't think it would be possible to appreciate her more—specifically, how unpleasant she had been—but he didn't point that out to her, just gave the woman her wages and sent her on her way.

Marcus nodded at Smithfield, then turned his attention to the other guests. The two sisters resembled Smithfield in height and coloring, and the last young lady—the one substituting for the husband—was, he noticed, blond and petite, with a curvy figure and a charming dimple that she seemed fond of exposing.

"Your Grace, may I introduce my sister and brother-in-law, Mr. and Mrs. Porter, my sister Mrs. Haughton, and our friend, Miss Lavinia Blake?"

Lots of names, lot of exclamations about what a lovely house he had, including the foyer, which he'd never much noticed.

Miss Lily certainly was a good instructor on polite conversation. The party shared a drink before going in to dinner and spoke about the weather, the Queen's latest appearancc, and other things he didn't care about in the least.

Eventually, he led them all into the dining room, where inevitably there were at least ten minutes spent on the beauty of the room.

If he were to be proper, would he have to start having opinions about interior design? If it weren't for Rose, he'd ponder doing something entirely shocking, just to liven up the party.

One thing Thompson had not decided—could not decide, actually—was where everyone would be seated around the table. Marcus was amused at the intricate machinations taken to place Miss Blake to his left, while Mrs. Haughton sat to his right, with Smithfield to her right, followed by Lily. It wasn't entirely proper, he knew, to have his governess dine with them, but he just wanted her there, he couldn't say precisely why. Mr. and Mrs. Porter sat on the other side, to the left of Miss Blake.

It felt very comfortable, even though everyone but Smithfield and Lily were strangers to him. He'd never actually had any of these kinds of intimate dinners; his parents had always taken Joseph, since he was the oldest and, his father would remind him, Marcus was "far too devilish" to be safe in company, so he had usually eaten alone, or with a tutor, until he was sent off to school.

He hadn't thought of those times in so long—deliberately, he knew—but now he let himself touch those memories, hoping he could find a family for Rose so she wouldn't have to endure those moments of loneliness. He'd need to; he didn't want any child to go through what he had.

And when had he become so maudlin, anyway?

He shook his head, and took a deep swallow of his wine.

He was aware that part of his mind was preoccupied with Miss Lily; where she was, who she spoke to, what type of expression she had. If it were up to him—which it was, honestly, but he wasn't *that* rude, despite what she might think—he would have canceled the dinner party and spent the evening as they had the night before, alone with her. Seeing if he could bring that pink sparkle to her cheeks, and reveling in her spiky retorts.

But that would not put him on his way to convincing proper society that he was sincere in his wish to be like them.

Not that he was. But for Rose, and the chance for him to explore his own happiness, he would try. No, damn it, he would succeed.

Which meant the only time he could say "damn it" was in his own thoughts.

"What is your opinion, Your Grace?" Miss Blake was addressing him, her voice a light, tinkling sound that made him think of chimes, or what fluffy clouds would sound like if they could talk.

He was not fond of either chimes or clouds.

"About what?"

He felt, rather than saw, Miss Lily frown at his tone. And felt guilty for knowing she was right. "About what, Miss Blake?" he repeated, this time trying not to speak abruptly.

"If the weather has been finer since the Queen's wedding, or if it is only my imagination."

Well, if that wasn't the most asinine question—not to mention proper, he hadn't forgotten Miss Lily's recitation of polite conversation—he had ever heard.

"That is difficult to answer, Miss Blake."

She smiled at him as though he had actually answered her rather than entirely prevaricated. Was this actually how young ladies conversed? He far preferred Miss Lily's direct way of speaking. Would this be what marriage to a proper young lady would be?

Perhaps he should just forego propriety after all. But there was Rose to care for now, and he did owe his title something.

He would need a woman, a *wife*, to teach his daughter about the weather, and conversation, and all those things that had not been part of his education. Eventually, even if he didn't need it right now.

With that in mind, he launched his next conversational assault. "Tell me, Miss Blake, what events have you attended since you've been in town?" Talking about Society events was safe, according to Miss Lily.

Stultifyingly boring, according to him.

Miss Blake simpered. "I have been to so many parties, each one has been wonderful. I do love to dance, although I like talking as well. I cannot decide which is preferable."

Marcus nodded in agreement, as though she had said something that was an actual opinion. He saw Smithfield bend his head to Lily's to say something to her, and when she bestowed a smile in return, he felt his fists clench.

But he had to force himself not to clench them because he was holding a soup spoon in one hand and gripping his wineglass with the other, and because it would be impolite to challenge his new best friend to a fistfight over a lady's smile.

"Your Grace," Mr. Porter said, thankfully distracting him from both soup and smiles, "might I ask your opinion on the Chimney Sweepers Act?"

Marcus was opening his mouth to reply when he saw Lily shaking her head imperceptibly. Right. He should not be speaking about politics in polite company, except— "I think it's an abominable practice to force children to work in such conditions. In any conditions at all, actually."

He saw Lily's shoulders slump. But if he could not speak his mind about such issues, then he did not wish to be polite. And, as she seemed to delight in reminding him, he was a duke, chafe at it though he might, and a duke was given more leeway to speak as he wished because of how very proper he was assumed to be.

An oxymoron that he wished he could point out to her so she could share the joke.

Besides which, it *was* an abominable practice, and at least he could look forward to arguing about that with his fellow peers at the House of Lords rather than taking a nap during the proceedings, as he had the other few times he'd attended.

But he couldn't discuss either oxymorons or abominable practices with her because Smithfield was engaging her in conversation again, and Mr. Porter was answering, so he had to pay attention to that, not how Lily's hazel eyes were sparkling gold, or how the gown he'd bought for her accentuated her curves and was cut low enough so he could see the swell of her breasts, which meant that Smithfield could see them, too, only more because he was closer.

Damn. His fists were clenching again. And he was silently swearing, too.

"Your Grace," Mrs. Haughton interrupted, before he could punch anyone, "I understand your charge is newly arrived to your household?"

Marcus nodded. "Yes, her mother—my cousin—has passed, and left her care to me."

He saw Lily nod in satisfaction out of the corner of his eye.

"And you have already gotten her a governess. How splendid."

Yes, she is, isn't she? "Yes." What was the proper

response to that? He would have to ask Lily when they were alone.

"I presume you will be sending her to school when she is old enough?"

Was that what people did? "Perhaps." An equivocal answer worthy of Miss Blake, even.

"And of course she will be useful when you have your own children."

Useful? What did that mean? "Perhaps," he said again, taking a bite of onion custard. It really was not to his taste. As this conversation wasn't.

But it would be a conversation that he'd likely have to endure if—no, when—he did return to polite society. Especially if he did decide to secure a wife who would tolerate her husband's natural child.

Tolerate. That was far too mild for what he hoped a young lady would feel toward Rose—he knew what it was like to be raised by parents who treated you indifferently, and he didn't want that for her. It was bad enough he hadn't been part of her life until now.

"I have to commend you on taking such a bold action, Your Grace," Mrs. Haughton continued, as she finished her portion of the onion custard. "Most men would not be so gracious about the responsibility of a young child."

"Rose," Marcus said through gritted teeth, "her name is Rose."

He saw Lily's mouth start to curl up into a grin, which she hid by taking a sip of wine.

"Rose, of course, what a delightful name," Mrs. Haughton said. The footmen then approached to remove the onion custard, leaving Marcus with a bad taste in his mouth. From the conversation and the food.

A few hours later, or so it seemed, he was filled with food he hadn't tasted and wine he had drunk too much of, and all he wanted was to see these people gone so he could be alone. Or not; he wished Lily to be there as well, although he wouldn't acknowledge that to himself, at least not more than once a minute.

She had spent the entire dinner talking to Smithfield, only speaking to the table in general when she was addressed, which was seldom—it was not customary for the governess to attend dinner at all, and if she did, she was supposed to remain silent.

Perhaps next time he invited people for dinner he'd provide gags for everyone so nobody could speak. At least that way he wouldn't have to endure the most banal of banalities he'd ever heard.

It would be very proper.

How different would it have been if it were just Rose and Lily? Much more pleasant, he knew that; for one thing, he wouldn't have had to eat things like potted lampreys and pigeon compote.

"Miss Lily, would you bring Miss Rose down to meet the company?"

"Yes, Your Grace." Lily stood and walked quickly from the room, returning only a few minutes later with Rose, whose cheeks were flushed red, as though very excited for the opportunity to meet new people.

"This is your Miss Rose," Mrs. Haughton said,

holding her hands out. Rose glanced uncertainly at Lily, then walked forward and took the outstretched hands. "You are so pretty. I can see the family resemblance," she said, casting an arch, knowing look at Marcus.

Marcus offered a tight smile in return.

"Miss Rose, I am Miss Blake."

"Blake starts with a B!" Rose exclaimed. Marcus's smile widened.

"It does! It might be my favorite letter, although I am not precisely certain," Miss Blake said, offering a warm, generous smile. At least she wasn't indecisive about being friendly.

"Miss Rose, I am Mr. Smithfield. Your governess has been telling me how smart you are." Smithfield looked at Lily as he spoke, and Marcus considered adding blindfolds to the list of things he would provide at the next dinner party he gave.

"Thank you, Mr. Smithfield," Lily replied.

There was a pause as conversation flagged, and Marcus realized he was the one who had to move the evening along. He had never been a proper host, although—as Smithfield knew—he had plenty of experience being an improper one.

"Ladies, if you will excuse us?" He rang the bell for Thompson, who bustled in as though he'd been listening at the door. "Thompson, please escort the ladies to the drawing room."

The ladies rose in a rustle of silk and exclamations, following Thompson out of the room.

At last, he'd only have to share a port with Smithfield and Mr. Porter and then they would all be on their way, and he could be done with this.

Only, a voice said in his head, *to do it all over again in the future as he continued his search for a wife.*

At least Smithfield was here, and not monopolizing Lily in conversation.

"That was very pleasant," Smithfield said, taking a drink from his glass. "I know this kind of thing is not your way, and I have to say I admire you for it." He paused, then checked that Mr. Porter was out of earshot. "There's been some talk, however, about who your charge is." He cleared his throat and took another swallow. "I thought you should know."

"Yes, I gathered as much from how your sister spoke to Rose." Yet another reason to find himself a respectable wife—if he were married to a proper young lady, the gossips would have nothing about which to speculate.

And he would have nothing improper to look forward to.

"And since you're a bachelor, and a duke, with gobs of money . . ." Smithfield trailed off as he gave Marcus a knowing look.

"Thank you for mentioning it," Marcus said, then finished his port, feeling guilty—twice in the same night, where he couldn't recall the last time he'd felt anything of the sort—for wishing Smithfield to the devil, just because he happened to be seated in a particular spot.

"Are you attending the Earl of Daymond's ball on Friday? The earl is that very distant relative I spoke of, we've all received an invitation." A pause. "Including Miss Blake." Who would probably just reply yes, Marcus thought, if he asked if she'd prefer sherry or lemonade.

"I'm certain I have, I am not certain if I plan to attend."

At his reply, Smithfield leaned in closer. "If you were to attend, and show yourself to Society, you would go a long way to dispersing all the talk about Miss Rose. Apparently, upon inheriting the title you have kept yourself to yourself far too much for the people who speak of such things."

And before then he hadn't mattered.

Smithfield's tone was dry, but his meaning was clear to Marcus: If he wished proper society to respect him, and not to natter on about who he had living in his home, he would have to present himself as a proper duke, one who might even get married to a proper lady; not a feckless duke who spent more time with his cats than proper company.

Or his daughter's governess.

In pursuing a lady's hand, a duke must keep in mind that although ladies' freedoms are much enhanced from previous centuries, a young lady will still be restricted by her parents' wishes. It is imperative, therefore, for the duke to ascertain that the lady is disposed toward him before disposing of her freedom by marrying her.

—The Duke's Guide to Correct Behavior

Chapter 13

Lily sat with the other ladies in the ladies' drawing room, which was the correct name for the Execrable Pink Room, counting the minutes until she could excuse herself and get Rose to bed.

Rose herself would likely argue about that, but it was obvious the little girl was exhausted, her eyes drooping as she munched on shortbread cookies.

"Miss Lily, my two children are just a bit older than Miss Rose. Perhaps you would like to bring her over for a visit sometime? I am certain my Sarah would love to show Miss Rose her dolls." Mrs. Porter did seem like a nice woman, and she had definitely enjoyed Mr. Smithfield's company.

Rose perked up at that and reached out to tug Lily's hand.

"Oh, that would be wonderful," Miss Blake said, her blond curls bobbing as she nodded her head. "There is nothing I love to see more than children playing. Unless," she said, tilting her head in apparent thought, "it is dancing and going to parties and eating ices. I love all of those things."

Wonderful, Lily thought, restraining herself from letting her lip curl. Was this the type of young lady from whom the duke would have to choose a wife?

Because if so, she was very glad she was not a duke herself, no matter what benefits might come with the position. Imagine having to endure this kind of meaningless conversation with the person you'd decided would be your partner for life?

"I thank you for the invitation, Mrs. Porter. I will inquire of the duke whether we might visit in a day or two."

"Splendid! And if you were to persuade the duke to accompany you, I know Miss Blake would be pleased to show him around the house while you and Rose visit."

Had she thought Mrs. Porter nice? Maybe someone thought Machiavelli was nice also.

"I will ask the duke," Lily said in a quiet tone. Who was she to deny the work of a master strategist? Plus the expression on Rose's face conveyed her eagerness to accept the offer.

After only a few more minutes the gentlemen rejoined them, and finally it was time for the guests to depart. Miss Blake couldn't decide if she thought the foyer or the staircase was more impressive, and it took all of Lily's willpower not to make the decision for her.

It was definitely the staircase.

Or the foyer.

Oh Lord, now she was doing it. Thank goodness they were all just about out the door. She was exhausted from the evening, having kept herself from speaking her mind or looking too many times at the duke. Not to mention talking with Mr. Smithfield, who'd spoken to her about governessing as though she was supposed to know what was to be done.

Finally the door shut behind them all. "Up to bed, Miss Rose," Lily said. Predictably, Rose protested, until the duke told her she had to get to bed so she'd have enough energy to go walking in the park with him the next day.

Lily shot a grateful glance at him, and he smiled in return, making her weariness disappear, to be replaced with—wanting.

"Miss Lily, join me in my study after Miss Rose has been put to bed."

Again? At this rate she would begin marking a trail in the carpet between where she was and his study. Where he was. "Certainly, Your Grace," she said, taking Rose by the hand as they began to ascend the staircase to the second floor.

"Tomorrow the duke said he'd take me out for a walk," Rose enthused as Lily was getting her dressed in her nightgown.

"He said he would take you for a walk tomorrow," Lily corrected.

Rose frowned. "I know that, I just said it."

Lily smoothed the curls off Rose's forehead and turned the sheets down so Rose could get into bed.

"Can we go see that lady's girl?" Rose asked sleepily. "I haven't played with someone in a long time. Not since before Mama got sick."

Lily's throat tightened. "Of course we can." She thought of Rose having to deal with a parent's death at such a young age—she had been eighteen when her father died, which was hard enough. Especially once it became clear that his fortune had died long before he had.

"Let me tell you a story to help you get to sleep," Lily said, smoothing the covers. She perched on the side of the bed and began a story of a young girl who was lost, then rescued by a prince with an exceedingly large nose.

It was not self-referential, she had to keep reminding herself.

Finally Rose was asleep and Lily slipped downstairs, her traitorous heart beating furiously.

The duke wasn't seated this time, but he was still accompanied by Orange, whom he held in the crook of his arm as he stood in front of one of the bookshelves. Orange looked as pleased as a cat could look, and it wasn't hard to see why—the duke was stroking his fur with those long, elegant fingers, and again it appeared that he had been speaking to the cat. Something about "soft fur" and "petting," plus he looked abashed when he saw her.

Orange seemed to know it was time to depart, since he leapt from the duke's arms and trotted off somewhere, no doubt to torment Stripey, as he was fond of doing.

The duke nodded at Lily and gestured toward the seat she'd previously sat in. "Would you care for tea?" he asked, walking to the beverage cart that had held brandy the evening before. He had removed his dinner jacket and cravat and was clad only in his shirt and trousers.

Tea? Interesting. *I care for many things,* she wanted to say, *including the removal of your clothing,* but instead settled for merely replying, "Yes, thank you, Your Grace." At his questioning look, she added, "Milk and sugar, please."

He handed her the cup and their fingers touched, sending sparks of feeling through Lily's body. If she reacted this way to just the touch of his fingers—goodness. What else might she feel?

"Charms to strike the spirit, and merit to win the heart," he said, sitting down a few feet away and raising his cup.

She clinked her cup against his.

"Did Rose enjoy herself?" he asked. "She certainly looked excited."

"I believe she did, Your Grace. Mrs. Porter asked if I might bring Rose for a visit. It seems she has two children of her own, not too much older than Rose, and she thought it would be pleasant to have them meet one another."

He snapped his fingers. "Of course! I hadn't even thought of finding other children for her to play with. How clever of you."

"Of Mrs. Porter, actually," Lily replied, taking another sip. "She also intimated that she would enjoy seeing you—that is, that Miss Blake could show you around the property while the children played."

"How did I do this evening, in polite company?" He sounded almost anxious, and she wondered, once again, what else his childhood had lacked. It nearly sounded as though it had been worse than hers—she'd had an irresponsible parent, but her mother loved her, as much as she was able to. It didn't sound that there was any love in his upbringing.

"You did very well," she said to him, "except for the chimney sweepers' discussion, but I understand why you took a stand."

He leaned forward in his chair. "Do you? And yet you would have had me stay quiet on the topic."

She bristled at the presumed accusation. "You asked me for assistance, instruction in how to navigate Society, and I am providing it. Just because I happen to agree with you on a controversial topic does not mean it is appropriate to talk about it in a polite setting."

"In a less polite setting, then?" he asked, waving his hand to indicate their surroundings. "What would you say then?"

He didn't sound accusatory. He sounded . . . interested. As though she had an opinion he wished to hear.

"It is deplorable." She thought about the children who'd accompanied their mothers to the agency, how little and scared they looked. Rightly so.

"It is, and since I seem to have developed a conscience lately, I am going to do as much as I can about it. What good is it being a duke if you can't change things?"

"Most people in your position would wish to keep things the same," she replied.

That eyebrow rose. The one that indicated his arrogance, his confidence, his certainty that he was right. "I am not most people," he said, keeping his eyes locked with hers as though daring her to challenge him.

That she felt she could was startling. That she felt he would like it was even more startling.

"True, you are not," she said in a wry tone. He smiled at her and took a sip of tea.

"Speaking of most people," he said, leaning forward to place his cup on the table next to his chair. "Miss Blake . . . is she representative of the type of young ladies I might meet in proper society?" It did not sound as though that pleased him, which conversely managed to please Lily very much.

"I could not say. I have not met many ladies in Society, either." Not since her father had died, and then she'd only met the families near his estate. Hardly the same company as that of a duke.

"The girl couldn't manage to express an opinion, and when she did say something, she had to punctuate it with a giggle." He met her eyes. "Thank goodness you are not like that, Miss Lily."

Not here, at least, she thought, recalling a time when one of Annabelle's exploits made her fall out of her chair with laughter. But he didn't know that about her. Here she was striving to be precise, prim, methodical—and not captivated by her employer. Not entirely, at least.

"I believe I will let you and Rose go to Mrs. Porter's on your own," the duke continued, arching an eyebrow. "I would not want to require Miss Blake to have to actually take a stand on anything."

"Your friend Mr. Smithfield had many opinions, at least. I found him very charming." Lily put her glass down on the table beside her. "Is he a particular friend of yours?"

The duke stood and turned to gaze out the window, giving Lily the chance to stare at his strong back and lower still. She'd never really thought about a man's backside before, but how could she not, when it was right here in her line of vision?

And it was a very lovely backside, she had to say, even though she wanted to giggle—ha!—at what the duke's face would look like if she told him, *Your posterior is quite remarkable, Your Grace.*

But that would be beyond improper, even for a woman who'd set on that course.

"Mr. Smithfield is my best friend," the duke replied. "I am pleased you like his company." But he said this in a voice that did not sound as if he were pleased at all.

"He told me about his family's shipping company," Lily said, "and was very kind to inquire about how I liked it here, and what my position had been before."

He turned toward her. She regretted not being able to see his backside any longer, but that momentary disappointment was more than made up for by his handsome face. "And do you like it here?"

More than I should. "Of course," she said, getting to her feet. "I like to spend time with Miss Rose and—"

"And me?" he asked, taking a few steps toward her.

This was dangerous territory. Risky.

But hadn't she told herself only a few days ago to take a risk? So she closed the distance between them, not sure what would happen, but knowing she wanted whatever it was.

Of all the things he'd expected, it hadn't been this easy capitulation. Not that he was complaining; many parts of his body were, in fact, rejoicing.

He took what she offered, leaning down to capture her mouth. He wanted her not to think about Smithfield, or anyone but him for that matter, and while kissing her might not necessarily achieve those ends—he wasn't entirely certain he was a good kisser—he knew that for the moment she was all he could think about.

Whether she'd think she should slap his face for his impertinence was something else.

But she didn't, thank goodness. And then she reached her fingers into his hair and held him to her so the immediate threat of slapping was put to bed.

As he wished they could be, but expressing that desire so soon after kissing her would likely get him slapped.

Her lips were soft, and warm, and so delicious, and he wanted to capture this perfect moment forever, this feeling of just being here with her, their mouths touching, her hands in his hair.

Her breasts pressed against his chest, and he congratulated himself on having removed his jacket so there was one less layer between them, not that he'd thought anything like this would happen. But if this type of thing was likely to happen he would be sure to keep his jacket off as much as possible.

He placed his hands on her arms, sliding his fingers up and down her warm flesh. Gently, softly, he licked at the seam of her lips, and she responded, opening her mouth to him so he could ease his tongue inside.

And then he gave into the experience, reveling in the taste and feel of her, and how she had taken her hands from his hair and had them now on his shoulders, gripping them as though to memorize their shape with her fingers.

She was tasting his mouth now as well, tangling her tongue with his, nipping at his mouth. His cock was erect between them, and he wondered if she felt it, knew what she'd done to him. Was doing to him.

He didn't have time to wonder, however, before she pulled away, a look of shock and astonishment on her face. "Oh, my, I didn't—oh, dear," she said, her cheeks flushing as pink as the walls of the loathed room, her mouth swollen from their kiss.

He put his hand out to her, but she didn't move or react, just stood there, a statue, but not a cold, stone statue; now he knew just how warm and soft she was, and he didn't think he would ever forget.

"That was unexpected," he said.

"It was." Her eyes were wide, gold sparks lighting the hazel.

"Did you like it?" He had to ask because he

certainly had, and he would hope they were in agreement on the matter. Because he would very much like to do it again.

"I did," she said, and now she didn't sound quite as shocked, for which he was grateful. "I should go now," she added, spun on her heel and headed for the door.

He stared after her, the feel of her still imprinted on his body, the way she had moved toward him, how she'd responded to him—both physically and mentally—as though he were worth something. A person she could discuss things with at one moment and then kiss at the next. He'd never known a woman with all those aspects. Either it was one or the other, but never both.

It was hard to say what ached more as she left him alone—his cock or his heart.

A duke will endeavor to please himself, first and foremost, because by pleasing himself he will therefore be pleasing everyone around him. Because an unpleased duke is not something anybody wishes to encounter.

—THE DUKE'S GUIDE TO CORRECT BEHAVIOR

Chapter 14

Lily fled upstairs to her room, something she seemed to be doing a lot lately, her heart pounding, her mouth soft and swollen, while her body was demanding to know just why it had to leave possibly the most pleasurable experience of her life.

Propriety was the best answer she had. It would have to do.

She stepped inside and pulled the door shut behind her, leaning on the wood. Her breathing was fast and loud in the quiet room.

Nor could she answer just what impulse had made her take those few short steps toward him.

And even though she really, really should, she just couldn't regret it.

It had felt so much . . . *more* than she had ever expected, even when she'd pondered what it might actually feel like. It was as though someone had described what it was like to eat a piece of stale bread, only to find, when one bit into it, that it was the most glorious chocolate cake ever, dripping with frosting and delightfully rich.

She could only imagine what the rest of it would be like. It would definitely be better than chocolate cake, she knew that.

What else might it be better than?

She walked into her room and sat down on the bed, and it seemed everything felt and looked different, as though the world was lit by fireworks.

She'd had her first kiss. No, not that, exactly; *had* implied a passive acceptance of the action, and once things had gotten started, she'd *taken* her first kiss.

From a duke, no less. If she thought of it, which she hadn't much, she would have assumed her first kiss might be from someone of her class, someone she'd met through the agency, or a neighbor. Not a gentleman who was only a step below the Queen, a man who had the power to change law, rule over counties, destroy a reputation by raising an eyebrow.

Imagine if he employed both of them, what type of destruction he could create.

Not to mention employing his virility, his commanding voice, his arresting good looks, and yes, his exceedingly nice backside.

And he had kissed her after having asked her opinion, and treated her—well, not nearly as an equal, she didn't think he was capable of that just because of who he was—but as someone with whom he wished to talk. To have tea with after the evening's festivities were over.

"You are a foolish woman, Lily Russell," she said as she unbuttoned her gown, the lovely new gown he had bought her. She hung it up carefully, then donned his nightshirt, not one of the night-gowns Mrs. Wilson had sent with all the rest of her new clothes.

It would be a shame to wear the new night-gowns just to have to wash them again, she thought, knowing she was employing logic equal to Annabelle's.

This didn't change anything, she reminded herself sternly. Kisses, to someone like him, were probably just one step above a handshake or a courteous smile. It didn't mean anything.

To him.

To her, of course, it meant a lot, but that was because it was her first. Perhaps she should go out and kiss other people, just to grow accustomed to it.

She giggled, like Annabelle, at the thought of how Mr. Thompson would look if she surprised him with a kiss.

She didn't think the duke would like it if she kissed his butler. The way he'd reacted when she'd spoken of Mr. Smithfield was proof of that.

But now she had to continue working properly for the man when she knew what his mouth felt like. What her improper feelings felt like.

She had definitely put herself into a very difficult position. In more ways than one.

Of course, the duke strolled into the breakfast room as though they hadn't shared a kiss the night before. Although how would he acknowledge it? He couldn't just walk in and say, "Hello,

Miss Lily, I see your mouth is no longer attached to mine."

To which, she thought, she could reply, "Your backside is really lovely."

And then they would be the Most Improper Duke and His Incredibly Inappropriate Governess.

So it was a good thing he acted as though nothing was different.

"What are you ladies doing today?" the duke asked as he sat down.

Rose answered before Lily could say anything. Although the only thing she could think to say right now was, *Reminisce about that kiss that shouldn't have happened,* and, *Go bury my nose in your nightshirt.*

"We're drawing today. Miss Lily says she is very good at rabbits. I'm better at horses."

"Perhaps I could stop by the schoolroom? See your horses?" The duke eyed the plate of sausages John was offering and shook his head.

"If you wish, Your Grace," Lily said quietly. Why did he want to visit the schoolroom now? Not that he didn't have a right to, it was his house, his daughter, his employee. But now? The morning after the kiss of the night before?

She couldn't think about it any longer or her head might split like one of those sausages.

"Are you going to draw, too?" Rose asked, taking another piece of toast from the table.

"If Miss Lily has enough pencils, of course."

Rose put her elbow on the table and rested her chin on her palm. Lily just as quickly gestured for her to keep her hands in her lap. "What animal do you draw best?"

"I don't know that I've ever been asked that question," he said in perfect seriousness. He got a crooked smile on his lips. "A cat, I think."

"I can draw a cat, too," Rose said, sticking her nose in the air.

"Then we shall have a contest as to who can draw the best cat, and Miss Lily will be the judge." Both he and Rose looked at Lily then, and she felt herself start to turn pink again.

"I shall be glad to."

"That is lovely, Miss Rose." It did look somewhat like a cat, in that it had a tail, at least. And was that—well, apparently it was a cat pirate, because it had on some sort of eye patch.

"How about mine, Miss Lily?" He held the paper up with a sly smile on his face. She circled around to his side of the table and took the paper from his hand.

That was even less of a cat than Rose's. At least Rose had given the cat some sort of defined shape. This was more of a cat blob, with whiskers.

"Interesting."

He leaned back in his chair and crossed his arms over his chest. "I have the feeling, Miss Lily, that you are not impressed with my artistic talents."

She tried not to smile, but she couldn't help it. He sounded so serious, and yet the warmth in his eyes and the slight grin that twisted his mouth told her he was teasing. She had rarely been teased.

She liked it. Not as much as kissing, of course, but teasing was definitely safer.

"Your Grace, I believe your cat is in need of some fur. And a tail. And paws."

Rose walked over to examine the drawing in question, and when she saw it, there was no mistaking the look of exultation on her face. "My cat is better," she announced, and both Lily and Marcus nodded in agreement.

Marcus took the drawing back and laid it back down on the table. "This was fun, even if I am horrible at it."

"Not horrible," Lily corrected, "merely abysmal."

They looked at each other and laughed, and Lily got that warmth all over her body, the one that had nothing to do with the actual temperature and everything to do with him.

"I was thinking about the other night," he began.

Not in front of Rose, she wanted to shout, but just clamped her mouth shut, staring daggers at him.

He chuckled, clearly knowing what she thought he was about to say. "About my interests. I was thinking I should develop more."

"Oh." Well, didn't that just flatten her sails. He hadn't been about to be inappropriate in front of a child. Or something.

"And maybe I should hire a drawing master. Or someone to teach me the piano—do you play piano, Miss Lily?"

The thought of sitting next to him on a piano

bench was almost too much for her. She might combust. She knew her face had gotten all pink again, she could feel the heat rushing to her cheeks.

"I'm going to draw a horse now," Rose announced, taking another piece of paper from the stack on the table.

"That will be lovely, dear," Lily replied, ruffling Rose's hair, then speaking to the duke. "I do play piano, Your Grace, but it strikes me that there are better things you could be doing with your time." Too late she realized what she had said.

He didn't speak, just regarded her with a knowing look in his eye, one eyebrow beginning its slow ascent up his face, his lips curling into a knowing smirk.

"That is," she continued, feeling breathless, "someone in your position likely has things to oversee and decisions to make. Weren't you speaking with Mr. Porter about some law or another in Parliament? And if you were to turn your attention to those things," instead of making my knees weak with kisses, "you would have an interest that was both suitable to your position and would also do good. Unlike," she added, picking up his drawing again, "your artwork."

He smiled at her joke, but then his expression grew serious. "You might be right, Miss Lily. I have not spent as much time . . . that is, I have not spent *any* time in maintaining my position. But perhaps I should look into things myself, that's what you're saying?"

He looked so sincere, so earnest, and so surprised at being asked to be a better person, it made her heart hurt a little. Had no one expected anything of him beyond his position, his looks, his ability to pour brandy without spilling it?

His attitude toward Rose, his obvious yearning for something more, even if he wasn't aware he was yearning, revealed what depths were underneath the impossibly good looks and title.

She was acutely aware that she might very well find his underneath even more attractive than his overneath.

She was only saying what he himself had thought a few days ago. But somehow, coming from her mouth, it seemed so much more real to him. There would be someone to whom he might be accountable, to whom he could talk about what he was doing.

Was that what he'd been missing? Companionship? No, not that, because he was never short of companions, and Smithfield seemed destined to be one of his best ones yet.

What was different about her?

Oh. Right. She was a *her*. Smithfield wouldn't look nearly as attractive as she did, and he doubted if even Smithfield would dare speak to him as she had. To challenge him with her wit and forthright opinions.

But that would all go away when Rose grew up or was sent off to school, at which point Lily would leave, too. What would remain for him then? He'd be older, that was for certain, but if he didn't try to make something of his life beyond simply being his title, he'd die miserable and alone.

Even if he did succeed in finding an amenable wife. And didn't that thought make him want to snarl, because he definitely did not want someone who had a claim to him—besides Rose, that is—in his life. He barely seemed able to just take care of himself.

"Are you all right, Your Grace?" she asked in a soft voice. He must have had a want-to-snarl expression on his face.

"Fine, yes, thank you, Miss Lily." He picked up his pencil and added a few straggling hairs to his cat picture. "I think your idea might be rather sound," he continued, keeping his voice light, "to try to engage myself. I had not really thought of it before," much, "and it would be far more useful to stand bills in Parliament than to attempt to draw a cat."

She snickered, and he felt his chest tighten. And other parts do other things, but he was in the schoolroom, and even Incorrect Dukes knew one had to act Correctly here, with children present.

He could swear her eyes were almost twinkling. "Yes," she said, "I do believe that if there were a list of things a duke should do, drawing cats—or attempting to draw cats—would rank just below learning to make the perfect blancmange or learning to knit."

"I will concede the knitting, Miss Lily, but surely blancmange would rank higher. A perfect blancmange is not to be trifled with."

She grinned more broadly as she delivered her

salvo: "We were not discussing trifle, Your Grace. That is much higher on the list."

He laughed and nodded. "Excellently done. And now I am hungry. Are you hungry, Miss Rose?"

She looked up from her drawing. It seemed her cat had morphed into an angry ball, since she'd expanded shape and added enormously fierce eyes. "Very hungry. Pie?"

"Let us see if the cook has any blancmange or trifle." He stood and held his hand out to Rose, who took it. What did it say about his life until now that this was likely the tenderest moment he had ever had? "Miss Lily, do you care to join us?"

"No thank you. I must tidy up here."

He nodded and took Rose by the hand, leading her down to the kitchen. Fully aware that what he wanted to taste most was the woman in the room he'd just left.

~~A duke must never forget just who he is. He cannot be seen enjoying himself excessively, expressing his opinion, or wearing clothing that is not faultlessly perfect for the occasion~~.

A duke may do whatever he wants.

—THE DUKE'S GUIDE TO CORRECT BEHAVIOR

Chapter 15

"What is your favorite color?" Marcus asked. He didn't think he'd ever enjoyed walking so much in his life. It was just the two of them, Rose having announced she wished to walk with the duke herself.

Not that she didn't like her governess, she had continued, but she wanted him all to herself.

Had he ever been wanted just for himself? It was a remarkable feeling. He held Rose's hand as they made their way through the park, the early spring chill just shivery enough to make them keep their coats buttoned. He spotted a few signs of potential spring; not enough to believe it was absolutely on its way, but enough so that there was hope.

Hope. He hadn't had that in a long time, had he?

"Red," Rose said, after a long pause. Long enough for him to nearly believe in hope again. "What's yours?"

Marcus thought of eyes that changed color, that flickered from dark emerald to warm hazel. "Green," he replied, giving Rose's hand a squeeze.

He'd initially forgotten that he had promised

he would take Rose out for a walk in the afternoon, and then was disappointed that his newest employee would not be accompanying him—but as they walked, silent for the most part, just being together on this not quite spring day, he didn't wish it any other way.

Rose was a quiet child, but definitely opinionated. She'd told him why she preferred cats over dogs (apparently it had something to do with the softness of their fur, but he wasn't clear on that point), why the letter R was the best letter in the alphabet (obviously!), and that she thought it was stupid for children to have to go to bed earlier than adults (that one he disagreed with).

She could give Miss Blake some lessons in decision-making, that was for certain.

And listening to her, and just *being* with her, made him feel that there was hope. Spring would come, and he would take care of Rose as best he could, and he would do whatever he needed to ensure her happiness and well-being. And if that meant spending time with her sometimes prickly, entirely enticing governess?

That was just an unexpected benefit.

He was looking forward to hearing her report this evening. He was looking forward even more to just seeing her. He knew he shouldn't want to kiss her, but he did nonetheless.

"And the only time was when I was little," Rose said, apparently completing a thought he had lost track of.

"What was the only time?" Marcus said in a soft voice.

"The only time I had an ice. Have you ever had an ice?"

Children really were resilient. Rose had lost her mother only a week or so ago, and here she was, chattering about ices and colors and animals. He wasn't so naive to believe she wouldn't have difficulty later on, but it seemed she had adjusted well thus far.

And for that he had his governess to thank. She'd proven beyond capable, and he congratulated himself on hiring her, even though—he had to admit—the only thing he had done was said yes when she presented herself.

He wished she would reciprocate in other yes-saying areas, but hadn't he just scolded himself for those kinds of inappropriate thoughts?

It seemed he was in need of guidance on such things. It was good, then, that he had an able assistant. Who was beautiful, even if she wished to hide it, intelligent, and witty. Who intrigued him more with each passing moment he spent in her company.

"There you are." He didn't mean to sound irritable, it just happened. And he'd been sitting in this room for nearly two hours, wrestling with ledgers, and tiny print, and orders for things he didn't even know he needed.

No wonder he'd always ignored all of this before. It was damned unpleasant, and if there was one thing in his life he was good at, it was avoiding unpleasantness.

But he'd been thinking about being useful since she mentioned it. He might as well, he couldn't continue just avoiding things. Look how well that had turned out. Or not.

"Sit down," he said, gesturing to the chair she'd sat in the night before. The night he'd kissed her.

Of course that thought made him wonder what else he could do with her here. Things that would definitely take longer than two minutes, or two hours, even—watching her come undone, that thick, dark hair flowing down her naked back. His fingers stroking her skin, making her tremble underneath his touch.

Much more pleasant than accounting, that was for certain.

But she looked even less . . . pleasant than she had when he first met her, and she'd been all spiky then, like an unruly hedgehog. Now she looked as though she were wearing clothing that was too tight—although he could see for himself that was not the case, more's the pity—or had eaten something that disagreed with her.

"Are you all right?" he asked, trying to soften his tone. He was almost proud of himself for noticing something was off—he didn't generally care about others' well-being, except now it seemed he did.

Which was only one of many changes wrought when Rose came to stay with him. Had Lily secretly hated his kisses? Was she worried he would abuse his position as her employer? He didn't know, precisely, how to address that topic, since to mention it would be improper, and yet to sit here together with all of it surrounding them was also improper.

If only he had someone who could advise him on proper behavior. The irony of it made him nearly smile, only he didn't want her to know he was thinking about that, even though he absolutely was.

"I am fine, Your Grace," she replied stiffly. "What did you require?" Back to the stiff-voiced governess he'd met only a week ago, which seemed forever. It was definitely better to return to a working relationship with her rather than muse about the softness of her lips, or the warmth of her body, or—damn.

He gestured to the papers spread out on the desk. "I've taken your advice, you see," he said, resisting the urge to ask about anything related to kisses, and the quality thereof, "and I am going through the past year's accounts." He felt the evening's frustration rise up into his throat. "And I can't seem to make sense of any of it. Not one bit." He looked up at her, directly into her eyes. She still looked hedgehoggish. "Will you help me?"

Well. She couldn't resist that, could she?

She got up from the comfortable chair, sincerely wishing he was a duke with a wart on his nose, not a handsome nose on his handsome face. It would make her life much easier. But he didn't. Or wasn't. Or whatever.

He had a half smile on his face, and she wished she could ask him what he was—or wasn't—smiling about.

But she couldn't ask him anything, because

asking him questions might make him ask her questions, like he had the previous evening.

Did you like it?

The words had whispered through her head ever since he'd said them. He hadn't sounded commanding, not then; instead, he'd sounded hesitant. Concerned. Worried about how she'd enjoyed her first kiss? But he hadn't known it was her first, had he? He might think she went around kissing all her employers, although that would have given him pause if he had considered the mythical vicar.

What did he think of her? She wished she could ask him, just as she wished she could ask why he couldn't seem to get a close enough shave on his cheeks, even in the morning, and if cravats felt so uncomfortable that he hated wearing them—he wasn't wearing one again tonight, showing that delicious expanse of skin.

But she couldn't say any of those things. She knew that, and yet the questions danced in her mind.

"What are you having trouble with in particular?" she asked instead, placing her hand on the top of the desk and leaning forward. His head was just near her arm, and she wondered what he would do if she stroked his hair.

Probably pull her onto his lap and kiss her senseless. So she probably shouldn't do that.

Even though she really, really wanted to.

"These numbers won't add up. I've tried them many different ways, and I get a different answer every time." His expression was aggrieved, as though the numbers were being difficult on purpose, and she tried not to laugh.

"I don't believe it is the numbers at fault, Your Grace," she said, drawing one of the pages near her. "If you don't mind?" she continued, gesturing that he should let her sit. He rose, but stood directly beside her chair, so she was acutely aware of him, his scent, the warmth of his body, everything there right beside her.

It was definitely distracting.

She shook it off, though, and looked at the long tiny columns. "Do you have a pencil?"

"That would help, wouldn't it?" he said in a dry tone. He handed her the pencil and her fingers touched his—what did the man have against wearing gloves, anyway? That was yet another question she'd like to ask—and the contact sent sparks through her, made her tingle in places he very definitely had not touched.

She swallowed. "Let's see, then." She bent over the paper, wishing she could better control her breathing, her heart rate—well, everything.

"I see. You forgot to include the second column here, in your calculations." She blinked as she kept looking at the numbers. "And for goodness' sake, do you have pixies working for you? Because this might be the smallest handwriting I've ever seen. No wonder you're having a difficult time."

"Good," he said, a strong thread of humor in his voice, "I was thinking it was because I was stupid."

She lifted her head to look him in the face, allowing herself to smile. "There's that, too, but the small handwriting doesn't help matters."

"So where did I go wrong, then?" At that, he leaned completely over her, and for a moment she was entirely and completely breathless. She was about to go terribly wrong—in such a right way—if she didn't remember who she was, what she was doing here, and what she should most definitely not be doing here.

She pointed a shaky finger at the second column. "Here. See how you should have added the hundred you got from these numbers to that one?"

He leaned farther in, and so help her, she just wished she could raise her face to his. To explore the stubble on his cheeks with her tongue, even though she'd never had such a perverse thought in her life before.

And was it so perverse, anyway? She simply didn't know.

One would think, she thought ruefully, that having worked in a brothel would mean that one did know such things.

All she knew was how to settle accounts.

With that lowering thought in mind, she did what she knew.

Lily rubbed her eyes and stretched. They'd been working on the accounts for about an hour—he'd drawn up a chair so he wasn't disconcertingly close to her. Perhaps only concertingly close, if such a thing existed.

He wasn't stupid, as he claimed, but he was far

too impatient for things just to be done, rather than working it through in order to get them done. She kept explaining it to him until at last they were both satisfied that he at least understood the rudimentary elements.

"I've had enough of this," he said then, stretching. She tried not to notice the strength and breadth of his chest as he held his arms over his head. Nor did she notice his bare throat, the tendons of his neck, how the dark stubble covered his cheeks, and how his mouth—that mouth that had been on hers the night before—had a slight curl to it, as though he were secretly pleased about something.

None of that. Instead, she reminded herself that she was just an employee, one who had plans of her own that did not involve him. The opposite, in fact.

"Then I might be excused?" she asked, beginning to rise from her chair.

His hand shot out and clamped her wrist, holding her still. That lip curled into an actual smile, not just a secretly pleased one. "After all that, we deserve more than tea, don't you think, Miss Lily?"

He didn't wait for her reply, just let go of her and stood in one smooth motion before stalking to the cart where the brandy bottle was. He poured as he spoke. "I would ask you to give the daily report on Rose, only I spent the afternoon with her." He picked up their glasses and put both of them on the desk, returning to his seat. "Should I report to you, then?"

He didn't wait for a response. "Miss Rose liked the walk, although she wished people took their cats out of doors as well as their dogs. She much prefers cats, you see," he added in an aside. "We didn't talk a lot—Miss Rose seems to like silence as well as conversation—but we had a wonderful time." He took a sip of his brandy. "I would like to take her out again next Tuesday, on your afternoon off. I think we will both enjoy that."

Lily took her own sip, this time anticipating the sharp burn of the drink. She did like it. "Of course, Your Grace. That is entirely your prerogative."

He frowned and set his glass on the table. "Look, could you dispense with the 'Your Grace' thing entirely when we are alone together, just us? I am reminded enough of my position, my difference from the rest of the world, I would like to be with one person who doesn't have to mention it every sentence."

"Yes, Your— Yes."

"Good. If you need to call me, you can always say 'Hey, you,' or 'You there,' or something similar. If only the two of us are in the room, I can likely figure out who you're talking to."

"To whom you're talking," Lily replied automatically, as though it were Rose speaking.

He laughed. "Of course. That. Thank you," he said, lifting his glass to her in a salute. He took a deeper drink then, and Lily watched the muscles of his throat as he drank.

"Rose and I are visiting the Porters tomorrow," she reminded him. "You did not wish to join us, did you? Miss Blake will be there," she added in a teasing tone of voice.

"I cannot decide what would be prefera—" he began in a clear imitation of the lady in question, then continued in his regular voice, "no, of course I won't be coming. Please do give my regards to the family. I hope Rose enjoys meeting other young children."

"I'm sure she will. She's been pretending that Mr. Snuffles is actually her brother."

That crooked smile creased his face. "Mr. Snuffles would make a better brother than most, I would imagine. He takes regular baths, doesn't speak much, and doesn't take up a lot of room."

"Do you have a brother, Your . . . ?" She gave him an awkward smile.

He shook his head and drained the liquid from his glass. "Not anymore. My elder brother died before he could inherit. Inheriting at all was such an unlikely event, neither of us had been prepared for it. But he had prepared for inheriting our father's responsibilities. Until he died." He sounded so distant, as though the misfortune had happened to another person. "And my parents did only so much for our family line, they were too busy with other things to sire more than just the two of us," he added.

"I did not have much company growing up, either," Lily replied, "but I preferred reading to playing anyway." She'd had a sister, too, who had died too soon, but she didn't want to share that, and he hadn't asked.

"That would explain why you are so good at your position, then. Reading would be a requirement for being an excellent governess." He got up to pour another splash of brandy in his glass, then returned for hers and did the same. "What else do you like doing?"

He doesn't mean it *that* way, Lily chided herself, even as she felt the color rise in her cheeks. "I suppose what most ladies like to do."

"That is the thing," he said in that impatient tone again, "I don't know what most ladies like to do. I should figure it out if I am to both marry a lady and raise one, shouldn't I? And don't tell me," he added, holding his glass out to her accusingly, "that I can just go through life without knowing because of who I am. That isn't fair to either me or the young ladies." A pause. "I am more—or less, depending on your viewpoint—than my title. I have only recently become the duke, as I mentioned." He shook his head, as though clearing away a memory.

His title might have been recent, but she couldn't help but guess that his commanding demeanor had come before he became a duke. It seemed like something he'd worn forever, not that he'd recently acquired.

"I like to read, as I said," she began in a quiet voice. "I like looking at people, at them having conversations, at their interaction. I like solving puzzles. I don't particularly like playing the piano, although I do love music. I think I would like to travel, if I ever got the chance." She looked up at him as she finished.

"Thank you." His voice was equally quiet, serious, and sincere.

A pause. A beat. A moment where she wondered just what would happen next, what she would do if he approached her for another kiss. Well, she knew what she would do, she just couldn't believe it of herself.

Thankfully—or not—that seemed not to have been on his mind. "I would ask you what authors you would recommend, but I think my reading time will be taken up with tomes that deal with things like proper business practices and crop fertilization."

"Sounds interesting." She took another tiny sip of the brandy. At this rate she'd be finished with it by midday tomorrow. *And you could spend more time with him.* The thought occurred even as she was trying to ignore it.

He grinned at her, shaking his head. "No, it doesn't. But if I am to understand what my employees are talking about, I need to read such books. And be able to comprehend the account ledgers. And all sorts of mind-numbingly boring things. And," he continued, holding his glass out toward her again, "when I'm not doing that, I have to learn how to spend time with a lady without offending her, or perhaps even persuade her that I have an inclination toward her."

Yes, the practice he'd spoken of. She would be giving lessons in the evening as well, it seemed. And even though she was the presumed teacher, look at how much she had learned: He was so much more than his title.

Even more than his bearing, his looks, his way of speaking. He was a Dangerous Duke in so many more ways than she'd originally thought—and she was in danger if she forgot why she was here and what she was doing.

A Duke must never:

Drink overly much, nor should he encourage young ladies to drink alcohol with him
Interact on less than a professional level with his employees
Appear in less than absolutely correct clothing
Seem bored or annoyed by his company
Kiss young ladies whom he has no intention of marrying.

—THE DUKE'S GUIDE TO CORRECT BEHAVIOR

Chapter 16

"Welcome, come in, Miss Rose, Miss Lily." Mrs. Porter pushed past the butler to greet them, an enormous smile on her face. "My girls have been in such a tizzy since I told them about you, Miss Rose. Would you like to go right on up to the nursery, or are you in need of refreshment first?" She addressed Rose, but she glanced at Lily as though she would answer.

Lily knew better than to try to answer for Rose. Decided opinions seemed to run in the family, judging by both the duke and Rose. "Want to go up," Rose said with a determined nod.

Mrs. Porter turned to the butler, who looked less daunting than Mr. Thompson. Still impressive, but not quite as supercilious. Perhaps there was Butler Training, and these men learned just the right degree of haughtiness to show, depending on their owner's position?

And if there was, then the agency ought to start training its prospective ladies' maids the same way. She would bring it to the attention of her partners the next time she went by.

"Take Miss Rose up, then, and Miss Lily and I will want tea in the drawing room."

"Oh, goodness, there is no need for that, Mrs. Porter." Lily was well-aware that a governess would not expect to have tea with the lady of the house. That the lady of the house seemed so eager for it meant something, something she suspected had to do with the duke. *Knew* it had to do with the duke. Because of Miss Blake, of course, but it could also be that Mrs. Porter was on a general information quest to help all the eligible young ladies in London.

Which Lily knew she was not, of course.

"I insist!" Mrs. Porter said, insisting. Lily had no choice but to follow her hostess into a drawing room off the main foyer (which was much less impressive than the duke's, but she did not think the foyer went to Foyer Training).

"So tell me," Mrs. Porter said almost as soon as they sat down, "all about the duke."

She definitely wasn't Machiavelli now.

"He is my employer." Which was the subtle way of telling her it was not appropriate for her to discuss him.

Mrs. Porter leaned forward and touched her on the arm. "But you can tell me something about him, can't you?" Apparently Mrs. Porter didn't understand subtlety, or at least chose to ignore it. "Is he courting a young lady?"

Not yet. "Not that I am aware of, but I would hardly be his confidante." Even though she was. Maybe she was secretly a very good liar, she just had to practice more. Now wasn't that a cheery thought.

"Then Miss Blake might have a chance." Mrs. Porter's face was smug, as though she had already secured the duke for her charge. Lily wanted to point out that Miss Blake was nowhere near the duke's social equal, that the two of them had met precisely once in a group gathering, and that the duke had promised he would never love the woman he would marry. But she doubted that Mrs. Porter would care about any of that. Just that Miss Blake would be Your Grace and take precedence over most other people. Oh, and she might have the power to express an opinion.

Or not. "Goodness, here you are, I was wondering where you had gone," Miss Blake said as she entered the room. "Or not wondered, exactly, but was thinking that you might have gone to the garden, but then again, you might just as well have come here. So I came here."

Miss Blake sat in one of the other chairs and began to remove her bonnet. "And I thought you might have gone to the garden, only I popped my head in there, and you weren't there."

The girl was brilliant.

At least Mrs. Porter seemed to think so. "Yes, here we are," she said with no trace of irony. "Miss Lily and I are about to have tea, would you care to join us?"

A pause. She would have to make a decision. Lily felt herself hold her breath, waiting for the outcome.

"I am not sure." Lily exhaled. "I had been thinking I might like some lemonade, only it is rather cold for that now, and tea would be nice, only if I have tea I will want biscuits."

And she didn't want biscuits?

"And I adore biscuits, only there are so many different types, and I can never choose just one to have."

Of course not. Even if the duke offered for her, how could she possibly accept? She would have to decide on one man for the rest of her life.

"Listen to this," Mrs. Porter said, her eyes sparkling. "Miss Lily says the duke is not currently courting any young lady."

Miss Blake sighed. "He probably has his choice of all of the young ladies in London, it would be so hard for him to pick just one."

Lily felt herself about to giggle, but stifled it so it just sounded as though she'd snorted. She wished the duke were here so he could share the joke—but then again, if he were here, it would be the answer to Mrs. Porter's—if not Miss Blake's—dreams.

Thankfully the tea arrived before Miss Blake could question Lily about whether she thought she'd had a cough or a sneeze.

Lily sipped her tea, wishing she had some brandy to put in it, listening to Mrs. Porter and Miss Blake discuss the party they were to attend that evening. The duke was to go, too, and Lily felt a pang at who he might meet there—some young lady who could express an opinion, who was pretty, cultured, of the right status, and who said she liked children.

She would never attend such an event in her lifetime, and she wished she could go, just to see the people, the clothing, hear the music.

To see him in his evening wear. Maybe even to dance with him. To—

The door opened again before Lily could even think about escaping to the terrace for a stolen kiss.

"Mr. Haughton," Mrs. Porter said, getting to her feet. "Clarissa isn't here yet, but we're having tea. You know Miss Blake, of course, and this is Miss Lily."

Lily stood, giving a slight curtsey. Mr. Haughton was a middle-aged gentleman who looked much like Mr. Porter, except he was blond. And was looking at her with a puzzled expression on his face. "Miss Lily is the Duke of Rutherford's charge's governess," Mrs. Porter explained. "And Miss Rose is upstairs with the children, so we are all having tea here."

"I'm not," Miss Blake chirped.

Mr. Haughton kept his gaze on Lily. "A pleasure to meet you," he said, drawing his eyebrows together in a near frown, almost as though it was not at all a pleasure to meet her.

"Thank you, sir," Lily replied. This was awkward. She had no idea why her appearance caused him such consternation.

"The governess?" he said, still with that frown. "You are the governess for the Duke of Rutherford?"

"Not *his* governess," Lily replied, even though she was sort of governessing him, but he didn't need to know that, "but the governess to his charge, Miss Rose. She is upstairs with the other children, and Mrs. Porter was kind enough to send for tea."

"Hm," he said, giving her one last, searching look before taking a seat. He took the cup Mrs. Porter had prepared for him and seemed to dismiss Lily from his mind.

That was just as well. It made her feel very uncomfortable to be so intensely scrutinized. Except for when the duke did it; then she only felt intensely something, but she didn't know what that something was.

"Did you have fun?" Lily asked Rose as they left the Porters'. She'd only had to endure another hour of inquisition from Mrs. Porter and an hour of indecision from Miss Blake.

She wanted never to answer another question again. Nor hear anyone debate the possible answer to a seemingly innocuous question.

Because really, how hard was it to decide if one wanted to sit in one chair or another?

Apparently very, very hard.

Lily had decided she wished Miss Blake would develop laryngitis.

"They had lots of toys," Rose answered.

"Mrs. Porter said you could return next week. Would you like that?"

Rose nodded. Thank goodness she did not suffer from Miss Blake's particular affliction.

In the midst of all the interrogation, Mrs. Porter

had said—several times, in fact—that the duke was to attend the ball that evening, and it seemed he had been very little in Society thus far. So not only was he unaccustomed to speaking with young ladies, it seemed he was unaccustomed to being polite at all. Interesting. No wonder he needed her help.

Needed her help to secure a young lady as his bride, a woman whom he'd want to be a mother to Rose. A woman he'd kiss. A woman he'd take to his bed and . . . do things to.

A woman who wouldn't be her.

Dukes should not fraternize with anyone who is not their social equal (with the exception of earls, but no lower than that). Which means, unfortunately, that the only people to whom they can be friendly is other dukes—of which there are very few—and royalty, of which there are fewer. Dukes need to recall their positions at all times, and not get distracted by a clever wit, a friendly gesture, or a kissable mouth.

—The Duke's Guide to Correct Behavior

Chapter 17

"If you'll just allow me, Your Grace," Miller began. He took another cravat from the stack and put it around Marcus's neck.

Like a noose.

The previous attempts were in a pile on a chair, their wrinkles and creases practically mocking Marcus for his determination to look proper, for one evening at least. Or so it seemed.

He waited, shifting impatiently, as Miller tied the fabric, smoothing it with a practiced gesture. Marcus resisted the urge to slide his finger between the fabric and his skin to give himself more breathing room. It would mean another attempt would have to be made, not to mention that he was about to go breathless, as it were, with no breathing room at all in his life.

He was about to take his rightful place, his dukely place, in society, which he had heretofore ignored, beyond taking advantage of his position for personal enjoyment.

He hadn't cared before, but now, with Rose's future happiness at stake, not to mention his own, he had to. And what was likely worse, he would have to do it with a smile on his face and pleasantries on his lips.

He wished he'd had more practice. With her. If he could get his lemony governess to smile, to regard him with approval, he could do anything. Of course he doubted that most young ladies were of the lemony persuasion, but neither did he think they would be as tempting to kiss.

"I believe this is the one, Your Grace." Miller stepped aside so Marcus could see himself in the glass.

His cravat was, indeed, correct. As was everything else he had on. He looked absolutely presentable, not like the sort of man who would lure young ladies in his employ to his study to drink brandy, nor the kind of man who even have thoughts about said action.

Excellent. Now he just had to persuade every member of Society—not to mention himself—that he was truly that kind of gentleman.

Thankfully there was a knock on his bedroom door before he could tear the cravat off and haul Lily to his study for some much-needed—by him—kissing.

"Your Grace, the carriage is ready." Thompson's eyes widened slightly and then he nodded, as though in approval.

Poor Thompson. The previous duke, according to all reports, had been one of the stuffiest men, his only oddness being his fondness for cats. Likely he even wore a cravat to sleep in, so it must pain Thompson to see him now holding the title.

"I'll be down shortly."

He allowed Miller to brush off some nonexistent lint, gave himself one last look in the glass, and headed downstairs to his doom. That is, the carriage.

"Glad you made it." Smithfield cast a glance at Marcus. "And you look so presentable."

Marcus grinned. "Don't look so surprised, I can clean up if I have to."

"If you have to, of course. That you wanted to is what is surprising," Smithfield replied, a dry tone in his voice.

The two men stood at the edge of the ballroom, couples whirling and dancing in front of them, a row of chaperones on the opposite wall, while servants passed nimbly throughout the crowd, handing out glasses of wine to the guests.

"I must have been an arrogant ass the night we met." Marcus plucked a glass of wine from one of the servants' trays.

The room was filled with people, none of whom Marcus recognized. Not surprising, since he'd made it a point not to be in polite company. Present company excepted, of course.

Smithfield uttered a bark of laughter. "You could say that. I got the impression you never did anything you didn't wish to, and so to see you here—you were most vehement about—let me see if I can recall correctly—'not changing just because I'm a damned duke'—well, to see you here being a damned duke is a surprise."

That did sound like him. But he'd be damned—so to speak—if he'd be entirely selfish at the cost of another person's happiness.

"Are your sisters here?" Marcus took another sip of his wine.

"Of course. They wouldn't have missed this party, not when a real duke promised to be in attendance."

Marcus cocked his eyebrow at his friend. "I can tell that event doesn't impress you."

Smithfield laughed again. "Don't forget, I've seen what you look like dancing with a cat in a corset." He cleared his throat. "That is, the cat was wearing the corset. Not you."

Oh. So that had happened. Interesting. And no wonder Stripey had bolted every time he'd seen him since.

"Your Grace, Mr. Smithfield." A small group had manifested in front of him, led by a gentleman who seemed to have been poured into his suit, it was so tight. "I am the Earl of Daymond," he said. "I am so pleased you were able to accept my invitation." The man bowed with an audible creaking of his stays.

Marcus reminded himself not to eat too much of the food being passed around.

"The pleasure is mine, my lord," he said without a trace of sarcasm.

He heard Smithfield smother a snort. So perhaps there was a trace there.

"May I introduce my daughter, Lady Lucinda?" The earl put his arm behind a young woman's back and propelled her forward.

She curtsied and held her hand out. "A pleasure, Your Grace." Lady Lucinda had blond hair that sparkled in the glow of the multitude of candles placed in sconces and candelabras on the walls and throughout the rooms. Her gown was a demure white, no doubt signifying her status as an eligible young lady.

Marcus bowed.

A silence. And then Smithfield's elbow nudged him in the ribs. Oh, of course—an eligible young lady.

"Ah, yes, Lady Lucinda, are you free for the next dance?"

Another woman, not Lady Lucinda, answered. Must have been the countess, who seemed to have taken the opposite approach to food as her husband—she was so bony she might have been a model for a scarecrow. "Yes, she is, Your Grace."

The lady herself, Lucinda, met his gaze and smiled, a hint of wryness in her eyes. "It appears I am, Your Grace. Thank you for the invitation."

And then the pack of them moved away, apparently having satisfied the courtesies and gotten the duke to dance with the daughter of the house.

Marcus exhaled. "Thank you for that, by the way," he said in a low voice.

Smithfield nodded. "Figured you were out of practice with this sort of thing."

Practice. He definitely needed more *practice*.

"The room is very nice," Marcus said. "Has your family owned the house long?"

Lady Lucinda nodded. So much for that conversation.

They were parted in the movements of the dance as Marcus racked his brain for more non-controversial conversation, but something that would require more than a head shake or nod.

"And is this your first Season?" he asked.

A shake this time. Damn it.

"Do you prefer chocolate or lemon ice?"

This time he got another one of those wry smiles. "You are determined to engage me in conversation, Your Grace."

Well. She was certainly direct.

"Lemon." And decisive. That was good.

But now there was nothing else to say.

He couldn't allow himself to think that this might be what marriage to an eligible young lady would be like.

Damn it. He'd thought it.

"And which do you prefer, Your Grace?" She tilted her head back to regard him. She had brown eyes, very pretty brown eyes, actually.

He preferred hazel. It was a good thing she hadn't responded with her own question about the most attractive shade of eyes.

"Chocolate."

She smiled. "Our first disagreement."

"Likely not to be our last," he replied without thinking. Damn.

She laughed. Thank goodness—he hoped he wouldn't have inadvertently offended her.

He really needed that practice. As in right now.

Unfortunately, he was at this party, and he had

to stay for at least another hour and dance and mingle and make idle conversation.

"I apologize for being so quiet, Your Grace," Lady Lucinda said as they turned and made the walk up the line of people to the next movement of the dance. "You see, I know that my parents will wish to hear every word we've said, and I don't have a good memory, so I thought if we limited our conversation it would be easier later."

"Perhaps we should write out our conversation in advance, so as to be better prepared?" He hadn't expected anyone here to be amusing. That was his own prejudice, one he had to admit to.

Not that he wished to marry Lady Lucinda on the basis of half a conversation, but at least it wasn't entirely painful.

She laughed again. She had a nice laugh, but it wasn't— Damn it. It wasn't hers.

They finished the dance in silence, no doubt so Lady Lucinda could accurately report what had been said. But it was a comfortable silence, at least.

He escorted her back to her parents, excusing himself as he saw Smithfield and his sisters.

"Your Grace," one of the sisters said. "You're here!" As though it was the most wonderful thing she'd ever seen.

No, probably the most wonderful thing she'd ever see would be Miss Blake making a decision. That lady was here as well, standing to the side and frowning as she viewed a tray of wineglasses. She had to be figuring out which one to take.

He couldn't bear it. He strode forward and took

a glass off the tray, handing it with a bow to Miss Blake.

"Th-Thank you, Your Grace," she said.

"It is nice to see you again, Miss Blake," he said. "May I ask if you are free for the next dance?"

"Of course she is," one of the sisters said. It seemed no young lady was capable of answering such questions themselves. In Miss Blake's case, he could understand that.

"Yes, I am," she confirmed, taking a sip from her glass. "Oh, this is good! I am not certain it is as good as the tea we had this afternoon, but I do like it."

Well, he was glad that was settled.

"I don't believe you've met my other brother-in-law, Mr. Haughton," Smithfield said, gesturing to one of the gentlemen. "He was unable to attend dinner the other evening."

"Pleasure to meet you, Mr. Haughton," Marcus said as he grasped the other man's hand.

"The pleasure is mine, Your Grace." The man looked as though he wished to say something else, but his wife—who was taller—nudged him and he snapped his mouth closed.

The music started up again, and Marcus knew he had to face the inevitable.

"This is our dance, Miss Blake?" He held his arm out to her, not giving her the chance to pick which arm she should take, and she hesitated only a moment before placing her hand on his sleeve.

He escorted her out to the middle of the dance floor, grateful that the movements of the dance would not allow for much conversation.

Yes, his first foray into Society was going spectacularly well.

"How is your Miss Rose?" Miss Blake asked, when she had a chance.

Rose. Her little face when she was talking so earnestly about cats, and how she stuck her tongue out of the side of her mouth when she was drawing, and how she'd held his hand on their walk.

"She is wonderful," he replied, knowing it was the most honest thing he'd said the entire evening.

"I know the children liked having her over. Miss Lily said perhaps she would come over again. Would you accompany them?"

He'd have to decide that, wouldn't he? And suddenly he understood some of what Miss Blake must go through in her every waking moment.

"I will consider it," he said after a moment.

He didn't have a miserable time after all, he reflected as he sat in the carriage a few hours later. But it hadn't been precisely fun; perhaps he would have to practice that as well. Having fun.

The thought of practice made him think, naturally, of her; not that he hadn't been thinking of her all evening.

And he wanted, no he *needed*, to see her. Now. That was a decision he didn't have to ponder.

A duke should treat a lady as though she were a lady. That is to say, as though she were a delicate flower, unable to deal with passion, strong emotions, manhandling, and cavorting of any kind. A lady who wishes to be treated otherwise must indicate her preferences to the duke in question.

—THE DUKE'S GUIDE TO CORRECT BEHAVIOR

Chapter 18

She tried telling herself that she was only in this room to retrieve something to read. Herself responded that she was a liar and that she should just admit that she wished to catch a glimpse of the duke when he returned from the Earl of Daymond's ball.

She continued to look for a book, refusing to even consider *Agricultural Practices in the Midlands,* Mary Shelley's *Falkner,* or Thomas Moore's *The Epicurean.*

Perhaps she would have to admit to herself that not only was she a liar, but that she had no interest in any kind of book at this moment. So much for liking to read.

Thankfully she heard the door open before she could wade through all the lies she was telling herself, and she pushed a book—she didn't know which one it was, but knew she didn't want to read it—back onto the shelf and turned to leave the room.

Before she could exit, however, he burst in, one

hand already ungloved, pulling his cravat off as he strode toward her.

A flurry of white fabric as gloves and cravat came flying through the air, and then he had her in his arms, her back pressed to the bookshelves.

"Do you want this?" he asked, heat in his eyes.

She couldn't speak, not even to tell him a book spine was poking her in the back. She just tilted her head back, closed her eyes and waited for the inevitable kiss.

Which, she realized after a few moments of eye-closed waiting, was not inevitable after all. She opened one eye, and he was still there, his face hovering above hers, the heat in his eyes not lessened, if anything even more intense.

"What is it?" she asked in a whisper. When she really just wanted to ask, *Why aren't you kissing me?*

"I promised I wouldn't ever use my privilege." His voice was rough and raw. "You have to tell me—'Marcus, I want this.' Otherwise I won't—I can't do something you might not want." He sounded so torn, as though it hurt him to say it and yet he had to.

Silly man. "Oh, so you want to know how it would sound when a young lady wishes for you to take liberties?" She smiled and raised an eyebrow, because two people could play that eyebrow game. She spoke in a low voice. "Marcus"—it was the first time she'd said his name—"I want this."

And even as the *s* of *this* had left her lips he was kissing her, his mouth warm and soft, his hands on her arms, almost tender, his palms moving on her bare skin.

She reached up to cup his cheek, feeling the stubble that had escaped his most dukely ministrations. It chafed against her fingers, but it was a delicious hurt, and she wanted to rub her face against his, to feel just how different he was from her.

For one thing, he was very male, and that fact was making itself known somewhere near her waist.

He still hadn't done any more than kiss her and touch her arms, and yet with all that seemed to be happening, she felt a smug sense of satisfaction that she had done this to him.

Although she had to admit he was having an effect on her as well, making her insides tremble, and her brain stop thinking, and her body wanting to engage in all sorts of activites she hadn't even dreamed of when flipping through the pages of *The Epicurean*. No offense to Thomas Moore.

She slid her hands around the back of his neck, anchoring her fingers in his hair, pulling herself up off the offending book spine and closer to his body.

His hard, lean body, with that lovely wall of chest pressing into hers (not that she knew if *she* had a lovely wall of chest, but he definitely did), and he intensified the kiss, sliding his tongue along the seam of her lips until she opened, softly. His tongue slid inside and she welcomed it, and him, and felt a rush of sensation all over her body as though she had been set on fire.

Which she almost felt she had.

Only there was no way fire could make her

feel this—delicious, this worshipped, nibbling her as though she were a rare treat, his tongue tasting hers, sucking her lip into his mouth. His hands had slid lower so they were on her waist, holding her to him, as though she'd wish to go anywhere—silly man!—and the hard warmth of his bare hands seeped through the fabric of her gown to her body. She shivered at the sensation.

Well. If she were asked now if she liked to kiss, she would have to say yes. Because she liked this an enormous amount, even more than new gowns, or brandy late at night with Dangerous Dukes, or seeing what a virile man's throat looked like.

She moved her hands down his back, feeling the flex of his muscles as he kissed her, devoted himself to her mouth. A part of her wanted to rip his shirt from his body so she could see what she was touching, but that would mean she'd have to concentrate on something other than what his mouth was doing, and she did not want to do that, not at all.

Not when it felt so incredibly good.

But people did need to breathe to survive, so eventually he drew away, panting, resting his forehead against hers, still with his hands on her waist, but his thumbs higher now, on her rib cage. She wanted so badly for him to put his hands *there*, there where she hadn't realized she was so sensitive.

Forget listing everything she knew about him; apparently there was a lot she didn't know about herself. Like how right it felt to be held by him, like this, and how much she liked it when he lightly bit her mouth, and how delicious it felt to have his hardness pressed against her.

All of that. Plus a lot more, if she could just clear her brain to think of it.

But he was still here, still breathing fast and loud into her ear, and she couldn't think straight.

"Why?" she asked after a few moments.

He chuckled, and she felt the rumble of his laughter against her body.

Suddenly she wished she were better at telling jokes so she could feel his laughter all the time.

"I couldn't stop thinking about you all evening," he said, speaking softly into her ear, "and it wasn't that the evening was bad, it was surprisingly not awful, but I kept wishing you were there so I could talk to you about the party, and the music, and catch your eye when someone said something ridiculous." He exhaled, and her skin prickled at feeling his warm breath. "Which was often.

"And also," he added, and Lily could hear the humor lightening his tone, "I knew I had to practice precisely what I must never do with a proper young lady."

Of course. Because she was not proper.

She took a deep breath and pushing herself away, against the bookshelf again, this time welcoming the stab from the book spine. A reminder of just how foolish and shortsighted she was.

"Did I say—" he began, taking his hands from her body, and in pulling away, leaving her suddenly feeling cold. "But I did say something wrong. I *did* something wrong."

She shook her head. "You didn't. I asked, you answered. It is fine."

He touched his finger to her mouth. "So lovely," he said. "I don't wish to hurt you."

You don't wish to, but you will.

If she had thought him virilely handsome before, it was nothing compared to how he looked now—a flush on his cheeks, his eyes heavy-lidded, filled with desire, his bare throat just inches from her mouth.

She was in so much trouble. And yet she knew this was not at all the worst kind of trouble she could be in. If she were honest with herself for a moment, beyond not wanting to read a single book anywhere, she'd have to admit that she wanted to find out what other kind of trouble she could get into, with him, in here.

What kind of trouble they could get in together.

Which was why she leaned up to kiss the side of his mouth and then scurried past him out the door and up to her bedroom—before she could be any more . . . *troublesome.*

That was definitely more than two minutes. And he'd liked it far better than what he'd always managed to do, in its entirety, within two minutes.

He thought of his evening as split into two segments: before he'd arrived home from the ball and after, Before Kiss and After Kiss.

Compared to this last kiss, the first one had been merely an aperitif. A sip of something pleasant, to be sure, but lacking the heady power of a snifter full of brandy or a satisfyingly rich glass of port.

But it was even better than any of that. It was . . . well, he didn't think he'd ever drunk anything so delicious as her mouth, the way she pressed her body against his, how she'd stroked his back, and the low moan he recalled, deep and soft in her throat.

Damn, he wished he could just stride up to her bedroom and take her, satisfy his body's urges—and hers—in a lot longer than two minutes.

Judging by how hard he was, his cock wanted that, too.

The thought of her in his bed was enough to make him take a few steps to the door, only to be stopped by his own conscience (his cock objected mightily). He had promised her he wouldn't abuse his privilege of who he was, and beyond that, it just wasn't right.

Things were easier, to be sure, when all he cared about was brandy and gambling and the occasional cat.

But those things didn't satisfy him. Not that he was satisfied—sexually, at least—right now, but he was satisfied in other ways. The way Rose held his hand and talked to him, and that because of her influence he was finally living up to his ducal responsibilities by examining the books, possibly even meeting with some of the people who managed his estates.

Hiring a housekeeper who was not the most unpleasant woman ever.

Redecorating.

Making this ducal mansion a home. For him. And Rose. And her?

When did he become a man who preferred being home to carousing? Cavorting, she called it?

He smiled at the memory.

He could pinpoint the moment precisely—when he looked into that little girl's eyes and saw emotions he recognized, and knew he was able to do something about it. About all of it. And would, if he could just prove to the world—not to mention himself—that he was the best and most proper person this tiny, precious creature had to take care of her.

And that did not mean taking advantage of her caretaker.

He tried to forget how Lily felt in his arms, against his mouth, and concentrated instead on the books he had gotten out from his library to take to bed.

And they would be the only things he would take to his bed.

That vow didn't feel quite as honorable a few hours later when he'd finished leafing through Charles Lyell's *Principles of Geology*—while no doubt a fascinating subject, it could not hold a candle to the "Principles of Lilyology."

Which he would love to explore in more depth. Perhaps even write Volume 2 of the series.

She was just down the hall. Just there. He could get up, tap on her door, and—no. No, he couldn't.

But what would happen if he did?

Marcus lay back on his bed, his hand sliding down to grasp himself. He'd managed to stop thinking about the After Kiss for a few hours, but now he was damned if he could think of anything else.

She'd be wearing a thin chemise—no, wait, she'd be wearing his nightshirt, her essence all over it. Because it would be too big for her, it'd be slipping off her shoulders, revealing her neck, her collarbones, the top of her neck.

He'd stand there at the door waiting for her to invite him in. He'd said he wouldn't presume, so anything that happened now had to be on her impetus.

"Come in," she'd say with a smile, turning to walk away from him, the shirt thin enough for him to see her back and the curve of her buttocks.

That the nightshirt was made of thick cotton in reality did not intrude on his fantasy, because this was his fantasy, damn it.

Anyway. He'd step inside, closing the door behind him. She'd walk to the bed and sit down, beckoning him closer. Of course he'd go, he wasn't an idiot.

He stroked his cock, feeling it get harder with each of her imagined movements. That he hadn't even gotten to see her underneath his own nightshirt was a testament to how poor he was at this kind of thing. But at least it had already gone on for five minutes, and he hadn't finished yet.

He'd sit beside her on the bed, he thought, and she'd slowly undo the tie of his dressing gown—damn, he'd forgotten he was wearing a dressing gown, and that was crucial in his scenario. He didn't want to be fussing with buttons and cravats and hose and trousers, he just wanted to get naked with her as she, too, got naked.

Dressing gown. Right.

She'd slide the dressing gown off his shoulders, putting her hands on his neck and pulling his mouth to hers.

And then they'd kiss, and he could slide his hands on her legs, up her thighs, pushing the nightshirt up so he could feel her skin against his palm. She'd groan, low and deep in her throat, for him, just for him, and touch his chest and his back and then reach for his cock, emitting a small sound of surprise at his size.

Because this was, after all, his fantasy. He didn't make a habit of comparing the size of his penis against other men, but he thought he likely was larger than most men, mostly because he was larger than most men in general. It stood to reason, if not scientific method.

Because a scientific method of gauging penis size would just be odd.

His hand moved faster and faster, gripped his length harder, and all he could think about was her, and the softness of her skin, and how her eyes would be blazing gold, and how her breasts would feel under his hands . . . his mouth.

How she'd taste . . . everywhere.

It was that image that brought him to a shuddering, satisfying climax, leaving him panting and sweaty and shaking in his bed, the momentary completion leaving him, contrarily, wanting more.

More that he couldn't take unless she wanted it, and more that if he took he would most definitely not be living up to the new standards he'd set for himself. Even by the old standards, that behavior wouldn't be acceptable.

It was going to be even harder—so to speak—to maintain a properly ducal decorum. Especially now that he knew he would have to do it for longer than two minutes.

A duke must have three things:

1. *A dukedom (of course)*
2. *The arrogance appropriate to his position*
3. *A larger than average . . . standing amongst his peers*

—The Duke's Guide to Correct Behavior

Chapter 19

"How do you take your tea, my lady?" Lily's entire body reacted when she heard his voice, even before she registered what he was saying.

Who was he talking to, anyway? She walked more quickly down the hall toward the schoolroom.

"Sugar. Lots of sugar." Her steps slowed as she heard Rose's voice. They were taking tea together?

She made her way to the door and peered inside. Rose and the duke were seated at the small table, the one where they'd done their drawings together, the duke's large frame bent over nearly double at the small table.

Rose was wearing a—was that, a cravat?—on her head, tied into a bow, and she appeared to have been slathering jam in copious amounts on her face.

The duke, not unsurprisingly, was not wearing a cravat.

She hadn't seen him since the night before, not since they kissed, not since she touched his back, felt the solid wall of muscle pressed against her chest, and had to remind herself that it couldn't happen again, not if she wanted to preserve the distance—tiny though it was—between them as employer and employee, not anything more.

It wasn't proper. It was delicious, enticing, intoxicating, and felt like wonderful madness, but it was not proper.

Perhaps she should embroider that on her handkerchief so she could refer to it when tempted.

Although if she did, she'd likely be looking at it every few minutes or so.

Enough, Lil, she reminded herself. She could not change the past, but she could guide her future.

She walked into the room, putting a politely distant smile on her face.

The duke caught her eye, a warm smile starting to curl his mouth up, but he froze, mid-smile, and Lily felt the catch of that in her heart.

"Are you having tea?" she asked, which was a stupid question, since that was clearly what they were doing.

Rose wrinkled up her face, showing just what she thought of her question.

Lily couldn't blame her.

"I told Miss Rose that we were both in need of manners," Marcus said. "Learning to do what was proper, and that you had been helping me in the evenings just as you teach Rose during the day." His tone was as proper and distant and respectful as it should be.

Why did that bother her?

"And so we decided to have tea together, to practice."

"Like you do," Rose added, of course not aware that Lily and the duke practiced things that would not come up in the course of polite conversation.

More like impolite actions. The exact opposite of polite conversation.

"May I join you?"

A silence as the duke looked at Rose. "This is your tea party, Miss Rose. Should we allow your governess to join us?"

Your governess. Reminding her again, even though he didn't mean it, of her position.

"Uh-huh," Rose said, reaching for the pot of jam.

The duke stood and held one of the small chairs out for her. "Please be seated, Miss Lily."

She sat, and she could have sworn he slid his fingers over the bare skin of her neck for just a moment, but he was back in his own chair before she could register whether it was what she had indeed felt. Not proper, she wanted to remind him.

"You take your tea with milk," Rose asserted.

"Let me pour the tea for you, my lady, the pot is still too heavy." The duke poured the cup, and then Rose put in so much milk the liquid nearly hit the top of the rim, making it nearly impossible for her to raise it without spilling.

Lily regarded the cup for a moment, then leaned forward and slurped enough out to make it safe to pick up.

"That action is not what polite young ladies usually do," the duke said, his tone laced with humor. Lily felt herself flush, reminded that slurping tea was the least shocking thing she had done that polite young ladies did not. "Although it is hard to imagine what a polite young lady would do when faced with that situation," he continued. "What would you do, Rose, if your cup was too full?"

Rose picked up her own cup which was blessedly only half full. "I don't know," she said with a shrug as she took a sip. "Spill it out?" She lowered the cup and reached for the sugar bowl.

The duke put his hand on her wrist. "I think you have enough sugar in that tea, don't you?"

Rose glowered but pulled her hand back. The duke patted her hand and leaned back in his chair. "What should we talk about at tea?" He shot a quick, amused glance at Lily. "The weather? The Queen? The elegance of this room?"

Rose shrugged again. The duke heaved an overdone sigh, humor lighting up his dark eyes. "Perhaps Miss Lily and I might converse so you can see just what proper young ladies and gentlemen talk about."

Only I am not proper, Lily thought. Not anymore, not since my father lost everything and I had to earn my living however I could. But for the moment she would play the part.

If only she were proper enough to even dream—but no, that was a very dangerous thought. He was her employer. That she had discovered she liked kissing her employer was improper, certainly, but there was no long-term harm in it . . . was there?

Except to her heart, and her reputation, and the very real possibility that he would be marrying some lady—a lady who was not her—and that she would have to see him with another woman, a woman who would take precedence in his and Rose's lives.

Wonderful. Now she was thoroughly depressed.

"Miss Lily?"

"Oh, of course. I am sorry." She sat up straighter in her chair and looked at him. "Had you asked me something? I was . . . I was thinking about something." About how this was the most untenable of situations, and yet it felt so comfortable, so right, being here. With him and Rose. About how his hands had felt on her skin and how she wanted to feel that alive, that wanted, again.

About how she had the chance to make her dreams come true, not the dreams where she and the duke were . . . doing things, but how she could elevate the agency's reputation so no woman would ever have to be forced into an unfortunate position again.

"I was wondering if you thought the weather will be fine enough for a walk tomorrow afternoon," he said. "All three of us. I cannot today, I have to pay a call on my host from last night."

"I cannot predict the weather, Your Grace."

He rolled his eyes, no doubt at her prim tone. "We are conversing, Miss Lily, not trying to predict anything."

That was the thing, wasn't it? She couldn't predict what would happen next, how she'd feel, what she'd do.

She felt as though she were standing on a precipice, and she could jump down or fly off. The results would be the same, but the journeys—oh, the journeys would be entirely different.

"In that case, Your Grace, I would say I hope it will be fine enough weather for a walk tomorrow. Miss Rose and I have been making a study of trees and flowers, and perhaps she can identify some for us."

"Excellent." He turned to Rose. "Does that suit you, Miss Rose? To take a walk in the park tomorrow?" He shot a glance at Lily. "I love to walk, just walk, don't you?"

Rose nodded, absorbed in the biscuit she seemed to have filched while the duke was not looking.

"Excellent," he said again. "It will be a pleasure to walk with two such lovely ladies."

His compliment, guarded as it was, still managed to warm her, making her aware that he was aware of her. That perhaps, if it were even possible, he had been thinking as much about her as she had about him.

In which case no wonder he didn't have a cravat on. He might well have lost his concentration, as she had, after last night. She was surprised she hadn't somehow managed to put her gown on backward, or forgotten how to speak.

He made her speechless and confused and wanting.

The exact opposite of precise, prim, and methodical.

And she wasn't sure she didn't like it much better.

A duke need never explain his reasons for not wishing to do something, but he should be prepared, if he is asked. And when he is asked, a duke can choose either to explain himself or to raise an eyebrow and stare at the questioner for his rudeness.

It is recommended to do the first, but much more common to employ the second.

—The Duke's Guide to Correct Behavior

Chapter 20

"I just don't know, Caroline." Lily sat in the Unfortunate Woman chair feeling as though she had earned the right to sit there. Unfortunately. Caroline sat in the chair opposite her in the office, an expression of concern on her striking features.

"But you haven't done anything worth doing, not really." Caroline drew back and blew a strand of hair off her face. "A kiss or two between two interested adults—that is not going to lead inexorably on a path of ruin, not if you don't want it to."

Oh, but she did want it to. She'd had more thoughts than she could fathom of going into his study and stripping him naked, unwrapping his cravat (even though it was likely already off), unbuttoning his shirt, undoing the placket of his trousers. She was a little fuzzy on what else he might wear. She hoped there wasn't much more, she didn't want to take too much time with it.

Sliding everything off so she could see the man underneath it all. She knew he would be gloriously, arrogantly naked, proud of who he was and what he looked like, as proud as he was when clothed.

Just—more unclothed.

"You don't want it, do you, Lily?" Caroline must have noticed her hesitation.

"No, no, it's just—well, I had no idea that kissing was so pleasurable."

Her friend laughed, and more hair flew around her head. Perhaps, Lily thought, she would purchase her a packet of hairpins for her next birthday.

"It is that. How do you think so many of us get into so much trouble?" Caroline's dark blue eyes danced as she spoke, but Lily knew her friend had been through more than she should have because of . . . trouble. It was what had been the basis for their partnership, their friendship, the bond of having to escape something that they were never truly part of.

In her own case, she'd had no choice; the only place that would take a female with no references but experience dealing with money was the brothel. She'd never thought her father's fecklessness would provide useful job skills, but she'd had to manage their money, as much as she could, from a young age. But even she couldn't withstand her father's determination to beggar himself and his family.

In Caroline's case, her downfall had been who she'd worked for—an artist who needed an assistant, someone who understood art and paint and the importance of quiet. An artist whose wife had seen a friendship and assumed the worst. Had blackened her name so thoroughly that Caroline couldn't find employment anywhere, unless she was willing to work in a brothel in the usual way.

But Caroline's experiences hadn't blighted her spirit, just dampened it. And now with the agency doing as well as it was, thanks to the duke hiring her, Caroline was as joyful as Lily had ever seen her. Caroline was not one for joy, usually. She was the mainstay of the agency, the one who bolstered everyone when they struggled, and who had the vision in the first place.

"What do you want to do?" Caroline asked in a soft, understanding voice.

Lily felt a wry smile curl her lips up, and she met her friend's gaze.

Caroline just laughed and shook her head. "You know you can't, not in reality. You can certainly think about it as much as you want. But to truly act upon it, you would have to be mad."

"Or an idiot."

"Or about to leave the country for parts unknown," Caroline rejoined.

"Or on the verge of inheriting so much money it wouldn't matter if I danced with my skirts held up to my knees in Trafalgar Square."

Caroline held her hand up to her mouth and guffawed, Lily joining her in laughing.

Both of the ladies quieted as they heard the bell at the door jingle, but resumed giggling as they heard Annabelle's voice. "Are you having fun without me? No fair," she said in an outraged tone.

She stepped into the office, garbed in the bright colors she favored. Today she was wearing a purple overcoat on top of a bright green gown. It was . . . well, it was eye-catching, that was for sure. Whether the individuals would wish their eyes to be returned after seeing Annabelle was a puzzle.

"Lily, how wonderful to see you!" Annabelle swooped down and kissed her on the cheek. "And Caroline is laughing! What have you done to her, Lily?"

She stood between them, her hands on her hips, her gaze darting between them in that bird-flittering way she had.

Lily reached her hand out and tugged on Annabelle's arm. "We were talking about my romantic life."

Annabelle's mouth pursed into an O and she perched on the arm of Lily's chair. "Does that mean you—and the duke?" She sounded absolutely delighted.

Of course. Because Annabelle never thought about the consequences of her own actions, nor anyone else's, for that matter, which is how she came to be unfortunate herself.

Caroline huffed. "She has to *remember her place,*" she said, emphasizing the last three words. "Because he won't." Then turning to Lily, she added, "And then where will you be?"

In his bed?

She didn't think that was what Caroline meant.

Luckily, the question seemed rhetorical, since Caroline continued talking. "You'll be on your own with a ruined reputation, and maybe worse. Not to mention the agency will suffer. As well as having your own heart broken," she added, as if in afterthought.

Well. That was all very bad, wasn't it? She'd been hoping that someone, somewhere, would say she could explore and have fun without risking everything and everyone she cared about, but that kind of ending was only in fairy tales, and she did not have a fairy godmother to care for her.

All she had were two strong young women who had fought the hardship sent their way and emerged better on the other side.

All in all, she preferred what she had. And that meant she could never have what she didn't have currently. Ever.

"Your Grace." The butler held his hand out as Marcus shook himself out of his coat and removed his hat. "The countess is in the drawing room, if you will just come this way?"

Marcus took a deep breath and followed the stern butler—not as stern as Thompson, but definitely stern—down the hall, a feeling of trepidation in his throat. Not that he should feel that way, he'd certainly paid calls before, except he hadn't done much socializing since assuming the title. He hadn't wanted to, nor had he needed to. Until now.

So while the prospect of spending the evening with men such as Smithfield, Collins, and the other men he'd spoken and drank with brought him pleasure, the prospect of sitting as he was inspected—and perhaps found wanting—by a group of proper ladies was enough to make him actually nervous.

No wonder he had eschewed it before. He hadn't realized just how ill-prepared he was to be a proper duke. To be a proper aristocrat, even. He'd had a succession of tutors, was given a few careless instructions as to how he should behave, but nothing more substantive. By the time he might reasonably have taken his place in correct society, his parents were dead, his brother didn't care, and he didn't want to bother with it. So he hadn't.

Which made this walk down the hallway feel as though he were on his way to his death.

Not that he was being dramatic or anything, he thought ruefully. This was hardly death, this was just—tea, and biscuits, and polite conversation. So death of a slower sort. Death by tea and talking. Death by boredom.

Thankfully, the butler stopped in front of a door before he could run away. The man flung the door open and held it wide as Marcus stepped through. "His Grace, the Duke of Rutherford," the butler announced.

The Countess of Daymond, the very thin woman he'd met the previous evening, rose and approached him, a very polite smile on her face. "Your Grace, what a pleasure. Thank you for the visit. Can I get you some tea?"

Tea. He really couldn't face any more tea. But it was the polite thing to do, so, "Thank you, tea would be fine."

"Or coffee?" she added. "I understand some gentlemen prefer coffee, although I cannot stand the appeal. So dark, and strong, and intense."

That was precisely why he did like it, but he wouldn't argue the point with her. "Coffee would be perfect, thank you."

The question of which beverage he would be drinking settled, the countess began to make the introductions. There were at least half a dozen ladies sitting in the room, all with teacups either in their hands or beside them on small tables, and he'd be damned—most certainly—if he could tell any of them apart. Except for Lady Lucinda, who was regarding him with that cool, slightly amused expression she'd worn the night before.

"You met my daughter, Lady Lucinda," the countess was saying, "and this is Lady Hall, of the Yorkshire Halls," as though that meant anything to him, "and Miss Charles and Miss Alice Charles—they are Lucinda's most devoted friends—and Lady Townsend, she is Lucinda's godmother. And that is everyone." She gestured to an empty chair. "Please do sit down."

Marcus sat, as instructed, feeling the weight of six pairs of eyes, twelve eyes in all, on him, wishing there was at least another male in the room so he didn't feel quite so on display. Especially since he knew just from the introductions that at least three of the women were unmarried, and therefore might be interested in snagging a duke. Would be interested in snagging a duke, since he could say without any modesty that he was one of the more attractive possible husbands a young lady could have. Or at least one of the most arrogant.

He wished Lily were here so she could take

him down a peg. He liked it when she got that wry, disapproving look on her face after he'd said something particularly peremptory or commanding. Or both.

But thinking about her was not going to get him successfully embraced by society, nor was it going to find him a wife, a well-bred woman who could ensure that Rose was able to navigate Society on her own, despite the stigma of her birth.

"Thank you for the invitation to the party," Marcus said, accepting the coffee the stern butler handed him. "Your house is lovely, and the weather remained tolerable." And with that sentence, he realized, he'd just used up all of his polite conversation. Uh-oh.

"You have just arrived in town, Your Grace?" the countess asked.

Actually, he'd been here for a few months, hadn't he? But if he said that, they would all wonder what he'd been doing, and that was not fit for polite conversation. "It seems so, doesn't it?" There. An answer Miss Blake would be proud of. Or not, if she couldn't decide whether or not to be proud of it.

"And what other parties do you plan on attending?" That was the other older woman, Lady Townsend, who shot a quick, knowing glance at her goddaughter, Lady Lucinda, as she asked the question.

"I am not certain," he replied. It was not to his benefit that he was mirroring Miss Blake's type of conversation.

"Do not pester the duke," Lady Lucinda said in

an amused voice. "He will be where he wishes to be when he wishes to be. Won't you?" she asked, regarding him with her wry smile.

He had to admit she was a surprise. A definitely pleasant surprise. She was witty, pretty, and eligible. Why did that thought not please him?

The conversation turned to the party the night before, including the quality of the musicians, an unnamed young man drinking a bit too much punch, and how the refreshments were so delicious each lady present declared that she'd had at least one more than she should have.

"Your Grace?" Lady Lucinda had somehow displaced one of the ladies who had been sitting next to him. He nodded, as though she might possibly be in doubt of his identity. Thankfully she didn't make note of that.

"I apologize for all the questions, it's just that there aren't very many dukes who normally grace our drawing room, and so of course we are all ridiculously curious about you. Especially," she added with a roll of her eyes, "my mother."

"Should we obtain a piece of paper and a pen so we might write down our conversation?" he asked, in a low tone matching hers, glancing over at Lady Lucinda's mother. Who was, indeed, keeping an eye—a gleeful eye, to be more specific—on the two of them as they talked.

Now he knew how the animals in a zoo felt. Maybe he should just put himself in a cage and allow Society to stop by to view him, perhaps poke a stick through the bars at him.

Although that wasn't fair. He was a rarity, he

knew that, which was why he'd kept himself away from this for so long. He hadn't wanted this inspection, not when he'd managed just fine not being inspected for most of his life.

Why couldn't his brother have just stayed on that horse? Then he'd have to be the one dealing with all of this. And would probably like it a lot more than he did, given how he and his brother were such opposites.

Lady Lucinda's voice interrupted his musings, thank goodness. "Biscuit?" She held a plate out to him, a gentle smile on her face.

She was rather attractive, he had to admit that. "Thank you," he said, helping himself to a particularly delicious looking treat. He popped it in his mouth, glad he could have some biscuits today, since Rose had done away with all the ones they'd had at tea.

Rose. Just thinking about her made him smile. He'd always liked walking on his own, but with her beside him, holding his hand, it elevated the solitary activity nearly into a joyful pursuit. Just as he'd been hoping for.

"I hear you have another inhabitant in your house, Your Grace?" It was Lady Lucinda's godmother who spoke, her voice cutting through all the other chatter in the room. "A young girl?"

There were several other inhabitants in his house, but one didn't count the servants, did one? "Yes. Miss Rose, my . . . ward. My cousin's daughter." The lie was getting easier to say.

"She has just arrived? And you have already hired her a governess?" The lady's voice was not approving. Not entirely disapproving, either, but Marcus felt himself grow defensive.

"Yes, I wish her to have a proper education." He finished the biscuit, but now it felt like ashes in his mouth.

"That is very Christian of you," the woman continued, as though he had done something incredible by taking her in.

No, I did something incredible and terrible not to know her before this, he thought.

"She should be grateful to you for the condescension," Lady Townsend said, before turning her attention to one of the Miss Charleses.

"Don't mind my godmother," Lady Lucinda said. "She has very firm opinions of what should and should not be done." Marcus hoped she never ran across Miss Blake, because one of them would likely not survive. "But it does seem . . . unusual for you to have taken in a ward, so soon after your own arrival."

"It is what had to be done," Marcus said, deliberately not explaining precisely what he meant. He felt his jaw tighten. He did not want to be defending his decision to take in a child who had nowhere else to go, who had his blood in her veins, who needed him.

"Of course," Lady Lucinda said in a placating tone, as though she knew just how irate he was getting. "Another biscuit?"

It is required of a duke—or any gentleman of good breeding and fortune—to ensure the title and fortune passes to a descendant upon the duke's demise. In choosing a bride, a duke—or any gentleman of good breeding and fortune—must look for a woman who possesses good breeding herself. Anything more she has to offer should be seen as bonus attributes.

—THE DUKE'S GUIDE TO CORRECT BEHAVIOR

Chapter 21

"You've already had five biscuits," Lily said as Rose reached her hand out again. For the sixth time.

Rose halted mid-reach and regarded her governess with one eyebrow nearly raised. It seemed the duke's daughter already took after him. In the most arrogant ways, of course. "But I am hungry," she said matter-of-factly.

"Then we can see what Mrs. Partridge might have in the kitchen. It is not good to subsist solely on biscuits."

Rose shrugged. "I never had many before. Mama usually just gave me what she brought home."

"Brought home from where?" Lily slid the plate of biscuits out of arm's reach.

"From the pub. She worked there. I stayed with Mrs. Tolliver when she worked, but she didn't have any girls my age. Just boys." Her expression showed what she thought of that. No wonder she'd been so pleased to play with Mrs. Porter's children.

"And what did your mama bring home?"

That shrug again. "Food."

Perhaps Rose was taking after Annabelle in the literal sense. But never mind the food, of course, what was more important was that Rose was talking about how she'd lived before without being questioned about it. Lily worried about the girl; she knew how hard it was to lose one's parent. In her case, she'd lost two, and even before her mother had died, it felt as though she was gone already.

It was what forced her to work at the brothel, and yet also what prepared her to survive by starting the agency. She hoped Rose would find some benefit as well in having suffered at such a young age.

"Mama always saved the carrots in the stew for me. I like carrots. And potatoes. And stew," she added.

"I like all those things, too. We should ask Mrs. Partridge if she would make us stew sometime. Would you like that?"

"Mm-hm," Rose said, her fingers reaching toward the biscuit plate.

Lily swatted her hand away. "Let's see if the kitchen has anything you'd like to eat—besides biscuits—and we will take a walk. Your father won't be home until dinner, I don't think."

Rose nodded enthusiastically. "I like walking."

Just like your father. Lily made a mental note to take Rose out as much as possible—she was thin and pale, and it didn't sound as though she'd had much chance just to be outside in the relatively fresh air.

Once outside, she took Rose's hand—the one not holding a warm piece of freshly baked bread—and the two of them walked to the small park where Lily presumed the duke had taken Rose before. It was cloudy but not showing signs of rain, and there was a mildness to the air that was refreshing after being indoors.

There were other governesses and children walking about as well, and Lily nodded to some of the other young women and their charges. It was so pleasant, she could imagine herself being happy at this position. It would make it all even better if the agency thrived because of this. Because of her.

"Will the duke keep me with him?" Rose didn't sound anxious about it, but it made Lily's throat tighten. That Rose had thought of it meant it had crossed her mind. Lily was startled at the ferocious response that unfurled inside her at the thought of him sending his daughter away.

It seemed he knew better than anyone what it felt like to be sent away, to be unloved. He couldn't do that to his daughter, could he?

"I am not aware of your father's plans, but it sounded as though he wished to get to know you. He would not have hired a governess for you if he planned to send you away, would he?"

"Maybe not. But that lady's girl, she said people were surprised he has me, and she asked me where I would go next. I told her I don't know."

If Lily's throat had tightened before, it now felt as if it were strangling her. She cursed whoever had spoken about Rose in front of the children.

It didn't sound that the girl intended to be spiteful, but if there was talk so early on from Rose's arrival, it meant many people were talking. The duke had been correct in his thinking—he would have to find himself a respectable wife soon to stem the flow of gossip.

Keeping gossip from tainting Rose's future, that was the most important thing. She would have to remind herself of that. Frequently.

"And how was your day, Miss Rose?" Marcus nodded at the footman, and the servant began to ladle soup of some sort from the tureen into his bowl.

"Good." Rose was definitely not one for over-explanation.

They sat in one of the dining rooms, not the biggest one, which looked like it might seat all of London, nor the small one they used for breakfast, but the one in between. This room did not seem to have been touched by the same hand as the one that had decorated the pink room, thank goodness; the table was made of a dark wood, and the walls were done up in gold paper, with maroon drapes. It was very cozy, though, for all that it was still a rather large room.

Marcus had squelched Thompson's wish to have a full phalanx of footmen waiting on them—it seemed ludicrous to have more footmen than diners—so there were only two, with Thompson popping in every so often to cast a stern eye at his underlings.

"Perhaps you might share more details, Miss Lily?" His governess—well, not his, but the governess he employed—sat to his left, wearing another one of the gowns he must have purchased for her.

He was very pleased with himself about that, if he did say so. The gown was some sort of dark plum color whose richness brought out the equally rich tones of her hair, and contrasted with her eyes, which were golden in the candlelight. Not to mention, since it was an evening gown, it was cut lower than her normal gowns, and he was better able to view the slope of her breasts and the creamy whiteness of her skin.

She shook her head at the soup and took a sip of wine. "We went for a walk in the park so that Miss Rose would not eat all the biscuits." She smiled at Rose as she spoke, and that warmth, the way the smile lit up her face, made Marcus momentarily lose his breath.

"I only had five," Rose asserted, dipping her spoon into the soup.

"Six, don't think I didn't see you grab another one as we walked out," Lily retorted. She met Marcus's gaze. "We saw many dogs, and children, and it seems that spring is on its way, finally. We'll be able to walk every day, as long as it doesn't rain. Miss Rose very much likes to walk."

He turned his head to smile at Rose. "Can we walk tomorrow?"

"Mm-hm," Rose returned, engrossed in devouring her soup as quickly as possible, it seemed. Marcus took a spoonful as well, and thought about how much better it tasted than the biscuits at the earl's house, likely because of the company.

It felt homey to be here, just the three of them. He didn't think he'd ever felt so at home before. So comfortable in his surroundings, who he was with and what they were doing. Eating dinner. Taking walks.

Kissing her.

But that, he thought regretfully as he darted another glance at her décolletage, should not happen any longer. It should not. Despite certain parts of his body arguing vehemently with him about that decision.

He needed to avoid temptation. It wouldn't be fair, to her or the woman he would eventually choose for his wife, the one asked to tolerate having her husband's illegitimate child in the household. She shouldn't also have to tolerate having a young woman with whom he had . . . dallied with in the household as well. But she was so good with Rose—Lily, not the unknown young lady to whom he'd be married—and he would not tear Rose away from another woman she cared for, not so soon on the loss of her mother.

He would have to step back from the constant wanting, he told himself again, the wishing he could explore her creamy curves, her lush mouth, to know what she tasted like.

Thank goodness he wasn't actually asking himself to step back, because if he stood up, it would be obvious just what he had been thinking about.

So. He had to step back. Figuratively, if not literally. "I will be going out after dinner, ladies. Miss

Lily, you won't have to make your report this evening." And he hoped he could remain strong the next time they met.

"Of course, Your Grace," she murmured, nodding in response to the next course. Was it his imagination, or was there a brief shadow of disappointment in those hazel eyes?

"But we'll walk tomorrow?" Rose asked. "And maybe have another tea party?" The girl's eyes were huge and pleading.

"Yes, sweetheart," Marcus said, leaning over to touch her cheek. "Our tea party was the best part of my day."

"Oh, I forgot," Lily said. "Mrs. Porter asked if Rose could come over again to play with the children. Would that be all right? Perhaps Friday?" She looked from his face to Rose's, her smile widening as she regarded her charge.

"Certainly. You like Mrs. Porter's children, then?" he asked Rose.

"Yes."

Lily looked as though she wished to say something, then bit her lip and averted her gaze. Interesting. What was she hiding? Marcus wondered.

Was there a young man at the Porters, one who was more suitable, more handsome, less arrogant than him?

Well, he could safely assume that any man she would meet would be more suitable and less arrogant. He might have to quibble about the more handsome part, since he knew he was attractive to look at, he'd been told so many times in his fornicating past. But being handsome didn't make him either more suitable nor less arrogant. Perhaps she'd told herself she had to step back as well.

Which just made him wish to follow her. Not what he should be wishing to do, not when he knew what he had to do. Not follow her. Not want her. Not do anything to her besides pay her salary and keep her at a distance.

He didn't need to have a report, or lessons in how to treat a lady every night, Lily reminded herself as she heard the front door close behind him. It was a good thing for her not to be in his presence in the evening, when Rose was put safely to bed. It was far too tempting to give in to his allure, to the charm underneath his blunt arrogance. To the want in his dark eyes, the way he touched her, as though she were both something precious and something to be thoroughly and completely handled.

She felt Rose's hand slide into hers. It felt wonderful, as though she was being useful, perhaps preventing this young girl from growing up to become an unfortunate woman. Rose would be one of the fortunate ones, as long as she herself could keep her head. "Shall we go up to bed? I can read you a nighttime story, if you like."

Rose nodded, then tugged Lily's hand toward the staircase. The two of them walked up, silent but companionable, Lily knowing that this girl's safety and happiness was more important than any fleeting desire. Or not fleeting, since she doubted she would ever forget him or what they'd done together.

In her room, Rose bounced on the bed, her hair flying everywhere, Maggie clutched tight in her arms. "He said we'd go walking, all of us, tomorrow. And another tea party!"

The girl was nearly as excited as Lily at the prospect. Not that she admitted her excitement; no, she was doing the opposite, instead reminding herself he was just a man, a handsome, witty, secretly charming, gentleman who was not for the likes of her. Even without her own unfortunate history.

"What would you like to read?" She had sent for a few children's books from the bookstore, since the duke's library did not include any. They'd gotten a collection of Perrault's fairy tales, which Lily recalled from her own childhood. Rose shared her taste in reading, much preferring the stories of dragons, fairies, and princesses to anything more mundane.

"Cind'rella," Rose said, getting into the enormous bed and pulling the sheet up to her chin.

Oh, Cinderella, the story of the lowly girl and the prince? Nothing that could possibly relate to her real life, could it? Wasn't she supposed to be forgetting all of this?

But Rose had asked, and Lily wanted to share the joy of reading and imagination with her charge. So she opened the book, found the story, and began. "'Once there was a gentleman who married, for his second wife,'" she began, losing herself within a few paragraphs to the magic of the story.

At last, after "'Cinderella, who was no less good than beautiful, gave her two sisters lodgings in the palace, and that very same day matched them with two great lords of the court,'" Rose was asleep, and Lily felt exhausted herself.

It was tiring not to be thinking of things all the time, nearly as exhausting as it was to remember everything she was supposed to recall; such as making sure Rose didn't eat too many biscuits, that her lessons were balanced with fun (not forgetting the duke's directive that Rose find happiness as well as schooling), that she not speak too much of her own past, that she did the best job she could so her own reputation would eventually help the agency.

All worthwhile. Nothing as purely wonderful as being kissed by a duke.

She would just have to live with that.

A duke must maintain his distance from all others, so as not to encourage false intimacy.

~~*A duke should be able to do what he wants.*~~

—The Duke's Guide to Correct Behavior

Chapter 22

The room looked about the same as the Earl of Daymond's ballroom had, which doubtless meant he should be thinking of things to say about it, at least things more than "This is a large room" and "Oh, look, there are windows."

But already he was fresh out of remarks on the room. Perhaps he should inquire more fully of Miss Lily what he could possibly say about something so unopinionworthy as a room.

He was interrupted before he could figure out what to say about the statues of coy-looking children placed in each corner, besides *Those are hideous.*

"You're out again, and even suitably dressed. I'm impressed, Your Grace," Smithfield said in a mocking tone.

Which made Marcus unsure whether he should pop his new best friend in the nose or merely bow in response.

He thought it would probably serve him better not to pop Smithfield in the nose, even though he was tempted. So he bowed.

"Thank you," he said, inclining his head. "I am taking your advice to heart, you see, appearing in public as my proper ducal self, nary a cat in a corset in sight."

"I have heard you have even paid a few afternoon calls. That takes far more fortitude than waltzing with a feline."

"Only one, and it was definitely more difficult to navigate those steps. Do all ladies say one thing when they mean entirely something else?"

Smithfield cocked an eyebrow at him. "When it comes to unmarried dukes, I'd be surprised if any young lady would tell the truth."

It wouldn't matter if you had warts and were bald. Any young lady would be cowed in your presence. Except for her. She was the one person—well, adult person, he thought, perhaps Rose would be the same—who wouldn't be intimidated by him, or more correctly, by his title. She didn't demand anything of him.

Except when Lily had said, *Marcus, I want this.*

"So if what you are saying is true, I should suspect all young ladies of lying? That is discouraging, to say the least."

"Not all ladies," Smithfield said, nodding to a young lady who was dancing by them in the arms of an elderly gentleman. "My sister's guest, Miss Blake, could not lie if her life depended on it."

"Nor could she state an opinion," Marcus added.

Smithfield chuckled, and nodded in assent. "That is certainly true. But at least you would never run out of conversation."

"Because she would be debating the various merits of each and every thing she might decide upon."

Smithfield nodded toward a young lady in the distance. "Lady Lucinda is a pleasant woman."

Marcus spotted her as well, noting her trim figure and calm expression. "She is that." A thought struck him, and he turned to his friend. "You are not interested in her, are you?" Smithfield's quick response cut off his words before he could continue.

"No, of course not, and besides, her father the earl is aiming much higher than someone in my position." His tone sounded rueful, and Marcus felt some emotion—he wasn't sure what it was—that made him not wish to pay the lady any particular attention. "Will I be wishing you happy, then?" Smithfield said in a terse voice.

"No, it is far too early for anything of that sort. Besides which, you've pointed out I've just made my first foray into Society. I don't wish to decide anything until I know what I might be in for."

Smithfield glanced at him, his gaze seeming—as it had the first time they'd met—to see through to his very soul. "I hope you find what you're looking for, then."

It was an eerie echo of what he had said just before Rose arrived into his life. He wanted to say that he'd found what he was looking for, a small child of perhaps four years who needed him. But that wasn't all of it, was it?

He knew that wouldn't be enough. Not for Rose, and not for him. He wanted someone to love her as he already did, someone who would care for her, and oversee her instruction . . . and take care of him, somewhat, as well.

Someone who would say what they meant, so he wouldn't have to always be deciphering what she truly wanted.

Someone who wanted both him and Rose.

Someone very like Lily.

The thought struck him before he could shake it off, and he wanted to growl his frustration out loud, but no doubt Smithfield—as well as all the other guests at the party—would think he was unfit for polite society, when he was working so hard on appearing as though he fit in.

Why couldn't she have been Lady Lucinda? Or any lady, actually, a woman of his own class where his interest in her wouldn't be scandalous?

Why did he have to be a duke, of all things, a personage so regal that everything he did was put under scrutiny and analyzed, as though he were a specimen under a microscope.

But it didn't matter how much he questioned, the answer was always the same: she was not, and he was. They could not be, not as they were, not together.

He excused himself and went to ask Lady Lucinda for a dance.

"It looks like rain." The duke peered out the window, a cup of coffee in his hand. Lily knew it was specifically coffee because he'd snarled at John when the poor footman tried to give him tea.

Rose hopped out of her seat and went to stand beside him. "No walk, then?" she asked in a sad, soft voice.

The expression on his face when he turned to her was fierce. Warm and caring, but also fierce. "No walk, but we will find something fun to do. Won't we, Miss Lily?" he asked, tilting his head up to look at her.

Her breath caught. "Of course, Your Grace, I am certain there are some indoor games we can play."

His eyes crinkled at the corners, just a bit, just enough so she could see them, but she doubted anyone who wasn't looking would. Thank goodness. "There are cards in the library." *Their* library. "Thompson can find them, and I might be able to remember how to play Snap. Or not. Do you know how to play, Miss Rose?"

Rose shook her head. "No. But Miss Lily can teach me, she's a good teacher."

The compliment along with the assumption that she would know how to do something warmed her heart, and she felt the prickle of tears come to her eyes. Silly, maudlin Lily, so very far from the prim, precise, methodical woman she was striving to be.

"It's settled, then. I will go find the cards, and we will convene in the drawing room—the pink room, that is," he said, "later this afternoon. Say around two o'clock? I have a few appointments before then."

Appointments, doubtless, to visit with young, eligible ladies who might be suitable mothers for Rose. Young, eligible ladies whose most unfortunate mishap would be losing a glove or having their hem stepped on as they danced. Not women who'd had to work in unfortunate places to make an unfortunate living, nor who had to hide their pasts to ensure their futures.

Nor women who would likely appreciate the duke's rough charm, or his inability to get a close shave, or wear a cravat, or ever wear his nightshirt to bed.

He would much prefer Miss Blake's inanities to this. This being listening as his various employees briefed him on the essentials of his estate; his finances, holdings, tenants, properties, and obligations. His whole ducal entirety summed up in three egregiously long hours.

Not that the hours were longer than regular hours; it just felt that way. He'd have taken any kind of treatise on agricultural practices or even the "Joy of Cat Dancing" to this.

But this was what he needed to do if he wanted to truly become the title he had assumed so reluctantly. And as he listened to the various dronings about crops and annual rents and repairs and investments, he realized that he now knew what being a duke meant. Still, if he turned his back on all of it, he would be an irresponsible coward.

He was many things, but he could not tolerate being that.

So he pasted a halfhearted smile on his face, took a few notes, nodded at what he hoped were the appropriate places, and knew that all of this was worth it. Not just to him, or to Rose, but to all the people who depended somehow on the Duke of Rutherford's vast dukedom.

"And if we convert some of the acreage from farms to industrial holdings, you will see a vast increase in your profits. After a few years, of course."

This droner, Marcus thought he recalled, was Mr. Waldecott, the estate manager. He'd been speaking for nearly an hour, and he held his hat clutched tightly in his hands as though Marcus were going to snatch it from him at any moment.

He nearly had, just to see what the man would do, but then remembered he was supposed to be more responsible, not more reckless. Damn it. He much preferred reckless.

Mr. Waldecott was the last of the trio of droning men to speak, thankfully. He'd already heard his banker Mr. Mitchell (tall, thin, wispy moustache, wan speaking voice), and his overseer Mr. Bird (plump, bald, a frantic way of speaking), make their statements on what the Duke of Rutherford—that was him, of course—had in the way of holdings.

He was very, very wealthy. He knew that much. But with all that wealth came an equal amount of responsibility, and he was determined to manage it all. Not just for Rose, although her arrival was the impetus, but for himself. To prove the man who was the Duke of Rutherford could be just as admirable as the title he held.

It was an even more terrifying a prospect than

having to be a good father. At least the latter job came with the promise of tea parties.

"It's you!" Rose popped out of her seat and ran toward the door, clutching the duke around his knees.

He looked over her head and smiled at Lily. "I am so grateful I am here, ladies. You don't know the horror of what I've been doing."

His courtship was going that well, then? Lily tried not to be glad.

"This way," Rose said, taking his hand and walking him back to the table. "You sit there," she commanded, pointing at the seat he'd taken last time.

"Yes, my lady," he replied with a grin, bending his long legs so he could sit in the too small seat. He should have looked ridiculous, but—no, he did look ridiculous, but he also looked so endearing, trying to accommodate his daughter's wishes.

"We found cards, Your Grace," Lily said, picking the pack up from the bureau at the side of the room. "Or rather, Thompson was able to locate cards." And had apparently been charmed enough by Rose not to completely glower when Lily asked him for help. Not completely.

"What will we be playing again?" The duke looked at her and Rose, his eyebrow raised in what Lily now knew was benignly questioning, not his arrogant commanding raised eyebrow. Not that there was that much of a difference.

"Snap," Rose asserted, her face revealing what she thought about him forgetting so quickly.

"Remind me how to play? Or actually, tell me how to play. I don't think I ever have before." His mouth tensed, briefly, and Lily added another item to her increasing store of knowledge of how sad the duke's childhood had been.

All three of them had been orphaned in their own ways, hadn't they? No wonder they got along so well. It felt . . . it almost felt as though they were a family.

Lily hastily picked up the pack of cards before she could follow that train of thought much further. "Of course. Do you wish to explain the rules, Miss Rose, or shall I?"

"You can," Rose said in a regal tone of voice.

"Snap!" An hour later, and Lily felt her sides were going to split from laughter. She hadn't won—Rose had won five of the six hands they'd played, with the duke managing to win the sixth—but she didn't know when she had enjoyed herself more.

Well, she did, but she wasn't supposed to be thinking about that anymore.

It had taken him some time—he said—to learn how to play, which meant that Rose got to lecture him on what he was doing wrong and how he could improve his play. Lily didn't miss the warmth of his smile as he regarded his daughter while she discoursed on the importance of shouting as soon as you see the match, and he'd caught her eye a few times, grinning at her in a way that melted her heart.

The two of them were so similar, it was remarkable to think that they'd only met a week or two before. From the raised, haughty eyebrow to the assumption that they were right and others were . . . less right, to the direct emotion they conveyed with just a change of expression.

She was looking at a family.

"Miss Lily? Are you all right?" His low voice sent shivers pulsing through her body, forcing her to shake away her memories of what had never been. He'd taken his coat and cravat off, of course, since it was just him at his own house and apparently that meant he needed to disrobe.

If only.

It certainly was a good way to get her mind off things she would rather not think about. There was that, at least.

Especially since he'd rolled his shirtsleeves up, exposing his muscular forearms and strong wrists. Really, how did someone like him stay so fit? What with lolling about and attending parties and just generally being a pampered duke?

She had no idea, but the fact remained that he *was* fit. She knew that firsthand from sliding her hand on his back and that his chest felt hard and strong against her.

"Yes, Your Grace?" She sat up straight in her chair, as though proper posture would somehow make her more proper.

"Miss Rose was asking if we could draw again."

"Since you did so well last time?" she asked, a teasing note in her voice.

He smiled in recognition of her jab. "I might

bow out this time, but Rose can draw while you and I talk."

Her stomach tightened. Talk about what? About sending Rose away and letting her go? About where she came from and that her references were false? About how she really, really wished there would be a heat wave in March in London so he would have to remove his shirt?

He must have noticed the tension in her expression. "About an event I wish to host. I thought you could assist me in the planning of it."

Oh, thank goodness. Well, thank goodness it wasn't the first two things. She still did wish there was a heat wave.

"Of course." Lily got up and gathered the drawing materials, placing them on the table in front of Rose, who immediately launched into drawing all three of the cats in the duke's house at a tea party.

"Over here, Miss Lily. I need to get the feeling back in my legs." The duke walked to the small sofa placed against the wall. He sat down and let out a pleasured groan. "Much better. We will have to purchase new furnishings for this room if I am to spend much time here. That table is not meant for someone of my size."

Lily's heart thumped at thinking about his size, and his breadth, and all of him. Those long legs stretched in front of him, his arm on the back of the sofa, revealing an expanse of skin at his throat . . .

Calm yourself, Lil.

It was fine to tell herself that, but faced with him, the wry curve of his lips, that mouth pressed against hers, those hands that had touched her as though she were precious, and yet were strong . . .

It was fine to look at him, wasn't it? Because if it wasn't, she should just leave now, because she didn't think she could ever stop looking at him.

"What do you wish to discuss?" She settled down beside him, her thigh nearly touching his, his hand draped behind her. His neck so exposed.

He withdrew his hand and she felt momentarily bereft. And then relieved, because it seemed at least one of them had not lost his head. He leaned forward, clasping his hands together, resting his forearms on his legs.

"I wish to have a party. But not the usual adult kind of party," he added, his expression showing just what he thought of those parties. "I want to have a gathering so that Rose can meet other children, more than just Smithfield's sister's children, where she can play and get to know the people of my world. Her world now."

"Rather like a coming out party? But for a four-year-old?" Lily asked.

He smiled. Nearly grinned, in fact. "Precisely. It is no secret that there will be talk about her, about who she is to me. I wish to present these people with the reality of her—a young, sweet child—so they know her."

For all that he was so arrogant and blunt, he was also naive. But that wasn't her place to say. Only— "May I speak frankly, Your Grace?"

He frowned. "As long as you stop referring to me as 'Your Grace.' "

Yes. That. "Well, Your— That is, I want you to

be prepared for some people in your world not to accept Rose, no matter how many parties you throw or how sweet she is." Or how arrogant and eyebrowishly similar to you she is as well. "You cannot hope to control everyone in your world."

He leaned against the sofa back and folded his arms. Lily was glad none of the nonaccepting people were there to see his face. "Then they shall have to deal with me."

"I—I wasn't going to say anything, but Rose mentioned that one of her new acquaintances has already said something about who she is and why she's living with you. Rose was worried you would be sending her away."

His jaw set. "Even more of a reason to make certain she will be accepted as much as possible." No mention of if or when he planned to send Rose away—but at least he was determined to do the right thing now.

"What kind of party were you thinking of?"

"Something children would like." He sounded as though he had no clue as to what that might be. Likely he didn't. "Did the vicar have events for his daughters?"

Lily nodded, finally not startled when he mentioned the vicar. That had happened often enough that she could almost picture her past mythical employer. "The girls had birthday parties, of course. They played games outdoors, and had food, and cake, and there was lots of running about." It was a lot like what she'd had when she was young, before her father died and she went to work. In a brothel.

That was definitely in the area of things not to share with your current employer. But the parties, she could discuss. "If you have good food, and pleasant company, and plenty of activities, all the children should have fun."

He waved a hand in the air. "I will ask you to arrange it all, then, since I haven't the slightest idea what to do."

"Me? Don't you have someone for that?" she asked, hearing her voice squeak.

He regarded her with a lazy rise of his brow. A new move by the eyebrow in question, and she didn't like it. It spoke of skepticism, humor, teasing, all far too dangerous to her peace of mind. "I have you. I pay you a salary, you are in charge of Rose's education and her fun, as I charged you earlier, and I wish you to handle the details."

Arrogant autocratic ass. "Fine," she said, folding her hands in her lap.

"Fine," he repeated, his voice holding that same wry amusement that was so stupidly charming. To her, at least.

He was her employer. She was his employee. Nothing else could happen.

But she couldn't stop herself from imagining all sorts of things that could happen if they were in different circumstances.

A duke's calling card must include his full name and all titles, not just say "Duke." But if necessary, "Duke" will do.

—The Duke's Guide to Correct Behavior

Chapter 23

"Will they all come?" Rose asked, her huge eyes even huger in her small face.

I hope so, Marcus thought. "Only the fun ones, sweet," he said, ruffling her hair. The past week had been a flurry of activity, from deciding what games to play, to what refreshments Partridge was asked to make, to constantly peering at the sky as though looking up frequently would force good weather.

And Lily had been there at every turn, organizing, managing, directing, but never commanding. Not like he did, at least. She was remarkable in getting people to do as she wanted, even Thompson, who had admitted to Marcus that she was a "tolerable addition to the household." Marcus didn't think Thompson would even admit he was a tolerable addition to the household, so that seemingly mild approbation was stunning.

As was she. They worked together, often in silence, and usually in concord, although there were a few times they disagreed; as when he insisted that she be present and in charge during the event, rather than he.

"How idiotic would it look if someone asks me a question and I just gape at them? Far better for you, who knows everything, to be who they ask."

"I don't see why," she'd said. "You could just stare them down with that eyebrow, or even two, heaven forbid, and they would slink away feeling foolish. They're going to just look at me and wonder why I am telling everyone what to do when I am only the governess."

He took her chin in his hand and stared into her eyes. "Don't ever say you are 'only the governess.' The governess, here at least, is a valuable member of the household. I don't want you to ever discount yourself so."

She drew back, swatting his hand away from her face. "Oh. Well. Thank you."

"You know you are important," he said in much softer tone. "To Rose and—and to me."

He couldn't admit just how true that was.

The day wasn't bright and sunny—it was London, so it couldn't possibly be—but at least it wasn't raining. And the smile on Rose's face when he saw her that morning was worth a million sunny days.

"You'll be there all day, Duke?" she asked, her voice pleading rather than with her usual peremptory tone (a tone which, if her governess were to be believed, was inherited from him).

Marcus took a sip of coffee and smiled. "Of course, sweet," he replied.

Rose nodded, as though that was entirely the answer she'd expected.

Which it probably was, given that she had asked the same question every morning at breakfast since he'd told her about the party.

Lily arrived in the room then, her normally tidy hairstyle less than tidy, strands of chocolate-brown hair flying in confusion about her face. It made her look more approachable, even more desirable, and Marcus had a few moments of imagining her in his bed with that hair draped around his throat. And other things.

He wished he didn't have such an active imagination.

"Good morning," Lily said in a distracted voice, only nodding when John the footman approached her with a cup of tea. Normally she had a few polite words for the servants, but it was clear the party was uppermost in her mind.

"Morning, Miss Lily," Rose said through a mouthful of toast.

That she did pay attention to. "We don't speak when we eat, Miss Rose," she said in her most governessy voice.

Rose swallowed, then tilted her head and gave her governess an inquisitive look. "Maybe you don't, but I just did."

Marcus tried to squelch his laughter, but it was impossible not to let out a chuckle or two, especially since Rose appeared genuinely flummoxed by her governess's lack of logic, while Lily was suppressing her own grin while still trying to look stern.

"Anyway," Marcus said, taking another swallow of coffee as he rose. "My friend Smithfield and his sisters—including his sisters' children—have promised to arrive just a bit early, so that means we have about two hours to do any last minute things that need to be done. Miss Lily?" he said, turning to her with a questioning gaze.

She took a visible breath, then nodded. "I believe we are ready. I will just go check with Thompson and Mrs. Partridge that all is in readiness."

"I will come with you," he announced, then winced inside as he heard himself. Could he not ask anything? He always seemed to be announcing, or commanding, or ordering. Never simply asking.

But if he did ask for anything, it would be for something he could not have.

He put his cup down with fingers that longed to touch her, to undo her hair even more, to place his hands on her neck, her shoulders, her breasts.

All over her.

"Of course, Your Grace," she said after a moment, her face starting to turn that delightful pink color. "Shall we go to the kitchens, then?"

Marcus placed his hands on his hips as he surveyed the goings-on. Rose was amidst a multitude of children, surrounded by a ring of caregivers, mostly governesses, with a few curious parents casting him sly glances when they thought he wasn't looking.

He'd given Lily leave to spend whatever she

liked on the party, and he was relieved to see there were toys for nearly every child to play with; Rose was playing Graces, and so far she was doing well, only dropping half the rings thrown to her. Her partner, one of Smithfield's nieces, wasn't faring as well, dropping nearly every ring. But the two of them were laughing with delight each time the ring went up in the air, so he considered it a success.

Marcus felt a clap on his back, and turned to see Smithfield's lean face to his right. They hadn't gotten a chance to talk, mostly because all the Smithfield women had filled up the talking space as they tried to agree which game Miss Blake would oversee.

She had ended up keeping watch over the cakes.

"This is a marvelous idea. Your governess's?" Smithfield asked, gazing at Lily.

Marcus felt his jaw start to clench. "No, I thought of it, Miss Lily merely executed it."

Smithfield snorted. "So you had the grand scheme and she implemented it? How very ducal of you." It was said in his normal mocking tone, and Marcus shouldn't have felt offended. But he was.

"She has done an admirable job. And it appears Rose is making friends, which is the entire purpose. She shouldn't be left just to her father and her governess." He spoke without thinking about his words.

Smithfield's expression changed to one of concern. "You know you can't acknowledge her as your daughter. Even to me. Everyone will know, of course, but if you say it aloud people will have to respond. And you might find your Rose is ostracized from some of these same children. Better to stick with your cousin story."

Damn. He wanted to rail against Smithfield, but the man was only telling him the truth. The same truth that Lily had said before.

If he had to be a duke, why couldn't he just make people do what he wanted?

Although if he could do that, he wouldn't be doing this today at all. He'd be spending the day with Rose and Lily, then having supper, then seeing Rose to bed, and then taking Lily to his bed for a much-longer-than-two-minute interlude.

"Your Grace, this is a lovely party. And what a clever idea!" It was one of Smithfield's sisters, he wasn't sure which. She drew another man forward, putting her arm in his. "You did not meet my husband, Mr. Haughton, when we dined with you. Your Grace, may I present Mr. Haughton?"

The gentleman in question bowed, and Marcus tried to recall what he was allowed to speak about. Not his daughter Rose, and he couldn't very well comment on the lovely room since they were outdoors. The refreshments? No, because he had provided them, and to draw attention to them would not be appropriate. Because if the people loved them, it would appear that he was desirous of compliments, whereas if they didn't, they couldn't very well say they didn't, not without running the risk of offending a duke.

"A pleasure to meet you, Mr. Haughton," he

said after a long silence. "I am so glad you were all able to attend my—my ward's party."

"Yes, my girls were ecstatic. Of course now they are demanding they have their own outing, but even if we did, it could not compare to yours," Mrs. Haughton gushed.

How could he possibly respond to that? It was as bad as the refreshment topic; if he said, "No it couldn't," that would be insulting, and to demur and say it could would just be a bald-faced lie, and he didn't want to lie.

Except under very specific circumstances.

"Thank you, Mrs. Haughton."

She didn't seem to notice his lack of response, however. "The thought of gathering all of these games and children and delicious food on such a spectacular day"—at that, all four of them looked up at the sky, which was not spectacular in the least, merely cloudy, but it didn't seem to matter anyway—"and having your ward make friends with all these delightful children. You are planning her future already, Your Grace? Finding a husband for her amongst these fine young gentlemen?" Now her tone was arch, and Marcus really wished he could say anything he wished to. But for the sake of Smithfield, who he had come to like, and the party—not to mention Rose—he wouldn't.

"Your governess. Has she been employed by any other families?" Mr. Haughton's expression was curious, as though something was nagging at him. Maybe his wife.

"A vicar someplace," Marcus replied. "Why?"

Mr. Haughton shook his head. "She just looks so familiar. I was wondering if I had met her before."

Marcus glanced at her, currently negotiating some sort of truce between a child who had apparently consumed quite a lot of cake and another child who was holding a slab of cake above his head.

She met his gaze for a moment, amusement lighting those hazel eyes to golden lights, and his breath caught.

He had purposely not asked her to visit him in his study for a while, instead spending the evenings alone with his accounts and books and other very dull things that were not her.

She seemed to have withdrawn as well, and he kept wondering if she had met somebody, a man who was far better suited to her than he was. The thought shouldn't tear him up so much, but it did.

And damned if he knew what to do about it.

Once he makes up his mind, a duke will pursue what he wants, without hesitation. And he will get it.

—The Duke's Guide to Correct Behavior

Chapter 24

"Miss Lily." The command—for that was what it was, there was no mistaking it—came from deep within the room, and she came to an abrupt stop.

"Your Grace?"

She could sense, rather than actually hear, his sigh of resignation at her continuing to use his title. She'd tried not to, but it was difficult to remember when she shouldn't and when she should, and she did not want anyone else to think an agency representative would be less than absolutely correct in their address.

Even if they were absolutely incorrect in their thoughts.

"Come in here." Another command.

Granted, it was the end of the very long day. The party had gone spectacularly well, with only one and a half vomiting incidents, two hair-pulling fights, and four tragic tantrums about not winning.

She walked to the room and stepped inside, holding her breath.

He lounged, as only he could lounge, in his chair, long legs stretched out in front of him, head resting on the chair. His hand dangled off the end of the armrest, his cravat dangling from his fingers.

His chest rose, and then he did as well, striding toward her, past her, to shut the door.

Putting them inside the room together as they hadn't been since she'd asked him—no, told him—she wanted this. Wanted him.

Her corset, even though it fit perfectly well this morning, suddenly felt as though it was constricting her all over. It felt hard to draw a full breath, and her lips were suddenly so dry.

He returned and stood in front of her, his dark eyes gazing down with an intensity she couldn't mistake. Nor, judging by the way his expression shifted, had he misjudged what her face must be saying.

He lifted his hand and placed his fingers on her cheek, drawing his hand back so his fingertips were just behind his ear. "Tell me," he said.

She licked her lips, and his eyes focused on the movement, his sharp intake of breath demonstrating his reaction.

She didn't break eye contact, even though she wished she could retreat—prim, precise, methodical, ha!—took a deep breath. Then spoke.

"I want this, Marcus."

Unlike last time, he didn't take her immediately in his arms. Instead, he slid his hand down her arm and took her hand, pulling her toward a sofa tucked into the corner. The sofa was small, just made for two people, and had the same worn, cozy look as the rest of the furniture This was his room, the only room—besides his bedroom, obviously—that was well and truly his alone.

Just as if he were escorting her off the dance floor and returning her, ever so gently, to where she had been before, he held her hand as she lowered herself onto the sofa, then took his place beside her.

His place. It was his place, deny it though she might.

They sat there in silence, not touching, not moving. It felt so right, so companionable, that Lily just wanted to sigh and lean back against the sofa and regard him.

So she did.

His head bent toward her, and he paused for a fraction, his expression still hesitant, which surprised her. He, who was so in command—and commanded—all the time, now the unsure one, when she was so sure, so certain of what she wanted. What she knew he wanted.

"Kiss me," she said, in a passable imitation of his commanding voice.

He smiled in recognition of her tone, that gorgeous mouth curling up irresistibly, and he lowered his lips to hers, pressing them against them in an almost tender kiss.

Which when their mouths met immediately blazed into something more, something far more. It felt to her as though the whole world had been painted in drab colors until it blazed to life, lit by his kiss.

She drew her hands up to his neck, wrapping

them around it, holding him closer still, so his upper chest was pressed against hers.

Her nipples began to ache, but not in a painful way; her breasts felt heavy, and wanting. She wanted more, wanted his body fully against hers, wanted him to never stop kissing her.

He was clasping her on the shoulders, and she uttered a growl of frustration deep in her throat before taking his hands in hers, sliding them down her shoulders, down her arms and onto her breasts.

Ah. That was more like it. It felt wonderful, to have his hands there. He wasn't doing anything with them, so she wriggled a bit, just enough for him to hopefully get a hint about what she wanted.

And then, yes, his fingers curled around the globe of her breast and his thumb found her nipple, which likely wasn't so difficult to find, since to her it felt as if it were about to burst through the fabric of her gown, even though that image, when it came to her, was rather awkward.

But oh, when his thumb began to move, to touch and caress her nipple, to rub so she arched her back and pushed even closer to him, she felt her mouth—still touching his, still warm and moist and wonderful—curl up into a smile, and she felt his mouth smile in return, and then she slid her tongue between his lips and licked, relishing the hitch in his breath as he reacted.

The pressure of his mouth got harder, and it seemed the intensity had increased also, as his tongue licked hers, and her lips, drawing back only to ravage her again.

Meanwhile, she was giving as good as she got, drawing his lower lip between her teeth and giving it a quick nip before again plunging her tongue inside his mouth. She realized she was gripping his shoulders so tight that she might bruise him, so she placed her palms flat against his chest, feeling the play and movement of his muscles under her fingers. And then she found his nipple and slid her finger over it. He raised his mouth from hers, and for a moment she was worried he was going to tell her no, and she would die never having known what his chest felt like, but instead he just said, "I want this, Lily," then lowered his mouth down to hers, allowing her hands free to roam all over his chest, to slide from his nipples—hard as well, which surprised her—down his sides, over his ribs, each area she touched hard and firm and, even though she didn't know for certain how she knew this, delicious.

Oh, and his hand was so warm on her breast, and his thumb was still gliding over her nipple, and it was almost enough, but not quite, so she withdrew one of her hands from his chest—sad moment though that was—and tugged on the shoulder of her gown, drawing it down her shoulder, at least as far as she was able.

He drew back and gazed at her, his eyes heavy-lidded, his mouth, his gorgeous mouth, just inches from hers. "Can I help you with that?" he asked in a husky voice that sent shivers down her spine.

She didn't answer, just shifted so her back was to him, and he took the hint, unbuttoning her gown and pushing it, no, practically shoving it down her shoulders as she shrugged out of her sleeves. When the fabric was at her waist she twisted back around, her upper half now in just her corset and shift. The expression on his face denied her even the remotest chance of embarrassment; it was wanting, yearning, lustful, hopeful, and desirous all at once.

She put her fingers—her now shaky fingers—to the ties of her corset and pulled, feeling the ease in her chest as the stiff fabric unfolded from her body.

Revealing her breasts covered only by her thin shift.

His gaze immediately went down, and he sucked in a breath and licked his lips.

And didn't that make her think of things she'd never, ever thought of? Such as his mouth on her breasts, his tongue flicking her nipple, kissing the underside of her breast, licking her skin.

Oh, goodness.

Her shift was cut low, and she drew it down so it was lower still, exposing all but the nipples in question.

The room was absolutely quiet, save for their breaths, which were faster, loud, and oddly sensual. It was just him and her in this room, together, and the solitude of it all made Lily feel as though nothing else existed, nothing mattered, outside this room. For right now, at least.

She would think of other things later on. Important things, such as her future, his future wife, Rose's happiness, what would happen to all of them. But for now there was the matter of her breasts, and his hands, and her hands, and his chest, and their mouths, and all of that put together into one—or hopefully more—glorious moments.

She reached her hand forward, a sly smile on her lips, as she began to undo the buttons of his shirt. As each button came undone, it seemed he did, too, his broad chest expanding and contracting with each deep breath. She undid the buttons, then yanked the fabric of his shirt to either side, frowning when she couldn't see as much as she wanted.

She pulled it up from the bottom hem and flung it off onto the floor, then gazed at what was revealed.

Well. That was all worth it, wasn't it?

She feasted her eyes on him, on the strong planes of his chest, the flat brown nipples, the light sprinkling of hair that covered his pectoral muscles, then retreated, then returned to mark a trail down his trousers to—

Well. And that was impressive as well.

She reached forward to put her palm on him, and he exhaled and closed his eyes, his expression one of pure enjoyment. "Touch me, Lily," he said in a hoarse growl, a low rumble that made her body tremble in response.

This, for oncc, was not a command, but an entreaty, and she obliged, sliding her hand all over his warm, smooth skin. His muscles shifted under her touch, and she stroked him with more confidence, then leaned forward to kiss him again. Keeping her hands on him.

He devoured her mouth, his tongue sliding

in and licking and sucking until she truly felt as though it was just them, or more than that, just their bodies, enjoying each other.

His fingers played around the neckline of her shift, then suddenly slid under the fabric, on her breast with nothing between them. And it must have looked odd, his arm bent up at a right angle as his hand went down to cup her breast in his palm, but it certainly felt wonderful, and besides, no one was there anyway—because that would be odd as well as shocking and reputation-shredding and all sorts of things she couldn't think of now—so she didn't care what it might look like, she just cared how it felt.

And it felt lovely. His hand cradled her breast, that clever thumb moving up to slide over her nipple, the sensation spreading throughout her entire body, including there, which she was surprised to notice. She'd not heard much of women getting pleasure from all of this, but she'd be very surprised if he was getting more pleasure than she was at this moment, because if he was, she had no doubt but that he would explode and die from happiness.

So far he had shown no signs of either exploding or dying.

What he was showing, however, was an incredible resourcefulness in the variety of ways he could both kiss her and touch her breasts. It was impressive, really, and she would have said that to him if he weren't kissing her so thoroughly, and if she didn't have serious doubts about her ability to speak at the moment.

The clock chimed just as Lily was trying to recall her own name, and they leapt apart, not very far owing to the smallness of the sofa, but apart nonetheless.

Lily felt wonderfully, achingly tender all over, and glanced over at him, hoping he didn't suddenly have one or both, heaven forbid, eyebrows raised in some sort of judgment.

But no, he was looking just as intense and passionate as before, his gaze holding hers as though never wanting to let go.

Don't let go.

He drew a hand—a hand that trembled—through his hair, and heaved a deep breath.

"We have to stop," he said, still in that low, throaty tone. As though he wanted to say something else and the words he did speak were pulled out of him reluctantly.

She knew they had to stop, even though she didn't want to.

She drew her shift back up, not breaking eye contact with him. Not wanting to run out in a mad panic, as she had the times before. She didn't want him to think she didn't want this. She did. They just—couldn't.

Not with everything at stake.

Apparently now was the time for the truth to come rushing in to disturb their sensual solitude.

The only question was, was it too late for her?

A duke's command is second only to the Queen's. And if the duke is persuasive enough, he might even be able to persuade Her Majesty that his command is far better than hers.

—THE DUKE'S GUIDE TO CORRECT BEHAVIOR

Chapter 25

Well, that could have lasted two hours and he still wouldn't have been satisfied. He tried to calm his breathing, tried not to reach for her again.

She turned to him and he did up her buttons with shaky hands. Had this all really just happened?

The erection tenting his trousers informed him that yes, indeed it had.

And his cock was importuning him to continue.

But he could not. It would not only not be respectable, it would be reprehensible. He knew full well she was an innocent—his governess, for goodness' sake—and he was not one of those men who would abuse his power for this kind of gain, even though he might abuse it to get strawberries in winter.

She was more luscious than a strawberry. And he knew he would want her in any season.

She turned back to him, her mouth swollen from his kisses—their kisses—her chest still moving up and down with her rapid breathing. Her body still just there, within reach.

"I should go," she said in a husky voice. One that sounded as though there were things she wished to say. Of course there were. He just hoped they weren't things like, *I quit, you scoundrel,* or *We will never do this again.*

Or *I don't feel anything for you beyond lust.*

"Thank you for your help with the party." It wasn't what he truly wished to say, of course, but he couldn't even figure out himself what he wished to say. Not even what he needed to say.

He was completely at sea about what to do next. Never, in his brief (in many ways) history of fornicating, had he had a woman in his arms who had appealed to him so. Who had stormed his gruff fortress, challenged him, made him want to take time—all the time in the world—with her.

It left him off-balance. Unsure about anything, even what he wanted to say.

She smiled, a mixture of shy and knowing, and that curve of her mouth was so alluring he just wanted to kiss her again.

Which he would want to do even if she were frowning, unless she had just told him she didn't enjoy his kisses. Then he might forbear the action.

But what was remarkable was that he knew, off-balance though he was, that she did like it. That she had felt as in the moment as he did. That if things weren't as they were, they would be further along in their exploration of each other.

"I will just go check on Rose, then," she said, getting up and pulling the sleeves of her gown up, straightening the bodice and smoothing the skirts.

Removing any physical indication of what they'd just done, even though it was irrevocably marked on his heart. Not to mention his very frustrated cock.

"Good night, then." He swallowed against the lump in his throat.

She was going to check on Rose. Rose, who needed his good name not to be scorned and shunned for all her life. Rose, for whom he had hired this woman, an honorable, respectable woman, to teach her what he could not.

"Good night," she returned, walking slowly to the door. The door opened and she stepped through, taking a piece of him as she left.

As it shut behind her, he leaned back against the sofa and rubbed his face with his hands.

The house was still when he finally emerged. He hadn't come to any sort of conclusion, not one that didn't involve things that couldn't possibly happen (her knocking on his bedroom door later, for example, was highly unlikely). But at least he wasn't in a torment of frustration, sexual or otherwise; no matter what happened, it was his uppermost duty to ensure that Rose's safety and future were protected. That was what mattered more than anything.

He'd never placed anyone above himself before. And no one had ever placed him anywhere in particular. Was this an essential part of humanity he'd missed out on? He suddenly resented his parents for their casual parenting even more. To think they'd had the chance to be a part of a child's upbringing, to guide him through life, to love him, and instead had chosen indifference, lavishing whatever small attention they'd had on his brother . . . well, now that he knew what they had missed, he felt sorry for them.

He walked slowly upstairs to the second floor, feeling as though his world had opened up and tilted upside down all at the same time. The hallway was quiet, a few candles left burning, since the staff knew of the master's late night habits, and crept, catlike, to his door.

Her door was several feet beyond, on the other side. To the right of where his daughter slept. The two most precious people in his life.

He couldn't knock on Lily's door, not without a good reason (and it was not a good reason that he just wanted to kiss her again). He had to summon his will not to do what he wanted to do most in the world, something he'd never had to do before.

He placed his hand on the doorknob and turned it, opening the door to his silent, empty bedroom. A part of him was disappointed she hadn't made her way here, but of course the other part knew that she couldn't have possibly done that, not without making a choice that was irrevocable.

Miller had laid his nightshirt out on the bed, since Marcus had told him not to bother waiting up. He was relieved not to have to interact with anyone, he didn't know if he could speak properly. Not without blurting something out that would, again, be irrevocable.

He'd put his shirt back on again sometime back then—he didn't remember doing it, but she'd taken it off—and now slid it off his shoulders, dropping it onto the floor. Wishing it were her hands removing it. His trousers were next—she hadn't gotten to those, more's the pity—and they slid down his legs so that he was clad only in his smallclothes. Those, too, he shucked, then drew the nightshirt on, the cotton fabric touching the places she'd touched. His shoulders, his arms, his chest.

It would be of no use touching himself tonight. Now that he knew how her fingers felt, how her breasts looked and felt, anything he did for himself would be a mere echo of what he'd actually experienced. Ultimately unsatisfying, no matter how much immediate satisfaction he was able to have.

Was this what the rest of his life would be like?

He snuffed the candle by the side of his bed and got lost in the darkness.

Rose had waited impatiently for him to come in for breakfast. Lily had also been waiting, but not driven by the same motives as Rose. How would he act toward her? Was he horrified at her behavior? Would he wish to dismiss her?

Did he want to do it again?

She hadn't slept much the night before, since there was so much to think about. And not think about.

Such as the look on his face when she drew back, that wanting, helpless, desiring look. Such as the way his chest was firm under her fingers, yet he flinched when she touched him. Such as how it felt when his tongue was plunged into her mouth, and when she was biting his lip.

All those things she spent much of the night not thinking about.

So she was relieved not to have seen him at breakfast, truly she was, only Rose would not stop popping up to see if he was walking down the hall, and Lily couldn't eat, and then she spilled tea all over the table because she was so distracted.

It was only when they were walking back up to the schoolroom that they saw him coming downstairs. Lily was relieved to see him properly garbed, even with a cravat on.

One more thing not to think about—how his throat had looked in the candlelight the night before, how his throat muscles worked as he'd swallowed.

"Duke!" Rose said, reaching out, putting her hand on his sleeve.

He shook his head, met Lily's eyes, then dropped his gaze to Rose. "What is it, sweet?" he asked, putting his hand on her head.

"The day looks fine, we should go for a walk," Rose said in her most commanding, dukelike voice.

He drew a deep breath before replying, and Lily felt her own breath catch. Would he say no, so as not to be with her? Would he say yes, so as to be with her?

Did she actually matter in his decision-making?

None of her questions could possibly have a satisfactory answer.

So she just waited.

"Of course." He pulled his pocket watch out of his waistcoat and frowned at it. "I am out this evening, and have some things to do before then, but we could all go now, if that suits." He glanced at Lily. "If that does not discommode your teaching schedule, that is?"

His tone was all it should be. Professional, cordial, direct. Nothing that indicated his state of mind. Not that he should speak in a way that did indicate it, not in front of Rose; but it was frustrating not knowing. Maybe nearly as frustrating as not getting to do all she wished to the evening before.

"It will be fine," she said. "We will adjust, will we not, Miss Rose?" It was cowardly, perhaps, to defer to her charge, but on the other hand her charge was more important than her own feelings. She was an employee here, she could not forget that.

"Yes! I will go get my coat." Rose scampered up the rest of the stairs, leaving Lily and Marcus alone.

"You slept well, I hope?" he asked.

She met his gaze and smiled ruefully. "Not very well, I must admit. I had a lot on my mind." And in my heart.

He looked relieved, as though he had been worried what she might say. How did someone so commanding and authoritative and handsome not realize the effect he had on people? Or person, actually, namely her?

"I didn't, either. We have some things to discuss."

Oddly enough, that didn't make her anxious, not in the same way his polite tone had. She could tell, just by the expression on his face, that he was feeling some of what she was.

Rose returned before she could reply, holding her coat and Maggie in her arms. "I'm ready!" she announced, stepping between the two of them on the stairs.

"Let us go," the duke said, shooting another quick glance at Lily.

The park was crowded, which was not surprising, given that it was actually sunny.

"I wish it had been this nice yesterday for the party," Lily said as they walked along the path.

"The only thing you couldn't control was the weather, and the rest of it was perfect," the duke said.

"Except for that one girl," Rose added, almost as an aside.

"What girl?" Lily and the duke spoke in unison.

"The one who called me a bastard." She shrugged, which she'd probably picked up from her father. If only her study of flowers were going so well.

"Did she say anything else?" the duke asked through clenched teeth.

Rose shrugged again. "No, just that. I told her to shut up."

Lily's throat grew thick. It was starting already—talk about Rose's parentage, and why the duke had taken her in, probably what he was planning to do with her, and that any young lady who was interested in him would have to take Rose into account—or not, if she could be sent away.

"You are right, Rose, but that is not all there is to it."

He put his hand on the girl's shoulder and squatted down so he could look directly in her face. Lily went to move away, but his hand shot out and grabbed her cloak, making her stay where she was.

"I was not married to your mother, but that does not mean you are not part of my life now. I love you. You are mine, and I—I am yours."

It was too intense a statement to be comprehended by a four-year-old, but it made twenty-four-year-old Lily tear up.

"Do you understand? I don't want you to ever think you are not welcome or loved in my home because of who you are."

"All right," Rose said, her eyes wandering past the duke's shoulder to where a group of children were playing. "Look, a few of the girls from the party are over there. May I join them?"

The duke nodded and stood. "Of course. Miss Lily can escort you."

Lily wiped her eyes quickly, then took Rose's

hand and led her to where the children were gathered.

"She didn't want me to stay right there. She wants to be able to see us, but not be right there." Rose had told her as much just as autocratically as her father would, and it had taken all of Lily's willpower not to laugh.

"Shall we sit, then?" the duke said, gesturing to a bench within eyeshot of the playing children.

"Certainly. Unless . . . unless you wish to return home and I can stay here, with Rose?"

He made a hmphing noise. As though she should know that was not what he would wish. "I'll stay here, unless you wish me to go?"

"No, of course not." Lily sat on the bench, shifting position as the cold crept through her cloak. She wrapped it tighter around her and watched as he sat beside her.

"About last—"

"We should discuss—"

They'd both spoken at the same time. "You go first," the duke said with a wave of his elegant fingers.

"Well. I just wanted to say that this changes nothing between us." She cleared her throat. "That I expect nothing of you, given what we—that is, what we did last night." She felt her face flush as hot as it ever had.

"Nothing has changed?" He did not sound pleased at her words.

She turned to regard him. "Your Grace, it is not

as though it can happen again. You know that. I know that. We, in fact, both know that." She turned to face forward. The trees were far less dangerous to look at.

"I wish—" he began, but she held her hand up.

"We cannot wish for what we cannot have. I have learned that a long time ago."

Silence for a few long moments. When he spoke again, his voice was ragged. "I thought I had, too. I grew up wishing for what I could not have: parents who cared, a brother with whom I had things in common, a purpose in life." She felt rather than saw him turn toward her. Was he finally telling her all the things she'd presumed from his comments? "I didn't think I could have anything I wished for until Rose—and you—walked into my life."

"Tell me about your life." She clasped her hands in her lap so she would be less tempted to touch him. "I know so little about you." That he'd spoken aloud anyway.

"You know who I am." He spoke in a low voice, a tone that resonated on her skin, to her bones, and within to her heart. "You know me."

It made her ache. It made her want to reach over and take his face in her hands and kiss him, show him with her actions just how she felt about him.

But she couldn't.

"My parents—well, my parents were not all that enthusiastic, I think, about having children at all, much less two boys. My brother was the older one, you see, and he was just like my father. At least in the ways my father thought were important. He was athletic, and stubborn, and proud, and took a dim view of people whom he thought were lower than him." A pause as he drew a breath. "And he thought I was one of those people."

Athletic, stubborn, proud? It sounded as though they had had plenty in common. But Lily did not point that out.

"And so my parents gave what little parental attention they had to Joseph. I was sent to school at an early age, and when I was home, I spent more time with the servants than with my family. I learned that if there was something I wanted, I was going to have to get it myself."

That explained a lot.

"And your brother?"

She felt Marcus's shoulders heave in a sigh. "It was only during the last year of his life that he was even the duke's heir in the first place. The previous Duke of Rutherford was childless, and had brothers who had children. No one expected that Joseph would be the one next in line for the dukedom. And then he died."

"So you were not raised to be a duke." He'd said that before, but she hadn't realized just how distant the likelihood was.

"Not at all. I was raised to be a gentleman, I suppose. But that was it. My father entrusted all his affairs to an estate manager, and then my brother. I was told to go away whenever I offered to help."

"That must have hurt."

He shrugged. A gesture that meant myriad things, just like his raised eyebrows did. Now it seemed to Lily it was a rebuttal of the pain he felt, that he still felt, at being cast out for no other reason than his parents' carelessness.

"I survived. And I did not suffer; my father was wealthy, I had the best schooling, I never had to worry about where my next meal might come from. Not like some people."

Not like me, Lily thought.

"Joseph was a fool." He snorted, a noise devoid of humor. "He became the duke's heir, and suddenly he thought he was invincible. Our parents had died by then, and he had no one but his younger unwished-for brother to try to talk him out of doing the foolish things he embarked upon. I warned him that the horse he bought was far too wild to ride, at least not without proper training, but he mocked me for being a coward."

The children's laughter drifted over to them, and Lily felt her heart warm at the sound. What he was describing was his past, not his future. Rose was his future, and he was ensuring his future was well taken care of.

"Joseph took Darkness out after he'd had too much to drink. He tried to jump a fence and was thrown. He was killed instantly. We had to put Darkness down, too."

She glanced around, not seeing anyone nearby, and took his hand. "I am so sorry."

He squeezed her hand. "It wasn't as though we were close. He was as indifferent to me as our parents were." It sounded as though he was trying to be nonchalant, as though it didn't matter, which just made Lily ache for him more.

"He was your family. Of course it is going to affect you."

"My family," he said in a musing tone of voice. "I have never felt as though I had any family. Not until now, with Rose."

A pause, as Lily wondered if he was going to add *and you.* She was both relieved and disappointed that he didn't.

"What was Rose's mother like? She hasn't talked about her much, except to say she worked in a pub."

Marcus removed his hand from hers and crossed his arms over his chest. "She was a—well, she was not a woman you would know, that is for certain."

Don't be so sure, Lily wanted to say. But she couldn't tell him of her past, of how just by being in Rose's vicinity she was jeopardizing the girl's future.

"She and I . . . kept company for a time, and when she told me she was with child, I arranged to take care of the babe. I hadn't expected—nor did I even want to—know my offspring." A snort that wasn't humorous. "In that way, I acted just as Joseph would, disposing of my troubles with money, and not thinking at all about the consequences of my actions. I'm ashamed of what I did."

"At least you made arrangements for her support. It doesn't sound that Rose was ill-treated or went hungry. She is thin, but she was not malnourished. And the few times she's spoken of her mother it has been with fondness."

There was a long pause between them as he let

out a deep breath. "I don't even remember what her mother looked like," he said. "It is odd. As soon as I saw Rose, I knew immediately I had to do the right thing. Or maybe not just the right thing, but the thing that would be best for her, since I knew it would also be best for me."

Which is why he was currently on the hunt for a proper young lady to marry, she thought.

A proper young lady.

Not a woman from a small town whose closest claim to respectability was a squire father who'd lost everything he ever owned. Not a woman who'd worked in a brothel.

Not her.

Although dukes should be cautioned against excessive emotion, they should also be certain to express their emotions if it seems that holding them in would cause an upset of the stomach or other such physical distemper.

—THE DUKE'S GUIDE TO CORRECT BEHAVIOR

Chapter 26

"Caroline?" Lily called as soon as she stepped inside the door to the agency. Rose was having a nap after spending a very long time at the park—she'd had no fewer than three invitations for later in the week, and she was smiling so much it made Lily's heart swell.

But all that playing made a little girl exhausted, especially after spending half an hour playing hide and seek with her father as Lily watched, trying not to giggle as the duke pretended not to see his daughter even though he was practically about to trip over her.

They'd walked home together, mostly silent, Rose between them holding each one of their hands.

Lily's mind churned as she reviewed everything he had told her. No wonder he was the way he was. And she'd been so wrong about him when they first met—he was arrogant, yes, but he was also so vulnerable, and so clearly in need of love, love he was getting from Rose. No wonder it was so important to him that she be taken care of and wanted as he hadn't been.

A different man would have repeated the same mistakes from his own upbringing, perhaps sending Rose away, or ignoring her while he was out enjoying Society.

By the time they reached the duke's house, Rose was yawning, the duke was consulting his pocket watch, and Lily knew she had to speak to someone about all of this before she burst.

"Your Grace," she said as they stepped inside, "would it be permitted for me to go run an errand? Rose will be taking a nap."

"I will not," Rose said in a peevish voice.

"And Etta can sit with her while I am away. It should not be more than forty-five minutes."

He seemed to take a long look at her, almost as though he could see the tumult inside her soul, then nodded and reached for Rose. "Come along, sweet, let us go upstairs and I will read a story to you while you rest—and not sleep," he said, shooting a quick, wry glance at Lily. "My engagement is not until later this afternoon."

"Thank you, Your Grace," Lily said, waiting as John the footman opened the door for her again.

She scurried down the steps and walked quickly to the agency, hoping Caroline would be there. And, even though she dearly loved her friend, she hoped Annabelle would not, since conversation with Annabelle invariably lasted at least twice as long as you thought it would.

"Caroline?" she called out, walking back into the office. No one was there, but the door had been open; perhaps one of them had just stepped out to the necessary? Lily sat in the Unfortunate Women seat, then sprang up again as the bell at the door rang. Just as it had only a few weeks ago, when the whole adventure began.

She heard footsteps, then Caroline herself walked into the office, jumping in surprise when she saw Lily. "What are you doing here? Is anything wrong?" her friend asked, stripping off her shawl and dropping it on the desk.

"No, that is—"

"You are all right?" Caroline's eyes scanned her face, then she exhaled in relief. "You are fine, it's just him, isn't it?"

Lily's mouth gaped open. It seemed Caroline needed to look at her only five seconds before gauging what was bothering her. So much for that career in gambling she'd been considering.

"Tea?" Caroline asked, turning to the small stove in the corner of the room without waiting for a response.

She busied herself with the kettle and lighting the fire ("Wretched match!"), and then drew the office chair as close as she could without actually banging into Lily's knees, for which Lily was grateful.

"Tell me what it is. And then I have a favor to ask you."

Now that she had her friend's full attention, Lily wasn't quite sure what to say. She thought she was falling in love with him? Caroline probably had already figured that out, since she appeared to be psychic. She didn't know what she would do when he married? Caroline would likely tell her just to bide her time until she could leave the position gracefully.

Why had she even bothered to come, when she could have had this conversation with Caroline in the comfort of her own bedroom, without Caroline even there?

Oh, of course. Because she wanted to say it out loud, have someone else understand just what was happening, maybe even offer some advice that she hadn't thought of inside her own head.

Fine, then, her own head said to herself. Which was confusing even without all the tumult in her brain.

"I—we've spent time together—"

"More kisses?" Caroline interrupted, arching an eyebrow.

Lily bit her lip and nodded. "And I know there's nothing I can do about it, he told me he is on the hunt for a suitable wife, a lady who can mother his daughter properly. It is not as though he has led me to have any expectations."

Actually, given that last time—when she had been the aggressor—perhaps she should have been concerned she was leading *him* on.

"But?" Caroline prompted.

"But . . . I don't know. That is the thing. I like him, I even think I—" If she said it aloud, she'd be admitting it, wouldn't she? Not that she hadn't already caught herself thinking it before, but it seemed that if she told Caroline what was in her heart, it would be a reality. She couldn't take it back, even if nothing ever came of it.

Fine, then. "I think I am in love with him." Not falling in love with him, or enamored of him, or charmed by him. No, she was firmly and definitely in love with him, and she knew that as well as she knew there was no chance anything could ever come of it.

Which Caroline should be telling her in about five, four, three—

"You know there is nothing that can really happen between you. You've heard enough of our women's stories to know that men say things they don't mean." Caroline glanced up, blinking rapidly, as though staving off tears. "You know from my own story that these things don't work out."

"I know," Lily said softly, reaching out to take her hand. This was what she really needed—the comfort of knowing a friend out there knew just what she was going through, and that she understood.

"I know you do," Caroline replied in a voice that nearly trembled. Nearly, because she hadn't broken down since the first time Lily had met her, long before they started the agency. Back when Lily had worked at the brothel—but not *worked* worked—whereas the brothel was where Caroline had come to work after coming afoul of a suspicious wife.

The kettle began to whistle, and Caroline sprung up from her chair, wiping the back of her hand under her eyes. "What do you want?" she asked as she poured the hot water into the teapot, before shaking it gently.

She turned around to face Lily. Her expression

was kind, but also held a warning that Lily knew the truth of as well. "What do you want?" she asked again, her gaze intent on Lily's face.

Him. "I don't know." Liar. You want him. "I think I just want things to be as they are, only they can't be, not with me feeling this way. I don't know how he feels."

"And you can't very well ask him, not without compromising yourself. Either your feelings or your position," Caroline said in a practical tone.

Caroline retrieved two mugs from the shelf, spooned sugar into each, and poured just a splash of milk in hers and more than that in Lily's. "So you just need to accept things as they are, as much as possible. Until something changes." She handed one mug to Lily. "He's looking for a suitable wife, is that correct?"

Lily nodded as her insides tightened.

"And when he finds one, that will be your time to search for another position. Luckily, you know some people who can find you something," she said with a wink.

Lily laughed, as she was supposed to, even though a part of her—a very large part of her, starting with her heart—wanted to cry. Caroline returned to her seat and placed her mug on the desk.

"Now that I have absolutely not solved your problem, I'll ask about that favor I mentioned."

Lily took a sip of tea, glad to focus on something other than her own incipient heartbreak. "What can I do for you? Please don't tell me you wish to marry a duke, because I don't think I can assist you there."

Caroline smiled, shaking her head. "No, nothing like that. Annabelle and I were talking about how we could help our clients, or even just the women coming here for assistance who we can't immediately help. And it is an awkward subject to broach, especially to someone you've just met, but we thought that if these women had access to certain things, it could help keep them from becoming even more unfortunate."

Though put in a convoluted manner, Lily recognized what she was saying. "You want to provide condoms?" she asked.

Caroline bent her head in a quick nod. "And neither Annabelle nor I knew even where to get them, and since you do, we were hoping—"

"You want me to buy them?"

Another nod.

"I can do that." Lily thought for a moment. "There is a druggist nearby who used to have them. I can go there on my way home. I'll bring them by when I come by next. Is that all right? There is no immediate need, is there?"

Caroline shook her head. "No, we can wait. Let me get you the money for them." She stood and went to the cabinet drawer where the agency kept its fees. "We knew you would say yes, so we went and took out enough from the bank." She counted out the money, returned to her chair and handed it to Lily, who put it into the pocket of her gown.

"The women will be so grateful."

Lily swallowed the rest of her tea, then glanced at the clock over Caroline's head. "I should be off, Rose will be waking from her nap in a bit."

She got up from her chair, smoothing her gown. "Thank you."

Caroline stood also. "For what? I haven't solved any of your problems, and I've only added more things for you to do."

Lily planted her fists on her hips and glared mockingly at her friend. "For being here, and listening to me, and knowing exactly what I am going through. For all of that. Thank you." Her tone softened. "For being my family."

Caroline smiled and opened her arms to take Lily in a hug. "Thank you, too. And be careful."

Lily felt the prickle of tears sting her eyes. "I will."

"Your Grace, thank you for attending our little gathering." The Countess of Daymond swooped in on him as soon as the butler had taken his coat and hat. Her expression looked startled, and faintly alarmed, as though a candle were right in front of her nose and she was blinded by the light.

Oh, dear Lord. Was the light him?

"Thank you for the invitation." He would have to get a damn secretary, wouldn't he, if he persisted in accepting invitations. A wife might also be of assistance, but he didn't think he could ask his new bride to see to his social calendar as well as his illegitimate child. Although she would likely prefer to see to the former than the latter. But there was only so much he could expect from a marriage.

The countess was still talking, and he had to remind himself to pay attention.

"And of course the Montgomery ladies are here, and my own Lucinda will be playing the pianoforte, and the earl has promised not to steal you away until you have taken a turn around the conservatory and seen the flowers. Do you know, I was able to hire the Queen's gardener's second assistant? Quite a coup, I know there were many other people vying for his services."

On the other hand, maybe he should remind himself not to pay attention. Or think about more pleasant things. Such as cold porridge, tight cravats, and finally reading the agricultural tomes that were beginning to gather dust in his bedroom.

"The Duke of Rutherford has arrived," the countess said as she swept into a large room that appeared to be housing a vast number of ladies. Dear heavens, were there any males here at all?

Marcus had more sympathy for the stud in a herd of horses. Or perhaps the rooster in a henhouse.

Or the only man in a group of women, likely some of them unmarried.

His cravat felt very, very tight.

"Duke," he heard a voice—thankfully, a male voice—say just to his right. He turned and was relieved to see Smithfield, whose smirk indicated he knew just what Marcus was feeling.

"Good afternoon," Marcus replied.

"Come this way, Your Grace, I wish to introduce

you to my daughter's godmother." The countess took his arm and drew him farther into the room before he could grab Smithfield and make a run for it.

"Your Grace, may I present Lady Townsend? She is Lady Lucinda's godmother, and she is my dearest friend." He didn't begrudge anyone having friends, but he didn't necessarily need to be informed of each and everyone's friends' status when he was introduced.

Or perhaps he was just grouchy.

He took the lady's hand in his and bowed. She gave him a thorough look, one that started at the top of his head, down to his feet, then back up again, which was when he recalled he'd met her before, to the same scrutiny.

And like before, he didn't know whether or not to hope he'd been found wanting.

"And here is Lucinda! Come here, my dear," the countess said, gripping his arm a little tighter, as though he were about to make a run for it.

Could she read minds?

"Your Grace," Lady Lucinda murmured, lowering her eyes as she dropped a curtsey. He bowed, and then was gratified to see, when she met his gaze, the humorous light lurking within. He did like her, certainly. Enough to make her his wife?

The countess took her daughter's arm in her other hand and drew her to Marcus's side. "Your Grace, you can accompany Lucinda to the conservatory. Mr. Ball is there to inform us all about the new plantings."

She spoke in a louder voice as she addressed

the many ladies—and two men—in the room. "Ladies and gentlemen, if you would be so kind as to follow the duke and my daughter to the conservatory, I would be delighted to show you the very rare and exotic flowers and plants we have imported."

A general rustling and clatter as teacups were put down, ladies stood up, and a queue—with Marcus and Lady Lucinda at its head—was formed.

He felt like a damn parade leader. At least no one had given him a banner that said Unmarried Duke Here to carry.

"I do apologize, Your Grace," Lady Lucinda said in a low voice as they walked down the hall. "My mother is . . . not subtle," she concluded in a wry tone.

"It is of no matter," Marcus replied.

They were silent for the remainder of the walk.

A short, earnest-looking man waited at the end of the hall, standing in front of a massive door, a telltale smudge of dirt on his face indicating that he was the gardener. He beamed as they all moved past him. The countess brushed past Marcus as she made her way to the front, and Marcus bumped into Lucinda, catching a hint of her scent. It was floral, naturally, and smelled lush and fragrant. She smelled nothing like Lily, the only other woman he'd been close enough to sniff lately.

If he thought about it, he would have to imagine Lily did not wear scent, as that was something proper ladies of fashion did, not governesses serving at the whim of their charges and their employers.

Something about that thought made him angry, but he brushed it away as the countess began to speak.

"Our conservatory will be, I hope, something special to see, and I am so glad all of you"—at which point she looked right at Marcus—"were able to join us for this little party."

She nodded to the gardener, who turned and opened the doors, then stepped aside so the countess could enter.

They all filed in, with nearly everyone exclaiming in delight as they walked into the room.

And it was impressive, Marcus had to admit; like his conservatory, the room had a multitude of windows, but that's where the comparison ended.

There were tables in a variety of heights set in clearly well-planned ways around the room. Statues were scattered throughout, young men and women clad in not very much clothing, all of whom looked absolutely delighted to be captured in stone and set in this room. Pillars were set in each corner, with hooks hanging from them, from which were suspended plants whose flowers cascaded down the sides. There were pleasant-looking benches on which to sit, a large cabinet holding an assortment of gardening tools—all of which looked to be kept in impeccable shape—and on a side table, trays with attractive looking pastries and other confectionary delights.

It was the kind of undertaking only a family with means and purpose could achieve. It was the kind of undertaking he would have scoffed at six months, or even six weeks, ago. But he could see now that in the right family, it would be a wonderful accomplishment, a delight and tribute to the passion of the family members.

The thought sent a stab of poignancy through him. He wanted the kind of family, the kind of emotion, that would inspire an effort like this one, even if the work was primarily done by the Queen's former second assistant gardener.

"It is wonderful," he said to Lady Lucinda, who was still at his elbow. Thank goodness she was not a talkative person, because he wouldn't have heard her anyway, so engaged was he in absorbing the beauty of her mother's conservatory.

He'd never paid much attention to plants, beyond the fact that they were the source for foodstuffs. But he had to admit, standing in all this splendor, that there was more to them than being the basis of bread, peas, and even onion custard.

"Mother is very proud of her work." Lady Lucinda paused, then cleared her throat. "I am very proud of my mother, even though she has been driving me crazy with her obsession." She chuckled. "I wish never to hear about the distinction among roses ever again."

Roses. Rose. His daughter, his bloom among the thorns of his life.

Dear God, when had he become so melodramatic? It must be the picturesque setting.

Or a bad poet had been lurking inside of him all this time. No wonder his cravat felt snug.

"Shall we find a place to sit?" Marcus didn't

wait for her answer, just drew her away from the crowd of chattering, delighted women and helped her sit on a small wooden bench tucked away between a statue of some nymph or another and what appeared to be a centaur. Or a badly sculpted thick-legged man.

"Thank you, this is nice." Lucinda turned her head to him. "How are you enjoying town? This is your first time in town as the duke, is it not?"

He nodded. "Yes, although I spent some time here in the past, before I inherited."

"It must be very different, to be here as the duke." She likely didn't mean to sound superior, as though it was infinitely better to be a duke, but it had to be inherent in someone who was raised in this kind of rarified atmosphere.

And she wasn't wrong, of course; it was on balance nicer to be someone who was deferred to, had power, wealth, and privilege. But it would be too easy for him to just have that and not do anything with it. As he'd nearly done before Rose came into his life.

Being a duke was work as well as rewarding. In the time since he'd paid attention, he'd realized just how much more he had to do. It was a challenge, and he hadn't had a challenge since . . . well, since that spoon-balancing time. And since meeting Rose. And Lily.

Meanwhile, Lady Lucinda was waiting for some sort of reply, even though he barely recalled what she had said to him in the first place. Oh, yes. Differences in life.

What could he say that wouldn't make him

sound like a pompous ass? Lily's voice came into his mind as clearly as if she were speaking into his ear: *Nothing, you already are a pompous, not to mention arrogant, ass.*

He smiled at the thought.

"I am older than I was, and so the things I do now for pleasure," he said, such as walking in the park with my daughter, or coercing her governess to lose her lemony demeanor, "is different from what I did five years ago, before I was a duke." He wouldn't mention what he used to do before. She was a lady, after all.

Although some of those activities had brought him Rose.

"I presume the same is true of you?" Nicely played, he imagined Lily whispering in his ear. Turning the conversation back to her, as though he were engaged in her reply.

Which, he reminded himself sternly, he was. She was so far the best option for a wife he'd seen thus far.

"Yes," she replied, on a laugh, "when I was here many years ago, all I wanted to do was to go to the music halls. I was mad for the pianoforte, and I even had dreams of becoming a musician myself. Can you imagine?" she said with a trace of bitterness in her voice.

He drew back and regarded her. "I could, actually. You are definitely more than you appear, Lady Lucinda." Well, that certainly, nearly, made his intentions clear. Not that he knew what his intentions were, precisely.

What were his intentions?

He felt a sudden wave of panic, glancing around the room, desperate not to continue the course of the conversation. "Tell me," he said in a different tone of voice, "which of your mother's flowers are your favorite?"

She hesitated, as though she were as confused as he by the sudden change of topic. Well, at least they had that in common.

"I do love delphiniums, and of course roses. In spite of my mother's obsession with them," she said in a wry voice. "But I would have to say that my favorite flowers of all are lilies. They're so triumphantly exotic, and colorful. And their scent! For my birthday last year, my father got me a perfume that smelt of lilies. It is my favorite." She chuckled a little self-consciously. "I am wearing it now."

As she spoke, she raised her wrist, inner part up, and he had no choice but to lower his nose down to her arm and sniff.

It wasn't unpleasant. In fact, if asked, he would have to say it was pleasant.

"Very nice," he said.

"And my mother promised we would devote a whole corner to the conservatory to lilies." Another self-conscious laugh. "No doubt that seems foolish . . ." she began.

"Not at all," Marcus murmured.

"But apparently lilies are difficult to grow, and Mr. Ball is one of the foremost experts in them, so that was one of the reasons Mama wanted him so badly. For me," she added.

"That is wonderful. Not foolish at all," Marcus said.

She smiled. "It is one of the privileges of our position, is it not? And you, you are in such a good position, you can do whatever you like."

Marcus smiled in return. "Such as commanding lilies to grow, or to demand strawberries in winter, or for the furn—"

He froze, mid-sentence. Strawberries in winter. Swapping all the furniture from one side to the other.

Having Lily. Marrying Lily.

Why hadn't he thought of it before? He was a duke, and with all the power his title entailed, he could do what he liked, even though it might—for a brief while—shock members of a society he'd only recently joined. Lily was the best possible choice for a mother for Rose, not to mention the best possible choice for someone to share the rest of his life with without loathing.

He should marry Lily.

He could make it right with the world he wanted for Rose. Just give people enough time to adjust, and then when a fresher scandal arrived, his marrying her would just be another oddity about him.

He could marry Lily.

And then he could garb her in his nightshirts all he wanted, and have the very distinct pleasure of stripping them off her, and sharing a bed with her, and maybe even bringing other little children into the world with her.

He would marry Lily.

Suddenly, he needed to leave, to be out of this house and on his way home, to speak to her, to tell her how he'd solved the problem in one easy solution.

She cared for him, or at least she liked being kissed by him—and she would not hesitate to argue with him if he were doing something that would be harmful to Rose. To their family.

She was the perfect wife.

A duke should utilize all of his available resources when in pursuit of a ducal goal. Not just his financial ones, although those may also be utilized. He should employ his position, his eminence, and most importantly, his eyebrows, to achieve what requires achieving.

—The Duke's Guide to Correct Behavior

Chapter 27

Lily stepped out of the agency, closing the door behind her. She had just enough time, she'd figured, to go to the apothecary and purchase the condoms. That had been one of her duties at the brothel, in addition to reviewing the accounts and, for some reason, handling the purchase of tea.

Her job skills when she left were balancing ledgers, knowing where to buy items for the prevention of pregnancy, and how much tea an establishment catering to a vast amount of men would go through in a month.

Not exactly skills for which she would be immediately hired.

Another reason to be grateful for the agency's formation. She was on her way to utilizing at least two out of the three skills. It only was left for a haberdasher or gentleman's tailor to hire her for her tea-gauging skills.

Something to look forward to, at least.

She rounded the corner to the shop, the memory of the last time she'd gone there fresh in her mind. By then she'd become a regular customer, so the owner of the shop knew to take her into the back office and conduct the transaction there. At first, when she went to the apothecary she had been heckled, not only by the shop's customers but by the assistants. The owner, Mr. Davies, knew the brothel was a good source of income, so he and Lily had swiftly worked out how they could best work together without embarrassment on either side.

A lady could not just go buying such things on her own, not without a lot of difficulty. Never mind the injustice that if a lady did not take care, she could find herself abandoned and with child. Men were the ones who were considered best able to purchase birth control, even though they were the sex less damaged by not having it.

She knew if she thought about it too much, she'd end up grouchy, and she didn't want that. Not when she had so many other things occupying her mind.

She opened the door and stepped inside, breathing in the aromas of the shop—camphor, turpentine, and the other smells from the various potions the apothecary carried. There were only a few people in the shop, and her eye was caught by a container with the words Cold Cream of Roses on it. She smiled, and took it down from the shelf, then headed to the counter.

Mr. Davies's back was turned to Lily as he reached up to a bottle with some green liquid inside. He placed it on the table in front of him before turning around, then his eyes widened in surprise, and old instinct, no doubt, made him glance to either side of her to ensure discretion.

"Good afternoon, Mr. Davies," she said. "It has been a while." Nearly two years, in fact. She was grateful to find him here after all that time.

"Good afternoon, miss," he said in a quiet voice. "Are you—"

She shook her head. "No, I am no longer employed there, but I do wish to purchase some items," she said, equally quiet. "And this," she added, holding up the jar of cold cream. Rose would be delighted to have something with her name on it, and Lily did like the smell of roses, if not that of her namesake flower.

"Of course," Mr. Davies said. He turned to one of his workers nearby and told him, "I am taking this customer to the office for a moment, please stay here."

"Yes, sir," the assistant replied, his expression unchanged. Not for the first time she reflected that Mr. Davies must have instructed his employees to maintain the utmost discretion, regardless of what was transacted in the shop.

Lily walked around to the side of the counter, waiting as Mr. Davies pulled out a large set of keys and jiggled the right one out. He unlocked the door, then held it open for her to step through.

It was more of a storeroom than an office, boxes and papers everywhere, filed in a way that only Mr. Davies, presumably, could figure out. He gestured to indicate she should sit in the only chair not filled with something, and she picked her way through the boxes, hoping she wouldn't accidentally knock something over. Especially not a box of condoms, because she knew she would blush so much she might accidentally catch on fire.

"Just over here, I think," Mr. Davies mumbled. "How many?"

Lily drew the money from her pocket. "As many as this will buy me. Plus the cold cream," she said, holding the bills in her hand.

He assessed what she held, nodded, and began rifling through one of the boxes. "Four, then," he said.

He turned back around, holding four condom packets in his hand. "I am glad to see you, miss, I was hoping you were doing well. It appears you are, and for that, I am glad." He sounded sincere, and it warmed her heart. She had left her position unexpectedly when her mother finally succumbed to her illness, the one that required expensive medicines, and she hadn't thought to let anyone beside her employer know where she went.

Another reminder, so soon on the last one, that she had friends and acquaintances who would help her and who cared for her. She felt her eyes start to tear up again, and had to immediately squelch the urge to cry.

Mr. Davies would likely be far more embarrassed to have a crying female in his office than to sell condoms to her.

He put them into a plain, discreet sack and handed it to her as he took the bills. He gave her some change, then went to the door and waited for her to follow.

"Thank you, Mr. Davies."

"Thank you, miss. Your custom is always welcome here," he said. He opened the door and Lily stepped through, holding her purchases close to her chest.

And saw Mr. Haughton's face, his expression changing to one of startled recognition as she walked around the counter.

"Miss Lily," Mr. Haughton said, his tone not nearly as polite as it had been when he first met her.

"Mr. Haughton," she replied, clutching her package tighter. As though he would take it from her.

He smirked at seeing that, and in narrowing his eyes Lily knew what he was probably thinking—that he knew what she was clutching. As he opened his mouth to speak, she felt her heart fluttering against her ribs. Was this what she'd feared?

"I knew I'd recognized you when we met before, only I couldn't recall where. Now I do." Well, at least he got straight to the point. "And you have the charge of the duke's ward?" And he stuck to his point, she had to give him that. "And you have been in company with my daughters and nieces?" His tone was outraged. "Does the duke know? Is that why he hired you? So you could be his—his—" With his voice rising, the growing panic in her chest blossomed into full-blown panic.

"No, of course he doesn't know," she interrupted.

Mr. Haughton straightened himself up as he

stepped closer to Lily, who had to remind herself not to step back.

"Listen, young woman," he said, his jaw tight. "I do not wish to cause a scandal for the duke, especially since . . ." He paused, and Lily could almost see the wheels turning in his head as he figured out how to phrase it. ". . . since he has just entered society and he is very properly looking for a wife." A wife who, if Mr. Haughton could manage it, would be Miss Blake. "So if you leave his employ within the next twenty-four hours, I will pretend you never existed."

Lily swallowed as she absorbed the import of his words. She could threaten him with exposure as well—after all, if he'd recognized her from the brothel, that meant he had been in the brothel as well—but somehow she knew that the damage would be done to her, no matter how others reacted to Mr. Haughton. She could threaten him, but a powerful man in Society would be able to damage her reputation, her future, the agency's future, far more than his brief moment in the sun of scandal.

Twenty-four hours. Twenty-four hours to disappear. From proper society, at least; she didn't think Mr. Haughton would care what she did, as long as she was no longer in his world.

"Well?" His tone was impatient, clearly irked at having to wait for a reply from someone so worthy of contempt. And she was ruminating again, wasn't she? She didn't have time to think.

She bit her lip and nodded. "Yes," she said in a whisper.

And darted around him and out the door before bursting into tears.

Of course, it was one thing to decide one was going straight home to propose to one's daughter's governess immediately, and another to actually do it.

First of all, she was not there. That was his first impediment. It was generally assumed that the person to whom you wished to propose should actually be in the vicinity for the proposal to occur.

Second, now that he was home, he wasn't sure what he should say.

Third was that she was not home yet. It had been at least five minutes since the last time he looked at the clock.

Couldn't she sense that he needed her here? That he wanted to change her life irrevocably, for the better?

Again, not that he knew what he was going to say.

A knock on the door interrupted his— Well, he wasn't thinking of anything at all, so perhaps it was interrupting nothing. "Come in," he said, straightening in his chair. If it was her, he still had no idea what to say.

Thompson opened the door and stepped inside. "Your Grace, Miss Rose has woken. Etta said you asked to be informed." Thompson accompanied his words with a bow, and then left, shutting the door behind him.

"Yes, thank you," Marcus said to the closed door.

He stood and stretched, feeling the slight soreness from having earlier crouched in a hiding position for over ten minutes. He hadn't been able to figure out if Rose knew where he was and was just extending the game or if she really could not see a six-foot-tall man hunched near a tree.

It was fun, no matter what. He hadn't played many games as a child, and so he was looking forward—probably more than most parents—to playing games with his daughter. To hearing her shrieks of delight as they played together.

And he'd shared his past with her, as well. That had been another new experience. He didn't speak about his parents, or Joseph, with anyone he was close to. In fact, he wasn't close to many people anyway. Except now he could say he was close to Lily. To Rose. Even to Smithfield.

So much had changed in his life. So much was about to change.

And all for the better.

He was smiling as he walked out of the library and leapt up the stairs to see his daughter.

Lily's steps slowed as she walked toward the duke's mansion. Her mind had been in a tumult since leaving Mr. Davies's establishment. Not only would she have to leave the duke's employ, and therefore him, but she would have to leave Rose. That would hurt her as well as Rose, who had suffered enough abandonment already. How would she tell the girl that she had to leave? She knew what she would say to him—she owed him the truth, difficult though it would be to tell him—but how could she tell Rose that not only was she not going to take care of her anymore, she was going to be gone within a day?

And how would she tell Caroline and Annabelle that their brilliant future was going to be jeopardized by her past? It was what they had always feared happening. That didn't make it any easier.

She walked up the steps to the no longer intimidating door, feeling as though her feet weighed as much as ten of those massive books on farming the duke had been reading.

The door swung open before she could raise the knocker, and Thompson poked his head out. "Miss Rose is awake, and she and the duke are asking for you. Come in," he said, in nearly a friendly way.

And she would have to leave Thompson, too, although that didn't sting quite as much. But still. She liked this house and the people who lived and worked in it. She didn't want to go.

But she had to.

She felt as though she was thinking in circles, starting with Mr. Haughton's accusatory tone, then cycling through all the people she would be disappointing, and back to Mr. Haughton.

She put her package under her arm, resisting Thompson's move to take it (because it seemed that would make her currently horrible situation even worse), and took her cloak off, allowing him to take that, at least.

"Miss Rose and the duke are upstairs?"

"Yes, miss."

She ascended the staircase, her feet now only feeling as though they weighed the same as five of the duke's farming books. She would get to see him, to see Rose, one last time. One last evening before she had to leave.

"Good night, Miss Rose." Lily tucked the covers around the little girl, feeling her throat tighten. As it had all evening, every time she thought about what was to come.

But she wouldn't waste her last few precious hours here with throat-tightening or chest-constricting or any other of the physical signs of duress.

She'd decided what she had to do, it was now just a question if she would be bold enough to do it. And if when he heard, the duke was so shocked that he wished to immediately relieve her of her position—well, it wasn't as though that would be a problem.

Rose turned onto her side and let out a soft sigh, the one that indicated she was more than halfway asleep already. Lily bent down to kiss her forehead, and smoothed a few tendrils of hair away from the girl's face.

And then returned to her room to prepare.

Marcus had spent an enjoyable if frustrating evening. He still couldn't figure out what to say, and then there was how to get her alone to say it—he didn't want to summon her to his library, as he usually did, because he didn't want to order her anywhere, even though she was his employee. He didn't wish to treat her as one.

So at the end of the night he was alone, in his bedroom, totally perplexed as to what to do. Go knock on her door? Slip a note into her room asking her to meet him somewhere? Wait until he blurted out some words or another, no matter where they were or what they were doing?

The last option seemed like the most likely one.

He was halfway through shrugging out of his coat when he heard the knock at the door. "Come in," he growled, resisting the urge to bite Miller's head off when he came in. He'd told Miller he would see to himself this evening—the last thing he wanted was company for his foul mood—so he didn't see why the—

The door opened and she stood there. Wrapped in a dressing gown, her hair undone and falling over her shoulders. Her arms were folded over her chest and she held something, some sort of package.

Her expression was—well, he couldn't read it at all. It appeared to be a mix of anticipation and anxiety. Likely other words that began with an A as well, such as agony, appreciation, and approachable.

Imagine if he allowed himself the rest of the alphabet.

She stepped in and closed the door behind her.

"You have not yet proposed marriage to anyone, have you?" she asked, biting her lip.

Dear Lord, he had not. And had no idea how to. "No," he replied.

"Good," she said, before he could open his mouth to force out words he didn't know how to say. "Because I am here to return your nightshirt." And she dropped the package she was carrying on the chair next to the door, opened her dressing gown and shrugged it off, all the while continuing to meet his gaze.

She was, indeed, wearing his nightshirt and nothing more. The fabric reached nearly to her ankles, and he wished he were shorter so the nightshirt would be shorter on her. He really wished he could see more of her legs; he supposed they were likely fine legs, nothing much out of the ordinary, suitable for walking and dancing and all sorts of things, but they were hers, and they were right there emerging from his nightshirt, and he didn't think he'd ever seen anything so deliciously erotic in his life.

Forget being able to ask her anything—he wasn't certain he could remember his own name.

"Marcus," she said in a low voice, "I want this." She stepped forward and placed her hands on his shoulders and tilted her face up to his. And then kissed him, sliding her fingers into his hair and tugging him to her.

Her mouth was so delicious. She was so delicious, only he didn't know that for certain, did he? He would have to taste her. Everywhere.

She opened her mouth and licked his lips, then her tongue dove into his mouth and tangled with his, licking and sucking and plundering.

He grasped her arms and then pulled her flush against him, her breasts pressed against him, his cock straining against his trousers. Dear Lord. This felt better than anything he'd ever had, and there were still a few layers of fabric separating him. The exhilaration of her being here, having come here as though he'd summoned her with his thoughts, sent his mind whirling.

Perhaps he didn't need to say anything. Which was likely a good thing, since his mouth was currently occupied kissing her and he didn't think he could speak anyway.

She drew back, a lazy, sensual smile on her face. "I am not wrong in presuming you want this, too?"

Marcus nodded his head, his wiser-than-he-was-at-the-moment hands moving to cup her beautiful breasts. And he would find out for himself, even though he already knew, that they were beautiful breasts.

"Good," she said, her fingers going to the buttons on his shirt. She slid out each button until they were all undone, then yanked at the hem of his shirt and drew it up over his head. That meant he had to take his hands off her body, but as soon as he was stripped to the waist he returned them, caressing the curve of her breast, running his hands down the indent of her waist to her hips.

Glimpsing the dark triangle of her sex under the white cotton. His mouth grew dry.

"Shall we move to your bed?" she asked, an amused curve on her lips. Apparently he'd been gawking. Not unexpected. It wasn't very often the object of one's obsession walked into one's bedroom wearing only a nightshirt. In fact, he'd have to say that had never happened. Especially not to him.

Marcus nodded again—still couldn't speak—and she took his hand and walked forward to the bed.

She sat on it, her legs dangling down to the floor, and he went to join her, but she pressed her hand flat against his belly, stopping him.

"First I should finish what I started," she said, licking her lips as she put her hand to the placket of his trousers. His erection tented his pants, and her hand brushed against him, making him flinch.

"I didn't hurt you, did I?" she asked, a note of concern in her voice.

He shook his head. "No, it feels good," he managed to rasp out. So he had not been rendered permanently mute, it seemed.

"Good," she said, then began to unbutton his trousers. One button, two, then three, and they were loose enough for her to pull them down his legs, and he stepped out of them, wearing only his smallclothes.

She ran her hand against him again, and he shuddered, feeling the touch throughout his entire body. Then she grasped the fabric of his smallclothes on his hips and shoved them down, freeing his erection and leaving him entirely naked.

"Oh my," she said, her gaze on his cock. Which appreciated the attention, he had to admit, but it would have preferred her touch again.

Thank goodness she seemed to want to touch him, too, since she stretched her fingers out and clasped him in her hand. He nearly came from that alone, but reminded himself he had more than two minutes—they had all night, they had the rest of their lives—and it wouldn't do to waste all this pent-up sexual energy by coming to orgasm now.

She withdrew her hand before his cock could argue his reasoning, and she lay back against the pillows—against the pillow he preferred, and he swallowed against the lump of emotion in his throat.

"You haven't returned my nightshirt yet," he said, running his hand on her leg as he got onto the bed.

She grinned, then sat up again and drew the nightshirt over her head, tossing it to the floor to join his clothing.

Oh, yes. Her breasts were beautiful. Just the right size for his hand to cup—he knew, he'd checked—and her nipples were rosy pink against the pale whiteness of her skin.

But it couldn't hurt to check again, could it? He leaned forward and slid his hand around the globe of her breast, feeling the warmth and softness of her skin. And then pushed her gently back so she was lying down again and he lay down next to her, on his side, his hand returning to its exploration of her body.

She rolled onto her side as well, so she was facing him, her hand on his hip, her fingers stroking his skin. He wanted her hands everywhere on his body, wanted to have her pet him, touch him, claim him.

He moved his hand to her hip now, running his palm on her curves, back on her arse, loving how round and lush she felt. Then he leaned forward to capture her mouth again, kissing her with an intensity that portended what they were about to do.

And this time, when she pressed against him, there was nothing between them, nothing but their skin touching, his erect cock snug against her belly, his chest against her breasts, his hands everywhere he could reach.

They kissed and fondled and touched until, finally, she broke the kiss and regarded him with a slightly dazed expression. "I arrived prepared," she said, then got off the bed to retrieve the package she'd placed on the chair.

She withdrew something from the package and held it out to him with trembling hands.

A French letter. A condom.

Dukes must be wary of involving themselves with people who wish to leverage their position at the expense of the duke's. If the duke is unmarried, he is to be extra cautious when dealing with young ladies, who almost certainly wish to entrap him into marriage.

Unless the duke wishes to be entrapped, in which case it is best to disregard this advice and proceed.

—THE DUKE'S GUIDE TO CORRECT BEHAVIOR

Chapter 28

She was entirely naked, in a duke's bedroom, carrying a condom. With an equally naked duke lying on his bed waiting for her.

If she weren't actually here, she would doubt it had happened. But she was, and there he was, and so there, in fact, they were.

She returned to the bed and scrambled up, glancing from the condom to his penis. Feeling skeptical one would fit inside the other.

Did condoms come in different sizes? She should know, shouldn't she, having purchased enough over the years? She didn't think Mr. Davies had ever offered a different size, but perhaps the clientele of the brothel had been lesser-sized than the duke?

Never having seen any examples of the appendage in question until now, she couldn't answer that definitively. Only she thought perhaps he was larger than usual.

"How is it you come to have that?" He didn't look appalled, or disgusted, or anything but curious. But he definitely looked curious.

"Well," she began, "I didn't want to return your nightshirt without considering what might occur. I like to plan things out in advance, you see."

His eyebrows rose as he pondered what she'd said. Then he shook his head and reached for the condom, sliding it on with barely an indication that it might not fit.

It did fit. Thank goodness. Because if she had to look at him and his skin and his body and all those muscles and the light hair on his chest, she just might die if she didn't get to do everything she'd planned.

Which included, scarily enough, his putting that large thing of his into her. But she would just have to trust it would fit. Look how wrong she'd been about the condom.

"Lily," he said, a slow smile on his face, "I want this. Come here," he said as he reached for her, wrapping his strong, muscular arms around her and moving so she lay under him. His body was a warm, welcome weight on hers, his penis hard between them, the hair on his chest tickling her skin.

She reached up to cup his cheek, then ran her fingers over his ever-present stubble. "I want this, too," she whispered.

At that, he lowered his mouth to hers and positioned his body so he was at her entrance. She would be more anxious about it, only he was already taking her breath away with his mouth, his tongue sliding into her mouth, his hands all over her skin.

And then his fingers at her entrance. He raised

himself up off her, just enough so he could stroke there. He touched her there, in the spot she herself had discovered could bring her pleasure. But his touch was very different from hers, not to mention there were two participants and one of them was the most handsome naked duke she'd ever seen.

Not that she'd seen any handsome naked dukes before, but the fact remained, it was him and she wanted him with an intensity that shocked her. She'd known it would be good, but she hadn't dreamed it would be this good.

And his large appendage hadn't even entered her yet.

He slid his fingers into her folds, and his face eased into a satisfied smile as his fingers touched her slick wetness.

He looked so pleased she couldn't even be embarrassed. Besides which, there was no room for any other feeling but pleasure right now. Later she could be embarrassed.

"Do you like this, Lily?" he asked, his voice a low rumble.

She rolled her eyes. "What do you think?" she asked with a soft laugh.

He grinned. "I want to hear you say it."

She reached around him to cup his backside. It was very firm, and flexed under her touch. "I like this, Marcus," she said, squeezing him for emphasis.

"Good. Because I have every hope we will be doing this for a long while," he said, lowering his head to her neck.

"Excellent plan," she agreed, then let out a low

moan as he licked the skin just behind her ear. He kissed her neck, then moved lower and took her nipple in his mouth.

Oh my. That felt wonderful. His tongue licked and sucked on her, and she felt the warmth and heat of what he was doing spread throughout her entire body.

Down there, plus every other place she could possibly feel anything.

He took his mouth slowly away from her nipple, and then took the other nipple in, as though he were comparing the two.

She moaned again, and arched, desperate for something, for some release of all the pressure building up throughout her body. How was he not inside her already? From what some of her working coworkers had said, men didn't do more than thrust inside until they released. But he, he was taking his time, as though he were savoring her. As though the eventual thrusting and all was but a part of the whole process.

So not only was he likely larger than the brothel's patrons, he was also more patient. She had chosen well when she had chosen this particular naked handsome duke.

Then he moved lower still, kissing her belly and touching her breasts and then lower still so that his mouth was where his fingers had been, and she held her breath, not entirely certain he would kiss her there but really hoping he would.

Because if his fingers felt wonderful, how would his tongue feel?

She only had to wonder for a few seconds

before she got her answer. He licked her with one long swipe of his tongue, and she bit her lip so she wouldn't moan so loudly that they were heard.

He followed that with several more long licks, and she couldn't stifle her moans. He lifted his head and met her gaze. "Do you like this?" he asked, his lips curved into a very satisfied smile.

She nodded, and thankfully, he didn't demand that she speak, since she didn't think she could. He put his mouth on her again, and now he was licking faster, right at that spot she knew would provide release.

Oh, and dear Lord, here it was, and she had a grip in his hair, and his hands were clasping her thighs and he was sucking and licking and blowing soft breaths on her skin that made her want to howl and moan and urge him to keep doing what he was doing, only she really couldn't speak, until finally, eventually, and all too soon, she exploded, feeling as though her whole body had shattered into a million different stars, all of which were falling through the sky.

When she finally recovered, he had moved up to lie beside her, one long leg over her body, his hands on her breasts, his penis poking her hip.

"Did you like that?" he asked.

So she whacked his arm and smiled at him. "What do you think?"

He smirked and raised an eyebrow. "I think you did."

"So now let's see about you," she replied, taking his penis in her hand.

A duke never boasts about his accomplishments.

—The Duke's Guide to Correct Behavior

Chapter 29

There was nothing so satisfying as bringing a woman to orgasm, Marcus reflected. He hadn't had much experience with it before, and he vowed to rectify that mistake as much as he possibly could in the future.

She gripped his cock, and he pushed into her hand. "What do you want me to do?" she asked.

"Stroke it up and down," he replied, then groaned as she did as instructed. It felt incredible to have her fingers sliding along his shaft, even with the condom sheathing him.

And, as it turned out, it was a damned good thing he already had the condom on. He couldn't wait. He needed to be inside her.

"Lily, you're killing me," he muttered, then moved so he was on top of her again, his cock at her entrance. He raised himself up on his arms and thrust, pushing inside her, past the barrier of her virginity, feeling her body tighten around him, hearing her gasp as he buried himself in her.

When he had gone as far as he possibly could, he lowered himself down onto her, panting, wanting to move but wanting, more importantly, to make sure she was all right.

"You have done this before, haven't you?" she asked in a humorous tone. "Aren't you supposed to move or something?"

Yes, she was all right.

He raised himself back up on his arms and began to thrust, in and out of her, the motion making her breasts jiggle in a delightful way. She had her hands at his waist and was watching what was happening down there, her lip caught between her teeth, her expression one of sensual engagement.

And then he moved faster, sliding in and out, building to his eventual climax, savoring each movement, each moment when their skin touched, when she moaned, the tightening grip on his waist, his hips.

One final thrust, then he spent and collapsed on top of her, his heart racing, his whole body feeling the impact of pleasure. She wrapped her arms around him and held him as his body shook with the tremors of his climax.

"Well, that was more than two minutes," he murmured into her neck.

"Pardon?" she asked.

He shook his head, as much as he was able to, given that his face was right against her skin. Her delicious, smooth, lovely skin.

And as soon as they were married they could do this anytime they wished. He smiled at the thought.

"Marcus?"

He raised up, the tone in her voice making him

think he was crushing her. "Was that all right? I mean, this and everything?" he said, gesturing to the fact that they were both naked in his bed.

Oh, how he liked the sound of that.

She swatted his arm. "Of course it was, I wanted it. I told you so. There need not be any worry on that score."

"What did you want to ask?" He continued without waiting for a response, "We'll have to tell Rose first, of course, and then we can put an announcement in the papers. But I want a quiet ceremony, no more than a few friends. I barely have any family, at least none that I care about, so—"

"What?" It sounded now as though not only had he crushed her, but that he had perhaps squashed two or three of her closest friends. Which he knew full well he hadn't. "We can't—I didn't know, you didn't say—we can't get married!"

His whole body stiffened. Well, except for that part. That part was still recovering.

"What do you mean, we can't get married? What was this all about, anyway?"

Too late, he realized he hadn't actually said anything. He'd just assumed, from her actions, that she wanted to be with him. Forever.

That she did not wish to be with him forever was therefore somewhat of a blow.

He rolled off her onto his side, propping his head up with his hand. Feeling ridiculous—he was entirely naked, spent and happy, but now the woman he wished to do this to every night had told him no. When he hadn't even gotten the chance to ask her.

"I—haven't told you everything." She sat up and wrapped her arms around her knees. She looked as though she were about to break, and Marcus felt a pang of emotion with which he wasn't familiar. He thought it might be empathy.

He reached up and stroked her back, his fingers trailing down her spine, then up again. It was a comforting gesture, one he didn't think he'd ever made before. Nobody had ever wanted comfort from him.

Money, whiskey, cat food, his bachelorhood, yes—but not comfort.

Her body began to shake under his hand, and he knew that whatever it was, whatever it was she hadn't told him, was more than she could bear on her own.

"What is it?" he asked, resting his palm on her back.

She moved off the bed, plucked her dressing gown from the floor and put it on, wrapping the sash tight around her. Then she wrapped her arms around her waist and returned to sit on the bed.

Not looking at him.

Her face pale.

His heart already sore.

"I know this was wrong," she began, her hand gesturing to indicate what had just occurred between them, "but I couldn't leave without it. It was selfish, I know."

Leave? First she had said no to a marriage proposal he hadn't tendered yet, and now she was leaving?

What could he have possibly done? He reviewed

his activities; no, there was nothing to which she could object, unless it was the less than professional way he treated his employee. But since that employee was her, he didn't think that was it.

"I was not honest about my past." She looked down at her hands, which were knotted together in her lap. "I never worked at a vicar's. I—I—" and at this she looked up, her eyes meeting his, so dark he would have thought he had imagined the gold glints he knew lurked inside.

"I worked at a brothel."

His stomach fell and he felt his mouth open in shock.

"That is, I did not *work* work in a brothel. You should have been able to tell that," she said with a return of her usual wry manner, "but I worked on the accounts. I was there for over a year."

"And?" He knew she was a virgin—had been a virgin—and he wanted to marry her, so how did it matter where she worked? Hadn't they established by now that a duke could do what he wanted?

"And you're an idiot!" she said, slamming her palm down on the bed for emphasis. But since it was a bed with a coverlet, it didn't do more than make a soft thudding noise.

"How am I an idiot? I am not the one who has just had relations with a gentleman who wishes to marry her and she tells him no, she cannot marry him, even though he hasn't even asked yet!"

Now she looked as though she wanted to slam her palm down on him. Which was better than looking as though her world had ended. Not much, but he much preferred Angry Lily to Disconsolately Despairing Lily.

"Have you ever, in your entire life, thought about the consequences of your actions?" she asked, her tone revealing her frustration. "It is not about us, Marcus. There is Rose to consider. How will people treat her if they knew that her governess had a disreputable past?"

He had no reply to that, did he? Because he did know how they would treat her. He'd already seen it in a few glances, one of Smithfield's sisters' uncaring words, Smithfield himself warning him that people were talking.

"People have already made reference to who she is to you," Lily continued. "The only way you can salvage her future is by marrying a proper lady." She uttered a snort. "I am neither proper nor a lady." Her tone softened. "The irony is, this situation, us, would never have happened if you had not been trying to do the right thing in regard to Rose. But you have to keep doing the right thing. You can't do something that would jeopardize someone else's happiness. A little girl's happiness," she added, her voice breaking.

"So that's it? You have to leave?"

"Somebody recognized me, Marcus. If I go now, I'll be gone before the talk can start." A pause. "I have to. For Rose. For you." Her tone was implacable.

He got up from the bed and retrieved his own dressing gown. If his entire romantic future was going to be ruined, he wanted it to occur when he wasn't bare-arsed naked.

"When will you leave?"

"In the morning. I'll bid a proper goodbye to Rose. And I will take the wages I am owed." She didn't ask, just knew he would not deny her that. She trusted him to do the right thing. She knew that about him.

And he? Marcus thought he'd known her.

Apparently he didn't.

"Of course." He sat rigidly on the bed, his whole body tense with emotion, with wanting to shout and order people to do things, as one was supposed to be able to do when one was a duke.

She nodded, not meeting his gaze, then stood, her hair falling forward to partially cover her face. Not that he wanted to see her expression; either she didn't care for him, so her expression was not as upset as he was, or she was as upset and there was nothing he could do to change her mind.

Either way, he could feel his loneliness return—the loneliness that had receded since she and Rose arrived—like a cold wave of anguish bursting into his soul.

He really was a bad poet.

"Goodbye." She nearly whispered, her voice was so quiet, and his throat tightened at the emotion he felt choking him. That he could do nothing about this, that she was right about what had to be done, didn't mean he didn't feel the pain of it.

And that he wouldn't feel the pain for a very long time. Perhaps forever.

She turned and walked out of his bedroom, soon to walk out of his life.

And Marcus leaned back against the pillow, still warm and fragrant from her, from them, and shuddered as agony and frustration washed over him.

No matter what might happen during the course of events, a duke must always remember that he is infallible.

Unless he is fallible, in which case he will behave as though he is not, and then his behavior will become the truth.

—The Duke's Guide to Correct Behavior

Chapter 30

He had spent half the night thinking about how to solve the problem, then a quarter of the night making plans, and then another quarter sleeping.

He would say he'd also spent a quarter of the night reliving what had happened between them, but that was too many quarters.

Which was why he was currently on his third cup of coffee as she stepped into the room, escorting Rose.

He knew Lily hadn't left yet—he hadn't paid her, for one thing—but he wasn't entirely prepared for the sight of her. Judging by her face, she had slept as little as he. Her eyes had dark circles under them, her face was pale, and even her gown looked woebegone.

Perhaps he was mistaken on that last point, but she looked as horrible as he felt. And still he felt his heart leap when he saw her, his chest constrict, and he wished he could just fold her in his arms and tell her he would make it all right.

But she wouldn't believe him.

"Good morning, Duke," Rose said, tilting her cheek up so he could kiss it.

"Good morning, Rose, Miss Lily."

Lily nodded, then went to the breakfast sideboard and got herself a cup of tea. That was it, nothing to eat. He stifled the words that wanted to pour out of him: *You have to eat something, you're about to leave this place, and I don't know where you'll go, or who you'll meet, or what you'll do.*

"Duke," Rose said as she sat down. "Miss Lily says she needs to leave. Can't you make her stay?"

He met Lily's gaze. I wish I could. "No, Miss Lily said she has to leave, and we have to respect that."

Rose stuck her lips out in a pout. "But who will teach me?"

Marcus swallowed. Not her, not anymore. "We will find someone, sweet." No one like her. No one can replace her. "Do you want to take a walk with me this afternoon?" Because if he didn't change the topic soon, he was going to shout his frustration, and that would only scare Rose.

"Mm-hm." Rose picked up a piece of toast and devoured it. She seemed all right—perhaps she didn't yet realize that this departure was permanent. Plus she'd already dealt with people leaving in her young life, maybe she had come to expect it.

He would never leave her. She was his to care for, his to protect. His to ensure she had as bright a future as she possibly could.

Which meant Lily had to go. At least according to her.

The final leave-taking was blessedly short; he handed Lily her pay, she curtsied, turned and left.

What took longer was what he did afterward. First he had to send a note to Smithfield to ask him to come right away; then he had to liquidate some funds so he would be ready for what he was preparing to do.

Then, once Smithfield had given him all the information, he had to write the correspondence in such a way to convey what he wished to do without offending anyone with his arrogant assumptions.

Not an easy task. He wished she were still there to advise him on how to be humble. But she wasn't, which was why he was doing all this.

The irony was not lost on him.

Finally, when everything was as prepared as it was going to be, he went for a long walk with his daughter.

Because Rose was the impetus for everything that was happening now. She wasn't the key to his happiness, she was his happiness.

And he knew their happiness would be increased if Lily returned to their lives.

"Lily?" She heard Caroline's voice in her ear. "Lily!" Caroline, presumably, shaking her.

"What is it?" She turned her head to look at her friend, not even trying to disguise her expression.

Which judging by Caroline's mingled look of sympathy and annoyance was the same desolate expression she'd had for the past week. Caroline's look, however, was beginning to edge more toward annoyance.

Was there a time limit on heartbreak? Lily certainly hoped so, since feeling this way was not conducive to living a productive life. Living any kind of life, actually, but she wasn't so foolish as to think she would just stop living because her heart was broken.

"Are the flyers ready for tomorrow? Annabelle has asked a few of our ladies to hand them out, as the members of the House of Commons are dispersing for the day." Caroline's mouth was a grim line, reminding Lily that the agency could not advertise that they had provided the governess for a duke's household since the governess in question was her, and she had left the duke's employ so abruptly.

Caroline and Annabelle knew most of what had happened—with the exception of the nightshirt's return—and while neither of them blamed her, the agency was definitely not going to be moving up in the ranks of the aristocracy as quickly as they had all hoped.

In other words, there was no yelping at the agency's office lately.

"I thought the flyers were going to be distributed on Saturday?" She had been moving in a fog since her return and knew it had taken her longer to do things. Just as it seemed now to take longer for her to breathe, or smile, or do anything that people did when their hearts had not been ripped out of their chests.

Of course, she was being melodramatic. Her

heart, she presumed, was still in her chest. It just felt as though it had been ripped out.

Caroline glanced up at the ceiling as though she were completely exasperated. "We talked about this." No, she actually was completely exasperated. "We agreed that after tomorrow's vote would be the best opportunity. The members should be in a good frame of mind, and will also be reminded that they might have to spend more time in the city, and will need help. We talked about this," she repeated, only this time more—exasperatedly.

Lily looked at the stack of papers on the desk. An ever-growing stack, papers for which she was solely responsible.

Wonderful. Not only was she completely wretched, she was also letting her partners down.

Perhaps later she could go take a dog's bone away, just to spread her misery.

And then the dog would bite her. That would take her mind off her heartache, at least.

"I'll stay late to finish them." It was not as though she had anything to do later on anyway, except for not eating the dinner she made and then not sleeping in the bed that wasn't his.

"Are you certain? Annabelle and I can stay." Lily heard Annabelle's howl of protest in the other room and nearly smiled.

"No, you two are working hard enough." And they were; it seemed Mr. Smithfield and his brother-in-law were not especially close, since Mr. Smithfield had stopped by the agency a few times and had even brought in some friends who needed staff.

The agency was surviving, and if things went as they were going now, in perhaps a year or two they could expand. Especially if, Annabelle put coyly, Lily's admirer, Mr. Smithfield, was able to persuade more friends they needed the agency's services.

Lily just rolled her eyes at Annabelle. She assumed that Marcus had said something about her departure, and Mr. Smithfield was just being nice. Besides, she thought she'd seen something in his expression as he spoke with Caroline.

"Be sure to leave by eight o'clock, then," Caroline admonished as she took her cloak from the hook on the wall. "Any later will be dangerous. I'd rather have you safe than all the flyers in the world."

Lily nodded. "I will," she assured her friend. She may have been wretched and slacking at her work and threatening to steal dog bones, but she wasn't foolish enough to walk home long after dark.

There were limits to her foolishness, after all.

The doorbell sounded long after Caroline and Annabelle had finished fussing over her and left, and Lily had shot the bolt to the door.

She glanced at the clock, relieved it wasn't yet eight o'clock, so she hadn't broken her promise to Caroline.

But who was coming to the agency at this hour? She didn't think it would be anybody she actually wanted to see.

Not that there was anyone she wanted to see. So never mind that caveat.

She rose, feeling her back ache the way it did when she had spent too much time hunched over her desk. The flyers were nearly all done, and she thought that she might only need twenty more minutes to finish them all.

Except there was someone at the door.

The bell jangled again.

And again.

Someone who was not going to leave until she responded.

"Who is it?" she called, already grumpy at having to deal with someone who was so persistent.

"Marcus."

She froze. The bell jangled.

His voice came clearly through the door. "Lily, I know it's you in there, and I also know you're alone."

A return to her old self might have had her asking him what she was wearing, since he knew so much. Too bad her new self was too occupied with what he was doing here, and how could she bear to see him, and all those things that her broken heart brought to mind.

And from the way it was constricting in her chest, she could safely say her heart was not, indeed, broken after all. Just in need of some mending.

"Are you going to let me in? It's starting to rain." He sounded as arrogant and autocratic as always, which is to say he sounded like the man she loved.

No, she meant, the man she used to love.

No, she loved him. Now. Still. Always.

But he didn't have to know that, did he? Neither one of them had told each other anything in the throes of passion except *mmm* and "Oh, yes."

"Fine," she said in a voice as far from passionate murmurings as possible.

She pushed the bolt to the left, then drew the door open slowly, holding her breath.

She'd nearly forgotten how tall he was, but the top of his hat went over the doorframe, and he'd have to duck to enter the room.

Which he did as she was gawking at him. He frowned, then took his hat off and shook his coat, spraying rain all over the wooden floor of the office. She stared down at the specks of moisture on the floor, trying to breathe, trying to remember what it felt like not to be in love with him so she could try to regain that composure.

At last, when she looked up, it was to find his eyes locked on her face, the intensity of his expression making her lose her breath all over again.

Perhaps she wouldn't have to speak to him, she would just asphyxiate in his presence.

"It is good to see you, Miss Lily." *Miss Lily.* They'd returned to that formality, despite how he was looking at her. It shouldn't hurt, but of course it did.

"Thank you, Your Grace."

She waited, the pause lengthening, then arched an eyebrow in imitation of his most intimidating look.

In response, his lips twisted into a wry smirk. Not intimidated, then.

"I suppose you are wondering why I am here," he said.

It was not really a question. And given that she was wondering why he was there, it didn't require an answer.

"I have a favor to ask you."

Her spine went numb. Would he ask her to instruct him how to behave with his new bride? Was he going to ask her to recommend schools to which Rose could be sent? Did he need her help with his infernal accounting?

Because the last item she'd had enough of, thank you very much. The agency's books were already in chaos, thanks to her . . . distraction. Caused by him.

"Well?" he said, again in that impatient tone that both irked and thrilled her. "Aren't you going to ask me what it is?"

"Aren't you going to tell me?" she snapped back, watching as his eyes widened at her reply. Of course. People did not speak to dukes that way, except governesses usually did not have relations with dukes as she'd had with him, which she would remind him of if he had the temerity to get all duke-haughty with her.

Yet, she had to admit, she did like it when he got duke-haughty. Or had liked it; that part of her life was done with, she reminded herself.

If she could just learn to breathe regularly, that is.

He clasped his hands loosely, as though he were a guard standing at attention. She saw the motion of his throat as he swallowed, then by habit noticed the dark stubble on his cheeks.

Stubble against which she'd rubbed her hand, her cheek.

Enough of that, Lily, she chided herself.

He lifted his chin and seemed to set himself in place. "There's something I want you to take Rose to."

And stopped. As though he didn't need to explain when, where, and most importantly, why she should do such a thing.

So she asked: "Why?"

He grimaced, and his jaw set. "Of course you wouldn't just do it," he muttered. He drew a piece of paper from his pocket and held it out to her, his gaze never leaving her face.

She took it from him, careful not to touch his skin, careful not to do anything that might let him know just how miserable she'd been the past week.

How miserable she was expecting to be the rest of her life.

The folded paper had a few raindrops on it, but it was still legible. *The Horticultural Society of London wishes to announce the opening of the Rutherford Gardens*—then lots of words that didn't matter, his name, and then: *An invitation-only ceremony to honor the donors will be held on March 21, 1840.*

She glanced back up at him, feeling herself start to shake. "This is tomorrow," she said. "And you will be there."

He nodded, then held his hand out. She folded it back up and returned it to him.

"Thank you. But I cannot go." Silence as he regarded her. A hot rush of emotions, tangled up anger, wistfulness, longing, love, and frustration tainted her words, spun them so she nearly spat out: "You know I cannot go, I had to leave your employ because I was recognized. If someone else recognizes me, if they say something to anyone, it will be the most delicious morsel of gossip your world can imagine—a dangerous duke's governess used to work in a brothel. Be realistic, Marcus." His name slipped from her tongue before she realized she'd said it.

"Rose won't go if you're not there. And I want her there to see me—see me doing something good. This is important to me. To us." He spoke in a low tone, one that traveled sneakily up her spine and settled somewhere in her chest.

Right where that treacherous, damaged heart was.

"I know Rose can't understand why I can't be there," she said, "but you can. You know what will happen."

He raised his eyes to the ceiling and huffed a breath out, as though keeping himself from saying something that would— Well, she had no idea what it would do, just that for some reason he wasn't saying it.

"You know yourself just how entitled the people in 'my world,' as you put it, are. They won't notice you. You can come just when I speak to the guests, and then leave when I'm done speaking. I just need to make sure Rose is all right."

She felt herself wavering, even though she knew it was a terrible idea. How could he even tamper with Rose's future like that?

He was even more arrogant than she realized, and she'd realized he was quite arrogant already.

It was good, then, that this would be the only thing.

Had she really just decided? She thought about it, and knew she had. Even though she was cursing herself for knowing she would give in to his request.

But if it was the only way for his daughter to see her father do something right in public—ironic though the whole thing was—she would have to do it. Later on he'd have a new governess, one who would be reputation-free, would likely not need to be clothed, or questioned, or—or kissed.

Or caressed.

Or anything else at all like that. He would have a wife, a proper lady wife, who would be able to touch that glorious chest, feel the muscles tremble under her fingers, make him lose his control and rake her fingers through his hair, down his back, and—

"I'll do it," she said, before she could think anything more detrimental to her current tenuous hold on not being entirely miserable. Partially miserable was a goal, at least.

A person should always have goals.

"Thank you," he said, relieved. "I promised Rose you would, and I couldn't bear the thought of going back and having to tell her you couldn't." He rubbed his hand against his cheek, just as Lily had been imagining herself doing.

"I will send a carriage for you at one o'clock, you can wait inside until it is time for me to speak.

I'll send John Footman to fetch you, and then you can leave right afterward."

It sounded as though he'd thought of her objections and was trying to answer them as best he could. As though he wanted to do the right thing, but there were two right things here—Rose seeing him, and her escorting Rose—and the two were contradictory and couldn't possibly coexist.

Could they? She could wear a large bonnet and borrow one of her friends' cloaks, not that his world had memorized her clothing, but at least there was less of a chance she'd be recognized. And thus far the only person who'd—

"One more thing," she said in as casual a way as possible. "Will Mr. Smithfield's sisters be there? His brothers-in-law?"

His gaze seemed to see right through her, but he just shook his head. "Not that I know of, it is a very limited guest list."

"Ah." Relief coursed through her, only to be subsumed in another wave of panic. "You are getting a replacement? This is only for tomorrow?"

An odd look passed over his features, so quickly she might have thought she'd imagined it. "I will not be needing you as a governess any longer after tomorrow," he said. "I promise."

She exhaled. "Well. Then, thank you. I will see you tomorrow."

She watched as he donned his hat and did up his coat, those long, elegant fingers she'd grown to love working the buttons with an alluring dexterity.

Unless she was just reading into that, and he had normal fingers doing normal things.

He touched his hat and offered a slight bow. "Thank you again. Rose will be thrilled you can attend."

And walked out before she could say anything.

Dukes always get the last word.

—The Duke's Guide to Correct Behavior

Chapter 31

He'd done it. He'd gone there, he hadn't blurted out what he intended to do, he had been himself, or the himself he was as much as he possibly could.

Seeing her had shaken him. He'd seen her everywhere he looked, since she left—was it only a week ago?—but seeing her in reality drove home just how much he wanted her. How much he needed her.

How much he loved her.

And that was why it was worth anything to him to have her again. For real, not just under the guise of returning borrowed clothing, or instructions in manners or accounts—although perhaps he could use her skills in that regard, since he was doing an awful job of it by himself.

"Your Grace, welcome back." Thompson had been even more rigid since Lily had left so abruptly. Even he had been affected by her.

And Rose. She was resilient, certainly, but she kept talking about "Miss Lily this," and "Miss

Lily that," underscoring just how much the child missed her, whether she knew it herself or not.

He hadn't bothered to find another governess. And he wouldn't, not right away, not without knowing if everything—that everything—would be all right. He couldn't dare think it wouldn't be.

"Tea in the library," Marcus ordered as he handed the butler his hat and coat, still damp from the rain.

"Very good, Your Grace," Thompson replied.

Marcus walked to the library—their library—and hesitated for a moment before entering.

It was the same room as it had been before, but it just wasn't.

He'd spent every evening in here since she left, staying up way later than he should, knowing that unless he were totally and utterly exhausted he would lie awake for hours, thinking about what they'd done in his bed. What he wanted to do to her.

It wasn't fair that he had been shown how it could be, how it should be, only to have it taken away. And he knew it wouldn't be the same with anyone else.

Not that he wanted anyone else.

He wanted her. And he would get her. He was, as she was so fond of pointing out, a duke after all.

Even though that meant nothing when it came to the society of the heart.

He really and truly had to admit he was a bad poet. And what was worse, if she were here, he would find himself spouting his bad poetry to her, just to see her face crinkle up in amusement or have her raise her brow in a mockingly derisive way.

He hoped he'd have that chance.

Thompson returned with the tea just as he was about to be concerned he was growing maudlin.

"If that will be all, Your Grace?" Thompson bowed his head just barely.

I am trying to get her back, Marcus wanted to shout. Only shouting at him, if momentarily satisfying, would do nothing more than bother both of them.

"That is all. Thank you," he said, leaning forward to pour his tea, hoping it would be the last night he'd have to drink it alone.

"I think she should wear the blue gown," Annabelle said, swatting Caroline's hand away.

Lily knew it had been a mistake to ask her friends to help her get ready, but what else was she to do? It wasn't as though she could dress herself, with shaky hands and distracted mind and butterflies in the stomach.

And once she'd told them, they wouldn't have listened if she wanted to be by herself anyway. Annabelle had to work through every possible ramification of what might happen, including the possibility of Lily discovering she was the long-lost heir to a remote German princedom, the only person who could accurately answer a riddle to receive a vast treasure, and that she could make plants bloom simply by walking by them.

Or all three.

Caroline merely snorted.

"It doesn't matter what I will be wearing," she said. "I am only coming out during the duke's speech, to ensure Rose can see and that she doesn't get lost. Then I will be on my way home." She frowned. "You two will be at the House of Commons today?"

Annabelle opened her mouth, but Caroline dug an elbow into her side. "Yes, we will. Thank you for finishing the flyers," she said. "What time is the carriage arriving?"

As though Annabelle hadn't mentioned it at least ten times during the past twenty minutes. "One o'clock."

"Of course," Caroline said. "We will be off just after you leave."

At last, after several more meandering conversations led by Annabelle, Lily was dressed—despite her own protests—in one of the prettier day gowns the duke had purchased for her. Caroline had done her hair up and Annabelle loaned her a bonnet, one that was attractive but still somewhat hid her face.

Lily gathered herself and glanced at the clock. Five minutes to one. She hugged her friends, took a deep breath and walked outside.

"Miss Lily! Miss Lily!" Rose came bounding up to her, dressed in the most beautiful frock Lily had ever seen, one that likely cost as much as her annual salary. Her previous annual salary, that is.

The duke walked up behind his daughter,

dressed more faultlessly than she had ever seen—from perfectly tied, straight, and white cravat, to elegant, well-fitting coat, to his sleek, clinging trousers, down to immaculate shoes, which would likely lose their pristine look within two minutes of walking around a garden—a garden full of dirt, of all things.

He must have shaved recently, since he had barely any stubble. Lily was selfishly glad no other young lady could see him in all his gloriousness with the addition of that stubble, which made part of her melt inside, now that she knew what it felt like under her hand.

"Miss Lily." Even his voice sounded formal and correct.

"Your Grace." She curtsied as she took Rose's hand. "When are you speaking?"

He drew a watch out of his waistcoat. "Five minutes, I believe. You will bring Rose up, close enough to hear?" He sounded anxious, and she felt herself soften at the reminder of how much he loved Rose. *Enough of that, Lil,* she warned herself. After today, she would never see them again.

And then she felt the tears start to well up. *Don't think about that now, either,* she chided herself.

So many things not to think of. What could she think of instead? How lovely the day was, how the rain from the previous evening had gone away, leaving a bright freshness to the air that could only augur spring. That the garden was truly lovely, with shaded areas and small benches placed precisely beside well-tended paths.

That the Queen was sitting on one of those small benches.

The Queen. As in, the queen Queen.

Oh, dear. Had she been worried about someone recognizing her before? Now she was terrified.

"Miss Lily, it is time. Could you escort Miss Rose up to the front?" His dark eyes met hers, nothing in them indicating he was aware of the abject fear and terror she was feeling.

So much for his being her true love, or whatever perversely romantic thing she'd concocted in her brain back when she was in the process of falling in love with him.

"Did you see the Queen?" Her voice wasn't a voice so much as a strangled hiss.

He took a nonchalant look toward the ruler of the entire kingdom and shrugged. "Yes, there was a rumor that she would be in attendance. Her Majesty is a great lover of nature."

He did not seem perturbed by her presence at all. Of course not, she reminded herself for perhaps the thousandth time, he was a duke. A duke was as close to royalty as a nonroyal person could get.

Whereas she—she was as close to a fallen woman as a nonfallen woman could get.

"Rose, Miss Lily?" The duke's imperious autocratic tone brought her back to the present. Where she was still on the verge of falling. "This way," he said, turning to stride toward a section where she saw a group of nonfallen women. There was a cluster of chairs, and a pretty young woman sat in one, a smile on her face as she beheld the duke.

Was this whom he had chosen to marry? This perfectly fine young lady with lovely clothes, a nice smile, and a trim figure?

There was nothing about the woman with which she could find fault. That might be the worst part of it all—she couldn't even hate her, this proper young lady who was entirely suitable. She just wasn't her.

An older thin woman stood and greeted the duke, then gestured for him to move to the front, where Lily assumed the patrons were sitting. She saw, then, Mr. Smithfield standing in the back row, smiling as he caught her eye.

Did he wink at her as well?

That was odd.

She couldn't think about that either, since the duke had moved in front of the gathering and begun to speak. His low, resonant voice wrapped itself around her body and made her want him all over.

"Ladies and gentlemen, thank you for coming this afternoon. We are all very pleased to announce the opening of the Gardens. We hope that this public area will provide a place for people to come enjoy the bounty of nature, even within an area as built up as London. People, no matter if they are dukes, chimney sweeps, or queens," and at this he bowed at Victoria, "deserve a place to come and find respite. Some greenery amidst the gray."

He paused, and a few people began to clap, thinking the speech was over.

"But," he said, sweeping his hands out in a

broad gesture, "more than that, it is a place where things live. Where things thrive. And that, more than anything, is what spoke to me, what persuaded me to become a patron of this fine undertaking."

Murmurs of accord, and even—did she hear it?—some comments on how remarkably handsome he was, standing in front of everyone, with all his height and looks and impressive nose and delicious voice and intense dukeliness.

Although that last could have been just her.

"Recently, I have been lucky enough to have undergone some changes in my life. I know that many of you know that I have just recently, and unexpectedly, come into my title. But that is not the luckiest thing." He gazed out into the crowd and found where Lily and Rose stood. "I have been lucky enough to find my daughter," at which a gasp rose from the crowd, "and she is the reason I wanted to support a place where things could not only live, but thrive. And be loved. As I love her."

Lily's heart was in her throat as she waited for someone to yell something, to say anything that would hurt Rose. No wonder he wanted her there—he needed to ensure that Rose was protected, but also so Rose could hear him say he wanted her, as he had never been wanted himself.

A pause, then a few people started to clap, joined by at least half more of the crowd. Not a complete approbation, but at least a mild tolerance. Lily let out a sigh of relief.

But he wasn't finished. "And someone else has entered my life as well."

Her spine tingled.

"She originally arrived to teach my daughter the names of flowers, such as we might find in this garden, and manners, and how to draw, but she's taught us so much more. Taught me so much more. This woman, this lady, is all that is intelligent, and refined, and polite, and I know that it might not accord with convention for me to have fallen in love with her"—at which point there was a crowdwide gasp, and then chattering, as everyone asked their neighbor who he could possibly be talking about—"but she has shown me how to live and thrive, and I cannot possibly live—or live happily—without her."

Startled cries from the crowd, while Queen Victoria seemed to almost smile. Marcus met Lily's gaze and his lips lifted in a slight wry curl, as though he knew she wanted to shout at him to stop but didn't dare.

"And when I had the chance to say something to her, I was tongue-tied. I was unable to say what I was feeling, and for that, I have the most profound regret. I am hoping I can say some of what I feel for her now, but I want to spend the rest of my life telling her what I feel, each and every day, until the end. And even that won't be enough." He straightened and looked directly at her, and Lily caught the shift as people turned to stare at the woman who was the object of the duke's affection.

"Lily," he said, "what is your damn last name? I don't remember."

"Russell," Lily replied.

"Lily Russell, I know you think we will not suit,

for reasons that aren't important. Here is why we will suit. These are the only reasons you should consider. You are the only person I wish to kiss first thing in the morning and the last thing at night, and all the times in between. You are the person I first think of when I wish to share a sorrow or a joy. You are everything I would hope for in a wife, a duchess, and most importantly, as a mother to my daughter. You are the only one I wish to live with and for, for the rest of my life."

He stepped forward, into the standing crowd, which parted for him as he made his way to her. When he stood just in front of her, he lowered himself to one knee. "Dearest Lily, in front of all these people, I want to tell you how much I love you. How much I want you to be my wife. Will you marry me?"

Lily froze, her hand going to her mouth in shock. The other hand still held Rose's, and she felt a tug on her fingers, then glanced down at the little girl.

"Answer the duke," Rose urged, then smiled. "He loves you, he told me."

Lily looked back at him, on his knee, thought about how his trousers were likely getting dirty, and how the crowd of his peers were probably wondering who she was, and that her past made her even more unsuitable than just not being one of them, and that maybe someone had recognized her and was spreading the story now.

But—did it matter?

Well, it did, of course it did, for all the reasons she'd left in the first place. But he had said it, in front of everyone. Did it matter now? Perhaps that was the right question.

"Can you give me an answer, Lily? Because my knees are starting to ache," he said in a return to that arrogant tone she had grown to love.

As she had grown to love all of him.

She looked down and lowered her hand from her mouth to touch his hair, his cheek. That stubble.

"Yes," she whispered softly, feeling as though her heart were going to burst through her chest.

He stood quickly, not even dusting off his now quite dirty trousers, taking her hand in his and holding his other hand to Rose.

"Let's leave," he said to her, so only she could hear him, "before the Queen has a chance to ask just what I meant by us being unsuitable." He began walking, Lily and Rose on either side of him, making their way through the crowd as people began to clap. Lily turned to see Smithfield leading the applause, his hands up in the air as he smiled at them, and she smiled back. She caught a glimpse, too, of Annabelle and Caroline, both of whom had wide grins on their faces and were also clapping. She nearly stopped, but Caroline made a shooing gesture—as of course she would—and Lily turned back around, seeing the duke's carriage just ahead.

They were all quiet in the carriage ride home, Rose because she was usually quiet, unless she was conversing about cats, and Lily because she was too stunned by what had happened to speak coherently. She couldn't say why Marcus was quiet, except that every time she looked over at him, he caught her eye and a slow, lazy smile curved onto his face, sending delicious shudders through her whole body.

So perhaps she did know why he was quiet.

They went into the house, Thompson glancing between her and the duke, then informing Rose that Partridge had just taken a fresh batch of scones out of the oven, and would she like to have some?

She would, and so she and Thompson left.

Lily stood, still in shock, in that foyer that had impressed her so much when she first arrived. And yet it was nothing compared to how impressive she found the owner. And she definitely did not wish to kiss the foyer senseless, nor did she wish to—

"Can we go into your library, please?" she said.

He nodded and took her hand, opening the door to allow her inside, then shutting it quickly and leaning against it, pulling her to him.

She felt his body, all of him, up against her, and the sensations of want and warmth and desire came flooding through her, but none as strong as the feeling of love.

Which, she recalled, she hadn't yet said.

"I love you, you know."

He kissed her, a quick affirmation, then drew back, a smug look on his face. "I know."

She stood on her tiptoes and rubbed her face against his slightly stubbled cheek.

"I did it for you," he said. "I knew you wouldn't

believe I was willing to do anything to have you, so I didn't even try. But I thought if I could just prove it to you, you would see that this—" He kissed her then, hard and fierce. "—this is worth anything."

"So you spent a vast amount of money just in order to be able to speak in front of everyone?"

He was silent as he considered this. Lily slid her hands around his waist and stroked her fingers on his back. "Not just in order to speak in front of everyone," he finally replied, "though that was the primary reason. But I also know how important it is for everyone to have a chance to grow and thrive under the best possible circumstances. Rose deserves that, and you have shown me how to do it. A ball is— Well, for one thing, Rose couldn't attend a ball, so it would have been that much harder to get you there, in practical terms."

She laughed as he continued. "And I wanted you where you fit best. I said when I first met you I could be called the Duke of Gardening, and now I really can. I have my Lily, and my Rose. A garden seemed like the right place."

"And speaking of the right place," she said, putting her hands to his cravat and slowly beginning to unwind the fabric, "I have had images of us here in your library, perhaps on the desk where you do your loathsome accounting? Or in that enormous chair where I sat when I made my reports on Rose's progress?"

He brushed her fingers away and tore his cravat off, dropping it to the floor. Then he pushed himself off the door and, before she could realize what he was doing, swept her up in his arms and strode to the middle of the room, then paused as he seemed to debate with himself.

He plopped her down in the enormous chair, then got on his knees on the rug in front of her, his hands on the arms of the chair, effectively trapping her.

Not that she wished to be anywhere but here.

"Lily, I love you. I want to make sure I tell you at every possible moment, since I couldn't figure out how to say it before when we . . ."

"Returned your nightshirt?" she said with a smirk.

"Yes, that. And I haven't come up with anything better to say than to just tell you, as often as possible, that I love you."

"That might prove inconvenient when we are in company."

"It will be good, then, that I plan to have you alone as much as possible," he said, leaning forward to capture her mouth with his.

Epilogue

"Just a few steps more, Mama," Rose said, leading Lily down what felt like a hallway. One of Marcus's cravats covered her eyes, and he held her other hand, the one with his ring on it.

"And here we are," he announced as Lily heard the sound of a door opening. Marcus put his hand at her back and guided her forward, into an area quite a bit warmer and with a different smell than where she had just been.

"Let me take it off, Duke," Rose said.

"Lean down so Rose can remove your mask," Marcus said.

Lily knelt and felt Rose's fingers fumbling in the loose knot Marcus had tied when they were in the foyer.

The fabric slid off and she stood up again, blinking as she looked all around at the splendor.

They were in the conservatory, but it wasn't the same place they'd been in a few weeks earlier. This room was filled to bursting with greenery, from huge spiky fronded plants to blooming roses, their scent redolent in the warm air, and delicate daffodils just poking up out of their small pots.

"Do you like it? The duke and I did it in secret, to surprise you."

The prickle of tears stung her eyes. "I love it. Just like I love you." She knelt back down and enfolded Rose in a hug.

"I love you, too," Rose said. She broke apart from the hug and looked up at the duke. "And Duke said there would be no lilies here, since you don't like them, which is funny, because I like roses."

Rose's logic did sometimes make a small amount of sense.

"Thank you for that. Roses are becoming my favorite anyway. This is so pretty, and what a surprise! Is that what you were doing when you said you were taking so many walks? I was wondering, since on a few of those days it rained, and yet you didn't come back wet."

"You were fooled, though, right?" Rose asked anxiously.

"I had no idea this is what you were doing," Lily assured her.

"Can I go water the roses?"

"Of course," Marcus replied. Rose skipped off, looking back a few times as though to make certain they were still there. She had adjusted well to her new, complete family, although she has asked when she might have a baby brother or sister.

Marcus just told her, very seriously, that he and her mama were working on that.

"This is lovely, " Lily said.

"As are you, my Lily. I don't need any other flower but you and Rose in my life. But it seemed a waste to have the opportunity to make things grow and not use it. Like I was living before you came into my life. I love you," he said, leaning forwad to kiss her.

"I know," Lily replied, kissing him back.

Next month, don't miss these exciting new love stories only from Avon Books

Say Yes to the Marquess by Tessa Dare

After years of waiting for Piers Brandon, the Marquess of Granville, to set a wedding date, Clio Whitmore makes plans to break her engagement. Not if Rafe Brandon—Piers's brother and a notorious rake—can help it. Rafe convinces her she'll make a beautiful, desirable bride. The only problem is he's falling in disastrous, hopeless love with the one woman he can't have.

Love Me If You Dare by Toni Blake

Camille Thompson is the best at closing deals. That's why a real estate developer has sent her to Coral Cove where the owner of the Happy Crab Motel is refusing to sell. No amount of money—or any other temptation Camille can offer—will convince Reece Donovan to give up the one link to his past. As a fragile romance grows, can Reece trust Camille with his secrets?

The Duke of Dark Desires by Miranda Neville

Julian Fortescue never expected to inherit a dukedom, nor find himself guardian to three young half-sisters. In need of a governess, he lays eyes on Jane Grey and knows immediately she is qualified—to become his mistress. Using the alias Jane Grey, Lady Jeanne de Falleron must find out which of Julian's relatives killed her family. But what if her darkly irresistible employer is also the man she's sworn to kill?

REL 1214